The Rebel Christian Publishing

ISBN: 978-1-957290-52-2 (eBook)
Print: 978-1-957290-53-9

Cover designed by Valicity Elaine

The Rebel Christian Publishing LLC
350 Northern Blvd STE 324 - 1390
Albany, NY 12204-1000

Visit us: http://www.therebelchristian.com/
Email us: rebel@therebelchristian.com

Contents

Beautiful Lies

A Dark Romance for Christian Women

By Valicity Elaine

A Rebel Christian Publishing Book

WARNING/DISCLAIMER

Author's Note

I owe no explanation for myself or what I write. But I do want to take a moment to make it clear that I am a Christian author, and this is a Christian novel. There is no foul language or graphic love scenes in this book, and it does include a message of Christ. The protagonist is a Christian woman, and through her testimony about Christ, others in the story are also introduced to Christ. All of that said, it is important you understand this is not a typical Christian love story in the least.

If you have read any of my other romance novels, then you probably have a good idea of what to expect from this point forward. For those who are new here, welcome!

Please understand this book was written for **ADULT** Christian women, specifically for women who are making the transition from dark secular romance.

Beautiful Lies takes place in the mafia world. I make no apologies for the fact that I did not shy away from the grittiness of our characters' lives. They are not perfect people, and neither are we. I will never try to hide that, but I will always honor God through it.

That is the message of this story, that Christ is with you

through the storm and no peace can be found without Him. The journey to Him may not be pretty, but He is always there by your side.

If you are a sensitive reader, I would not recommend you continue with this story. While there is no foul language or graphic sex, there are themes that sensitive audiences may find offensive. Please take a close look at the topics below and decide for yourself if you want to continue down this journey. For those who move forward, you have been warned.

This book is for readers 18+ and will include topics/themes including, but not limited to…

- Murder/gang violence
- Distribution of illegal substances
- Arranged marriage
- Infidelity
- Kidnapping/hostage situation
- Suicidal thoughts

Prologue

Luca

This is the sin I carry.

It's my little brother named Mario, a kid with braces at age fifteen. He's been begging us to get them removed for a month now. He's never cared about the braces before. I suspect there's a pretty girl involved. But I like the braces, they make him look like the innocent kid that he is. Instead of the prince of the Italian mafia.

It isn't easy being the youngest son of Vincent Vittore. Neither is it easy being the oldest.

I make it a point to keep Mario shielded from the worst of our world. He isn't blind. He knows who he is and what his family does, but I won't let that stop him from living a life as close to normal as possible. My father believes it's stupid. Says Mario shouldn't be in a private Catholic school learning the Lord's Prayer. He should be involved in the business, shadowing me as I take care of my father's work.

I understand what he's saying. Mario is a Vittore. One day, he'll have to step up. One day, he'll have to learn the business. Just like me. But I learned at fifteen, and I wouldn't wish that experience on any kid. Especially not my own little brother.

Does a fifteen-year-old really need to learn about shipments of cocaine? Freight trains full of living cargo. The flesh we sell when the drugs aren't enough. Does a teenager need to see what happens in my father's cigar lounges?

I learned with a smile on my face and a groan tumbling from my lips. I learned with my eyes rolled to the back of my head, drowning in a fog of ecstasy. I won't say it wasn't *fun*. But it certainly wasn't worth it.

When I look at Mario, I don't see a gangster. I don't see the next don of the mafia. I see a kid who's itching to get out of the car so he can join his friends before classes start.

Mario's face is pressed against the glass of the passenger door, his breath fogs the view as he practically pants in excitement. "Can I go now?" he asks, not even looking back at me.

I drive Mario to school when I've got the time. Still trying to be the father our real papa should be. But Vincent had an appointment, so I took the kid instead. I didn't mind.

"Hold on a sec," I say, tugging Mario's sleeve. "Let's talk for a minute."

When he turns from the window, he rolls his eyes at me. I can't get mad when he's got dimples the size of quarters in both his cheeks. Even when he isn't smiling. He looks like a chipmunk, fat face and round nose. I'm still waiting for him to finish that awkward stage of puberty. I'm waiting for the day I wake up and his chubby cheeks have somehow morphed into a square jaw and grown a beard. He's taller now, and he thinks that one hair on his chin is impressive, but his confidence deflates each time his voice cracks.

"What's up, Luca?" he says, knee bouncing impatiently.

I raise an eyebrow. "Got somewhere to be?"

"Just school. Friends."

His phone lights up in his hand and he smiles when he glances at the screen. Definitely a girl.

"Special friends?" I say.

"Nah. I don't know." He shrugs. Lets out an embarrassingly goofy laugh. The sound makes me laugh too.

"Mario, whoever she is…" my voice trails off.

How do I tell him this? How do I explain he shouldn't let himself get too attached because any good girl would run screaming if she knew who the Vittores really were. How do I tell him our father has already started having dinners with Dante Rossi, a fellow general in our mafia. He's even taken calls from the De Lucas in New York. Their princess ran away a little while ago, but I hear the Italian Rose finally returned. Even so, she's too old for Mario, and that little runaway stunt has ruined her reputation. Her loyalty.

I'm not interested in a withered rose.

But what I'm interested in doesn't matter. I'm the underboss of the Italian mafia. I will have a marriage arranged by my father, something that will benefit our organization. So will my sister Serena, and so will Mario. He might be fifteen, but he's old enough to sign a contract. It won't be fulfilled until his chosen bride is eighteen, but both parties will be expected to honor one another. Basically, his bride will remain a virgin and Mario will end whatever flings he has before the wedding date.

This girl who's got him grinning will never be more than a flashing text on his phone. That's the sort of life we live in this organization. I never said it was great, but it can be beautiful, if you're willing to look beyond the lies.

"What is it, Luca?" Mario leans toward me.

I sigh. "You like this girl?"

He can't hide his grin. "I mean. She's just a girl. Not like the ones you snag."

He could literally be talking about any woman in the city at this point. I'm not very discreet about my love life. But I never thought Mario noticed anything.

Speaking of women—my own phone buzzes in my pocket, but I ignore it and clear my throat. "Mario, you've got to be careful."

He wrinkles his nose. "I know how to use protection."

"I wasn't talking about that," I say flatly. "I meant… You're a Vittore. That means our lives are different from the ones your friends at school live."

He seems to understand, staring down at his hands with a contemplative look on his face. I know this isn't the first time he's thought about this. But it might be the first time it's really clicked.

Mario swallows. Clutches his phone. "Luca… What's

something you regret about your life?"

What the heck. He's too serious for a fifteen-year-old. But I answer anyway.

"This life doesn't have room for regrets, Mario. You get the job done and move on. That's all you can ever do in our world."

"Okay," he says slowly. "What's something you fear?"

I scratch the stubble on my jaw, a peppering of dark hair that stands out against my olive-toned skin. "I fear for you guys. You know? Like, if something happened to my family, and I couldn't do anything about it. I couldn't stop it." I shrug. "I guess I have a fear that one day I'll look back and say I wasn't enough."

Mario doesn't respond. He just sits there chewing his bottom lip. Thinking.

"What's going on, Mars?" I say slowly.

He seems to snap out of it, flashing his cheery grin so I can see all of his shiny braces. But it looks forced.

"You know you can talk to me, right?" I say. "I'm the underboss. There's nothing I can't fix for you."

Mario nods. "I'm good, Luca. You did help me, actually."

"How?"

He looks up at me, like a kid staring at his father. "You made me realize I *am* enough."

Enough for what…

I want to ask what he's talking about, but the school bell rings loudly enough for me to hear in our car outside. We both jump and Mario curses.

I whack him in the back of his head. "Language."

He rolls his eyes. "I've heard you say worse."

"I'm more than twice your age. I can say whatever I want. Now get to class."

Mario swings the door open and then leans into the window after it's shut. "Thanks, Luca. I'll see you later."

"You're welcome, kid."

I watch him jog toward his ridiculously expensive private school. A herd of other rich brats descend onto the lawn and walkway, but I can make out Mario's bright yellow backpack in the crowd. I'm not his father, but with us being so many years apart, it's hard not to feel protective of him. Especially in this awful world we live in. Whenever I drive him to school, I always watch him until he's inside.

But I didn't that time.

My phone buzzes again and I can't resist any longer. I dig it out of my pocket and glance at the screen, grinning wider than Mario had when I see the picture I've been sent. It's a babe I hooked up with the night before. Don't even know how she got my number, but I'm glad she did.

I glance back up at the school to check on Mario, but he's gone. There are a hundred other kids out there, so I figure he made it inside. With a stupid smile on my face, I put my car in drive and speed home to the girl I left in bed.

That's the sin I carry.

I carry the weight of my brother's last words. That he would see me later. I carry the guilt of checking my phone when I should've been watching. I carry the sin of failure. I carry my greatest fears.

I was right there. I was ten feet away. And he was taken right from under me.

I carry the shame that when it mattered most, I truly wasn't enough.

1

Morgan

When I was a little girl, fairytales taught me that happiness could only be found in misery. Think about it, Cinderella was basically an abused prisoner before she met the prince. Sleeping beauty pricked her finger because some hag was jealous of her. Snow White actually died—oh my gosh. Even Jane was chased through a forest by ravaging gorillas before getting rescued by Tarzan, and she wasn't even a princess. That wasn't even a fairytale! But the lesson is the same.

Pain is beauty.

But that's the beauty of pain, don't you think? After a little suffering, your prince charming will come along. Like a reward. Except, that's not really how it works. Sometimes the pain never ends, you just learn how to cope. The idea of a happily ever after is a lie. But it's a beautiful lie. A lie so sweet on my lips I'd rather swallow that than honey. I'd rather whisper the curse of fairytale love than face the truth in this dark reality.

I can't think of a more beautiful lie than true love.

"Stop being gloomy, Morgan." I pinch myself as I march down the block. I'm heading home from work, trying to block out the maddening negativity that comes with an overworked, underpaid crap job.

"God is love, right?" I think aloud, trying to change the subject to something lighter.

My pastor says God is love. But I grew up without an ounce of love in my life, hopping from foster home to foster home. Each awkward goodbye was met with an equally awkward introduction as one more family fell victim to my cute dimples and decided to give me a chance.

I was awful to my foster families.

Like a little gremlin, I destroyed the house, destroyed their trust, and destroyed any hope of ever getting adopted. I was angry and mean and tired of being given back. Kicked out. Abandoned. So I started things off with an attitude and a chip on my shoulder. No point in building hope that wouldn't last.

I know I deserved to be abandoned. I never gave any of those poor foster parents a chance. The nicer they were, the meaner I became. If you cut open my chest, you wouldn't find a heart. You'd find a little monster with fangs.

I think it's still there, tamed and subdued by a God I gave my life to a year ago when I was released from the foster system and set loose on the world. The world kicked my butt. I no longer had a hopeful pair of foster parents to take me in and give me a place to stay until their faith in me dwindled. I had the clothes on my back and a check from the trust fund my foster home had set up for me. 1500 dollars to my name—in a city like Benton, exactly 45 minutes from the Big Apple, that wouldn't last long at all. I had to get it together, and quick.

Eventually, things worked out well enough. I'm a waitress at a diner so cruddy it should be closed down, and I've been attending Bible study a record breaking three weeks in a row.

I'm trying.

This whole love thing is tripping me up, but I force the thoughts away when my phone vibrates in my pocket. It's a cheap burner phone from the dollar store. I've got to put minutes on it and everything, like it's 2008 again. I can't afford an iPhone, okay?

The name on the screen makes me roll my eyes. Travis Williams, my *sort of* boyfriend. He's a little cheesy, but I met him at church, so I figure he's safe. Right now, I don't have much of a social life. I'm trying to lay low because I got myself mixed up in awful business and taking chances with strangers could be the difference between life or death right now. I'm not being dramatic.

Six months ago, I witnessed a murder.

I was walking home from Bible study when it happened. The weather was awful, it'd started raining hard, so I ducked into an alley to take cover. I had no way of knowing that someone was getting beaten in the back of that alley until it was too late.

When I lifted my head and wiped rain from my long lashes, I found myself staring at five white-haired men as they stomped a teenager into the concrete. They were too distracted to see me, and I was too afraid to look away—not even when one of the men pulled out his gun and shot the kid. In the head.

Since then, I've been on the run. Well … I spent two weeks in a witness protection program, but I got paranoid about being hunted down and killed, so I skipped town.

I grew up in the system. I know better than anyone that the police cannot protect me from the men who murdered that kid. They weren't just random thugs. They were men dressed in nice suits—which could only mean they were involved in organized crime. Gangsters. Mafiosi.

Where I'm from, the mafia is not a legend of old. They're very real and very present in Benton, New York. And if my suspicions about the identity of that kid's killer are true, then I could be in serious trouble. I witnessed an assassination and my testimony in court could put a lot of powerful people behind bars.

I don't trust the police to keep me safe. So I ran away and decided to survive on my own as best I could. That's how I made it through the foster system, dodging abusers hidden in plain sight, barely escaping smiling foster parents who would have touched me, hit me, or done worse.

I learned at an early age that the best way to survive is not to take any chances, so I certainly didn't take any with this.

Except … I've been living on the run for six months now. Hopping from motel to motel, holding down a dead end, cash-paying job, using the money to do little more than survive. Buy clothes from the thrift store, buy food—only canned because I can take it with me in a pinch—buy new documents so I can legally change my name.

The only smidge of freedom I allow myself is church. I don't go as often as I should, but I go enough to give myself a passing dream of a social life. And so that someone will remember me when this thing inevitably blows up.

I know it's dangerous to develop any sort of meaningful relationship with anyone, but I'm dying for human connection. I've been doing this for six months now. Looking over my shoulder and living like a street rat can only last for so long before you start to wonder if it's all worth it. I don't know how many more cans of beef stew I can survive off, or how many more nights I can spend in the motel room I rent by the week.

Getting close to Travis isn't a good idea, but he's a corny little church boy. I trust him.

We've been texting and calling for about a month, and last week I let him kiss me. He'd driven me home from work and didn't ask for gas money, so I felt like I owed him. In my defense, I'd eaten leftover Greek salad from work with plenty of red onions so I was happy to smack him with my fresh breath if it meant I wouldn't have to walk home like I am right now.

A smile wiggles across my face as I stare at the screen of my phone. I wonder if Travis will give me a ride home tonight.

"Hey," I answer the phone, hoping I sound happy to hear from him. I'm not super attracted to Travis, but he isn't pushy, and he gives me rides—and also doesn't complain about onion breath. I feel like there's potential here.

"Hey, little ghost," he says teasingly. That's his very weird nickname for me. My name is Morgan Blank. That's not the name I was born with, but I changed it when I got new documents. I picked Morgan because there are millions of Morgans; if any mobsters are looking for me, they won't track my name down that easily. And I picked Blank because I'd never been adopted and had never met my real parents as a kid. I felt like I was literally a nobody. So Blank seemed like a fitting last name.

I told all of this to Travis. Even the part about me being on the run. I know it was dumb, but like I said, I'm tired of living like a ghost. If I get caught, I want someone to know why. I want someone besides those gangsters and the police to know the truth and to know who I am.

I didn't tell Travis my real name, but he also didn't ask. I honestly don't think he believes any of it, which works out for me. He said the story behind my current name was *funny*. According to him, I'm a ghost because I belong to no one—I'm dead inside and neither heaven nor hell will take me.

It's probably the craziest thing I've ever heard, but he'd bought me 500 minutes so he could talk to me on the phone that night, so I obliged his stupid story and didn't mind the nickname.

Potential, okay?

"Hey, Travis," I say into the phone. I don't have a nickname for him. He's just Travis.

"Where are you right now? I stopped by the grocery store. I was thinking I could come over tonight and you could make me dinner."

I fall silent. Travis went to the store to pick out things for *me* to cook for *him*. In my own kitchen. I mean … My fridge has an orange bell pepper and a container of leftovers from the diner inside of it right now. I'm not going to complain about cooking Travis dinner if it means he'll stock my motel room mini fridge. It's like an even exchange. I think.

"Sure," I finally say. "I'll cook dinner. What'd you have in mind?"

He chuckles into the phone. "How about lasagna?"

"Sure."

Whatever.

"I'll see you soon, then. When will you get home?"

"I'm walking from work. Maybe thirty minutes."

He sucks his teeth. "I'm hungry now, Morgan."

"You can come pick me up."

"Actually, I'm on the other side of town. At the store. You know?"

I fight the urge to sigh. "Then I'll see you when I get home."

"So, you're going to make me wait outside for you?"

"I'm not giving you a key to my apartment, Travis."

He's been dropping hints since we kissed, but I don't care how many groceries, minutes, or whatever else he buys for me. I will never share my home with anyone. It's a tacky motel room with a mini fridge, a microwave, and an electric stovetop I bought from a garage sale. The shower is stained and smells like fungus. The blanket is threadbare. But it's my haven. The one sliver of space on this earth that is mine. Just mine. Proof that I exist.

I won't split that with some guy who's so desperate he'll suck onion fumes out of my throat just to say he got a little action. There's potential with Travis, but not *that much* potential. Let's be real.

"If I had a key, I could go in and put up all the groceries for you," he offers in a singsong voice.

"And start dinner as well?" I grunt back.

He sighs. "I'll be parked out back. Call when you get here."

"Alright. See y—"

He hangs up. I'm not even mad. I just want my stupid groceries.

I frown at my phone before I tuck it away in my back pocket. As soon as it's gone, something cold and wet plops onto my shoulder and I groan. Perfect. It's raining now, and I've still got another half-hour of walking to do. I pick up my pace while it's still a light drizzle, but after a few minutes, I start getting hit by more and more of those fat raindrops, so I break into a light jog. I'm wearing combat boots and ripped jeans with an oversized flannel. Comfortable but not something I want to run through the rain in. Still, I haven't got a choice.

As a new Christian, I'm learning not to be superstitious anymore. But this weather reminds me way too much of what I went through six months ago. Don't get me wrong, it has certainly rained since then. I've even had to walk home in it a few times. But something is in the air today, something I cannot place my finger on.

For now, I tuck my chin as it really starts to pour. By the time my raggedy motel comes into view, I'm soaked and *so* not in the mood to deal with Travis. But I don't see his car in the parking lot. He must have gotten tired of waiting on me.

As I walk through the front doors and nod hello to old man Whinnie who watches the front desk, I check my phone and see a stack of messages from Travis asking why I'm taking so long. I text him back.

Home now. Where r u?

I tuck my phone under my arm as I unlock my door. Travis replies almost right away, and I giggle when the phone buzzes under my pit, tickling me—but my laughter is caught in my throat when I push my door open. Instead of walking into my little haven, I'm shoved inside from behind. I hit the ground hard, my phone slipping from my grasp, and then I roll to the side so I can try to defend myself. But my attacker is faster than me.

As soon as I glance up, I see the bottom of a boot, and everything goes black.

2

Luca

Something smells awful. Sour. Rotten. The smell is bad enough that it wakes me from my slumber. With an angry groan, I sit up in bed and very quickly realize I am not alone. The sheets rustle beside me, black silk falling away to reveal a smooth, feminine thigh.

I have no idea who that thigh belongs to.

I lean over and sniff the bundled-up person next to me. The smell isn't coming from this woman. She smells like fresh flowers. I get a good whiff of it when she rolls over and the covers shift to reveal a second woman beside her.

It's at this moment that I realize I might have drunk too much last night. My head starts to ache as snippets of the night before tumble into my foggy memory. I groan and toss my legs over the bed—that's when I find the culprit of the awful smell. It's a puddle of vomit I nearly step in.

I wrinkle my nose, gag at the awful smell, and then gag again at the smell of my own morning breath. This is not a great way to start the day, but I've got to keep going. If the time on the glowing clock of my bedside table is correct, then I'm very late for a very important meeting right now.

In two minutes flat, I stumble into the bathroom, splash water over my face, take a shot of mouthwash, and then toss on a nice enough shirt and my freshest slacks. By the time I walk out of my room, I look good enough to fool the servants who offer me food as I take a shortcut through the kitchen. I know my father won't be fooled, but I also know he won't say anything.

Lately, we've been doing this thing where we entirely ignore all the massive problems in our lives. Like the fact that I drink too much. Or the fact that he's a dying old man. We also ignore—

My blood freezes when I round the corner to leave the kitchen. It's Mario, leaning against the counter as he scrolls through his phone with a stupid grin on his face. I know without even snooping that he's looking at something he shouldn't, but when he glances up, he plays it cool, even winks as he waves at me.

"Morning, Luca. Can I get a ride to school?"

I swallow thickly. "What the heck, Mario…"

He stands there, still grinning. Still waiting for an answer. A ride to school.

When I blink, he vanishes. And his image is replaced by a gush of tears that blur my eyes. *He's dead*, I remind myself. *He's dead, Luca. And it's your fault.* That last bit sneaks into my mind unbidden, a whisper against my soul, like a curse I can't escape.

I wasn't enough, the voice sings.

I take a deep breath, clutching my chest. I need to get it together before I enter that meeting. My father may not comment on my tardiness or my appearance, but he will certainly say something if I walk in babbling like a fool.

I *feel* like a fool. Seeing visions of my dead brother. Being haunted by his ghost. I can't sleep without reliving the nightmare of that last car ride. In reality, it was a peaceful day. The most relaxing nightmare I've ever experienced. But it haunts every waking moment of my life now. Mario's last words play on repeat. His grin bubbles to the surface of my memory. Sunlight skittering across the kitchen tiles reminds me of the flash of his metal braces. His bright smile.

See you later, Luca.

I pinch the bridge of my nose. Count to ten. And then I run my hand over my hair and head into the meeting room.

When I walk inside, everyone glances up in surprise, but the shock settles into a welcoming nod as I mumble an apology and then take my place beside my father. He says nothing. Just keeps his dead eyes staring forward, focused on Antonio Caruso who sits across from us.

In an instant, my hangover falls to the back of my mind. My nightmares hush to dark whispers. And I become the man I was raised to be. There's no time for regrets in this life. All you can do is get the job done and move on.

I force myself to focus on this meeting. Force myself to remember that I am the underboss of the Italian mafia. I am my father's chosen heir.

I suddenly feel at home.

Antonio Caruso pours himself a glass of wine and then reaches for a little slice of cheese from the display in the middle of the table. He looks very fat as he does it. Plump little fingers like seasoned sausages grasping for free food. I suppose I cannot blame him, the Carusos are flat broke, he's probably hungry. And even I must admit, the wine is good.

It's a signature bottle from our vineyards in Verona. My grandmother runs the production, tasting a grape from each cluster before giving the OK for plucking. Technically, she isn't my grandmother—she's my father's older sister but she's more than fifteen years older than him and raised him like a mother would. That's why I call her my grandmother because that's all I've ever known her as.

Regardless, she's an eighty-year-old woman with a bent back and gnarled, arthritic fingers. It was those swollen fingers which personally packaged and shipped this bottle to her brother—my father—Vincent Vittore, for his sixty-third birthday this year.

The bottle sits beside Antonio as he *inhales* cheese and olives from the charcuterie board. If I squint, I can make out the oily fingerprints he left on the neck of the bottle. My eyes slide down the glass to rest on the cork he discarded on the table like the cap to a Coke bottle.

Do you know how corks are made?

They come from seasoned, boiled planks of wood cut specifically for the purpose of becoming a cork. Corkwood is special. You cannot use any tree in the woods for this purpose.

You cannot even use certain parts of the tree for a cork. It must come from the phellem layer of bark tissue. The best corks are punched by hand, but no matter how you punch it, it must be dried and then sorted to filter out the best quality.

A cork is significant. Because the quality of the cork can sometimes determine the quality of the wine. If someone cares about the wood which seals their liquid, then you can trust they care about the very grapes which were grown to produce the wine in the first place.

It's the smallest part of the product but it holds the most responsibility. Corks do not merely seal a bottle shut, they prevent oxygen from entering the bottle, which could damage the wine and alter the flavor. Then decades of aging would be reversed.

But even deeper than that, more intimate, more *beautiful* is the fact that a cork oak could take up to 25 years to produce corkwood. The trees I grew up with, running through the sunny vineyards of my grandmother's home while they stood sentinel on the outskirts of our property—those trees are the ones we harvest our corks from.

I climbed those trees as a boy. I hung from their thick branches, counted the splinters in the wood and picked their crinkled leaves in the fall. Those trees grew up with me and the grapes and the bottles in our cellars too. All of us aging, maturing together. I am as much a part of that bottle and that cork as they are a part of the livelihood of the Vittore name.

And now that bottle is being caressed by the greasy hands of Antonio Caruso as he fills yet another glass. He takes a long pull, sucks the flavor off his teeth, and then leans back in his chair. His eyes land on my father who sits silently beside me.

"I think this is a good deal," Antonio says.

Of course he thinks this is a good deal. I've missed the first half of the meeting, but even I know this deal benefits no one but him. At that thought, I slide my gaze over to my father. Vincent Vittore sits as tall as he can in his chair, I bet Antonio hasn't noticed the dark circles beneath his eyes or the way the skin around his cheeks seems to sag now.

Sometimes, I look at my father and wonder when he turned into an old man.

He does not return Antonio's smile, instead, he slides a thick contract across the table and says, "If you are pleased, then..." the rest is left unsaid, and we watch in silence as Antonio licks his lips and reaches for the papers. He quickly scans them and then passes them off to his lawyer who sits beside him, munching on a wheat cracker.

The lawyer coughs, wipes crumbs from his fingers, and takes the contract. "Oh, yes," he says quickly, "this should work."

I clear my throat and feel my father stiffen beside me. He knows I do not like this.

This meeting is an arrangement for my sister's betrothal. She's 24 years old and controls 10 percent of the Vittore organization, she has a degree in business administration and has been working under my father for the last three years. Serena *should* make a lovely bride. As I *should* make a wonderful husband.

I moved here when I was a teenager, didn't speak a lick of English and had never left my grandmother's farm. Now, I run 30 percent of the Vittore business. Throughout my twenties, business was booming. That was why my father allowed my little sister to go to college. In this business, women do not educate themselves. They grow up as spoiled princesses and are married to rich men who expect an heir and a docile attitude. Nothing more.

You don't need a degree to listen to your husband or pump out a son. Most girls in this life are raised under strict standards and married off at 18. Old enough to be a legal adult but young enough to still be a virgin.

My sister Serena is neither young nor virginal. That's exactly why she has no charming marital prospects. That, and the fact that she's educated and runs 10 percent of my father's organization. Mafiosi do not like women like Serena. She is too headstrong. Too old to tame and too experienced to be fooled or impressed. Their wealth and power have no influence over a woman who stands side by side with one of the most powerful men in Benton, New York. Although her husband would have every right to put Serena in her place, no one would dare raise a hand to the daughter of Vincent Vittore. Or the sister of Luca Vittore.

A year ago, Serena's singleness was a joke of the family. My father was proud of her and openly bragged that there was no man in this country who could ever hope to claim his spoiled little girl. But then the diagnosis came in … and our grief doubled when my little brother was taken from us.

That was the nail in the coffin. When Mario died, everything about my father—everything about my *family*—changed. Now, my father won't shut up about his two remaining children getting married off and settling down.

I've been sent on countless dates with a string of eligible women. They were all obedient little flowers, but I'm not ready to get married—much to my father's chagrin. Serena, on the other hand, hasn't had as much ease in avoiding these sticky situations. While my father was liberal enough to allow her an education and even gifted her a small percentage of the family business as a woman, when he realized his life would be cut short, and then Mario's life *was* cut short, he decided to put his foot down.

"I want to see you married and I want to see my grandchildren before it's too late," he'd explained.

Serena managed to escape a few marital arrangements because of her age and because she'd tainted her virtue two years ago, but now we have a serious offer on the table and my father has just handed over the marital contract. He's really going to do it; he's going to make Serena marry this fat little man.

Antonio Caruso is the younger brother of Romeo Caruso, the leader of the Caruso family. Perhaps some starry eyed 18-year-old who doesn't know what she's getting into would be pleased to marry him, despite his size and his age—a ripe 46. But the Carusos are broke. They are beneath us. Always have been.

There is order in the mafia, a code that we live by, if you

can believe it. Some families outrank others, some families are honored not for their money or power but for the simple fact that they've been in this business for longer than the United States has existed. Our organization goes back centuries, and some of the older families are still alive and kicking today, despite all the changes and crackdowns of law enforcement over time.

But the Carusos are neither rich nor powerful, and they certainly haven't been in the mafia long enough to justify an arrangement with the Vittore princess. For as long as I can remember, they have been poor; mostly offering their sons as security guards and grunt men to higher ranking families within the organization.

Antonio has a bastard son who shines my father's shoes on Sundays before he goes to mass. That's how insignificant they are. Which means a woman who runs 10 percent of the Vittore business is a goldmine for Antonio. He doesn't care that Serena is educated, old, and lost her virginity two years ago. He wants her for nothing more than her name and money. Despite this very obvious fact, my father is willing to give Serena to this man. He is that desperate.

I shouldn't be surprised. There are only three things any wise man should fear in this world. The wrath of God. His wife's temper. And cancer.

Vincent Vittore has 18 months left to live, that's if he responds to chemo well enough. After that, I will bury him and take over the business. Permanently. Somehow, he wants Serena and me to both find a spouse and pop out a baby in that short amount of time. He is ready to hand us off to anyone at this point.

Poor Serena, I think, as I watch Antonio reach for a bowl of olives marinated in oil and herbs. He eats them right out of the porcelain bowl with his fingers while his lawyer reads the contract. I watch as he chews with his mouth open and exhales though his nose, making the whiskers of his unruly mustache flutter.

He smacks his lips. "When can I see her?"

My father goes to reply, but I cut him off, "Serena would like to maintain her privacy until the wedding day."

Antonio frowns. "Privacy? She's my woman—"

"Not yet."

Antonio's eyes narrow on me. "Hand me the pen." He opens his palm, greasy fingers wiggling as he nudges his lawyer with his elbow.

"Sir, I haven't finished reading—"

"I didn't ask you that," Antonio snaps. "Pass me the pen, I'm ready to sign."

"But, sir, there could be a clause—"

Antonio shoves to his feet and snatches the contract from his lawyer's hands, but before he can dig an ink pen from his pocket, the door swings open and Serena herself strides in.

Antonio is momentarily stunned—we all are—not only is it uncommon for a woman to enter the room during a business meeting without permission, but Serena isn't supposed to be here right now. I made sure her schedule was full so this meeting would be over by the time she returned from her duties today. Her presence here could only mean one thing.

While my father has buried his illness and his grief in this stupid search for the perfect husband, my little sister and I have spent our time searching for Mario's killer. It didn't take long to find him. We have connections throughout the city, even men on the police force who report to us. But not every cop is on our payroll. Some cops in this city still believe in justice and play by the rules. My father lets them live because he admires their foolish hearts. *Someone* should stick up for justice, right?

Since Mario's death, my father's light-handedness has bitten us in the rear. My brother's killer is in custody. Safe from us. He's awaiting trial like a normal prisoner and will stand before a judge and jury to have his fate handed to him.

His fate is a silver bullet in the barrel of my gun. But I can't give it to him while he's being guarded by these righteous policemen.

The only hope I have is in some eyewitness. That's the only scrap of evidence police have against the man who shot my brother. I'm not surprised, since I know the men responsible are Bratva garbage. Members of the Russian mafia.

Under normal circumstances, I would hunt down my brother's killer myself. I would start a war with the Bratva until my need for vengeance is met. But my father is old and cautious now. He doesn't want to risk a war he may not live to see finished. He wants to close his eyes on this life like a normal old man, with grandkids running around while he rocks in his comfy chair.

He wants to die as if he never lived as a mafia boss.

I get it. I do. But I am not my father. I don't like depending on the police. I don't trust they can do their jobs right. That's exactly why Serena and I took things into our own hands when the cops on our payroll reported the eyewitness as missing six months ago.

The one sliver of hope we had of getting justice for Mario simply disappeared. And police had no answer for it. How on earth they let a witness disappear from *witness protection* is beyond me, but the fact that Serena just entered this very private meeting without permission could only mean she's just found some information on the case.

We all stare as she makes a beeline for my father, her eyes focused entirely on him. I know she's come to relay info to me, but she's already disrespected the chain of command by interrupting us, it would be unforgivably disrespectful for her to speak to me instead of our father. So I sit back in my chair and pretend not to notice when her eyes shift to me for half a heartbeat. It's a quick look, one a stranger would interpret as a simple glance around the room, but I know Serena well enough that we can speak without using words. Whatever she's going to tell my father is truly for me.

Serena's black dress flows around her long legs as she walks, making it appear as if she is gliding across the room. I barely hear the click-clack of her six-inch heels, I'm too distracted by the stressed look on her face. Her eyebrows are drawn together, her red-painted lips are pressed into a tight line. Even a few strands of her thick chocolatey hair have fallen loose from her bun. She doesn't swipe them away as she stops before our father and leans down to speak to him at eye level.

Her voice is low so only he can hear, but I pick up snippets of information. "Police … Mario … investigation—"

My father's eyes grow large, and he clears his throat. "Excuse me, gentlemen, but this meeting must be cut short."

"Cut short?" Antonio waves the contract around. "I was just about to sign, and Serena is here now. We can sign together."

My father stands and Serena takes his arm. Together, they walk to the door without even looking back at Antonio. That leaves me to respond to Mr. Caruso when he snaps his head in my direction. He's so fat, his cheeks quiver with the motion.

"What is the meaning of this?"

I sigh, stand, and straighten my tie. "Mr. Caruso, we will finish this another time."

Until then, I've got to find the little rat who managed to elude police for six months.

3

Morgan

My head aches when I blink into consciousness. I am not in my motel room anymore.

My memory comes back in a violent storm, flashes of the attack playing in my mind as quick and painful as bolts of lightning. My skin prickles as I see the heavy boot crashing into my face again. I feel that dreadful panic all over. Sweat dapples my forehead like it's 80 degrees in the middle of October.

And then I hear footsteps.

I'm not locked in my memory anymore; the sound of those steps is *real*. Someone is coming toward this room. Panic bleeds into raw adrenaline, and for the first time, I glance around the dim space. With escape screaming to the forefront of my mind, the only thing I register is the set of glass double doors blocking entry to a stone balcony. I can climb out of here and escape.

My legs tremble as I swing them over the high bed, I have to leap down to the soft carpet, landing with an inaudible thud.

I'm not sure if the bed is exceptionally high or if I'm just pathetically short. Either way, I wobble to the double doors and gasp when my shaky hands grasp the cool metal—it's locked.

That means I've got to fight. There aren't any weapons around that I can see, so I run to the bedside table, heart pounding faster than the steps I hear, and yank open the drawer. The only thing I see is a hardcover Bible. Honestly, that'll do. It's heavy and sturdy and good enough to scare the devil.

I grab the Book and run barefoot to the door, tucking myself against the wall just in time to hear the soft click of the lock. Huh. So I was locked inside.

I stare at the knob as it slowly twists, willing my breathing to slow down so I can remain calm. I've spent my life dodging sketchy people and the last six months running from murderers. I can face whoever is coming for me now.

I see a glossy black shoe enter the room; it's followed by a long leg that stretches into a tall man.

It's too dim to make out any significant features, but I can tell money when I see it. He's wearing a crisp shirt that hugs his frame as if it were made for his body alone. He takes up a lot of space, but not in a way that makes him seem so big, his presence suddenly makes me feel *small.* I can smell his cologne from here, rich and savory. Hints of allspice and oakwood. But it's the way he walks that makes my gaze narrow. He walks in like he's got every right to be here, only stopping once he realizes the bed is empty. That's when his rich boy demeanor shifts into something darker—something dangerous.

In an instant, this well-dressed man becomes a predator. His sharp eyes flit through the room as he hunts for me, checking every crevice. Except the spot behind him.

On bare feet, I step forward with the Bible raised. He glances back, but I'm already mid-swing.

His voice is deep enough that I feel his grunt in my bones when the hit lands. He stumbles sideways, and I throw the Bible at him and dash for the door. I make it two steps before my hair is in his hands.

I scream as I careen backwards, feet kicking up, arms flailing. A strong arm wraps around my middle and I'm suddenly lifted into the air. I get a front row view when a long leg whips out in front of me and kicks the bedroom door shut. I am locked inside with him.

My fear turns to anger, it churns inside of me and rumbles out like a volcanic eruption. I twist my body and shift away from the strong arm that holds me. The motion is quick enough to catch my attacker off guard, and his grip on my hair loosens. I turn and tackle him, and we roll like alley cats.

He hisses something in a language I don't understand, but you don't need to study a new tongue to know cursing when you hear it. I'm on top of him, clawing at his eyes, screaming like I've lost my mind. I was kidnapped and transported to God knows where. My only chances of making it out of here alive is killing this man. So I fight with every intention of taking his life.

And I quickly realize my greatest effort is simply not

enough.

In a fit of anger, the man bucks his hips forward, throwing me off balance. Then he grabs me by the back of my neck and rolls us so he's on top. He pins my legs with his own, then reaches for my clawing hands. I scream and try to bite him, but it's pointless. All I manage to do is piss him off.

He lets out a feral growl when he's got my hands pinned above my head, my body pressed into the carpet beneath his heavy weight.

"Stop fighting!" he shouts in my face.

English. It takes my brain a moment to register that he said that in English.

"Let me go!" I shout back.

He leans back enough for me to see his face, the anger in his eyes. It's a mottled look of rage, but it doesn't seem aimed at me. I mean, yeah, he's probably mad that I whacked him over the head with a Bible, but the look on his face is more insulted than hostile.

I stare at him. "What do you want from me? Why did you kidnap me?"

"Do you know who I am?" he asks.

The answer is obvious.

"You're one of the men from the alley. Six months ago."

One of the men who killed that kid. And now he's finally hunted me down to finish off the only person who could put him in prison for life.

A fleeting look of confusion passes over the man's face—and in that brief moment, he lets his guard down. I yank my hand free and almost smile at the surprise on his face before the heel of my hand connects with his jaw. He grunts and curses in that language again, releasing my other hand. That gives me the chance to shove him backwards and crawl to safety across the room.

I know it's stupid, but I yank on the balcony doors again, angry, frightened tears burning my cheeks. *Please, please open!*

The man behind me sighs and says only one word. "Effervescent."

The calmness in his tone wraps barbed wire around my heart. The voice is deep, the sort of smooth timbre you hear in dreams, strong and stern as the mighty oak outside the balcony doors. When it reaches my ears, it curls around my fears and shakes them loose. Just like the burnt ochre leaves outside, the guard I've built up breaks and falls away. His voice is an autumn wind, and I am a crumpled leaf, defenseless against its subtle might.

Do not mistake me. It isn't the *sound* of his voice that shatters me. It's the word he's just said. *Effervescent.* That's my name—my *real* name. Before I ran away and changed it to Morgan Blank.

Whoever this man is, he knows who I am. Which means I am most certainly screwed.

"Effervescent Storm," he says from across the room, as if to prove that he wasn't throwing random vocabulary out there. He does know who I am. He's somehow found my full name and then he found me.

I am trapped with someone who knows what he's doing.

With a gasp, I yank on the balcony doors again. My eyes blur with frantic tears. *I don't want to die!* That's the only thought in my head.

"It's locked," says the man, like I don't know this.

I let out a yucky sob that almost sounds like a burp and place my forehead against the glass. I'm so sweaty, my head actually slides to the side and makes that squeaky noise you get when you clean your windows. It makes me feel 100 times more pathetic.

"I had my men check the room for anything you could use as a weapon," the man explains, then he chuckles, and I hear the sound of material shifting. He must have stooped to retrieve the Bible I beat him with because he says next, "Apparently, the Word of God really is a weapon."

I don't say anything, I just keep my head pressed against the cool glass and focus on my breathing.

"Turn around."

It's a command I'm not stupid enough to disobey. So I take a deep breath and turn to face this stranger. His clothes are disheveled from rolling around on the floor with me. There's a dark spot on his jaw that will likely bruise. The sight of it almost makes me smile despite the situation. If he kills me, at least I'll die knowing I fought hard enough to leave him sore.

But … now that I'm really looking at this man, I realize he looks nothing like the white-haired men I saw in that alley. He's a little younger, and he's got chocolate brown hair and olive skin. His jaw is square and strong as his broad shoulders. He looks like he could go another round with me and not even break a sweat. I wonder if he's even hurt, even though his chin is starting to bruise.

"Are you going to kill me?" I ask without thinking. Because it doesn't really matter who he is, he still kidnapped me.

The man's face freezes, like this thought has honestly never crossed his mind. Then the muscles of his mouth twitch and he makes what I can only assume is supposed to be a smile. I won't call it that, because it vanishes so quickly I wonder if I imagined it. Now his brows are flattened across the plane of his smooth forehead, and he's tilting his head to the side.

"Do you know who I am?" he asks for the second time.

"One of the men I saw six months ago," I say for the second time. "Or someone who works for them."

His expression darkens, and when he speaks, his voice is not a strong oak-like timbre, it's the hiss of a viper. "The Stepanovs. They're the ones you're talking about."

I blink once, waiting for that word to make sense to me.

"Russian mafia," the stranger says.

It clicks. Their nice suits, and white hair—*not white*, I correct my memory. It was platinum blonde. Like the snowy strands of silk you'd see on a pretty albino. Suddenly, their mysterious accents have a proper name and category. They weren't strange foreigners, they were Russians. And the accent of their victim…

I look up at this man with his olive skin and dark brown hair. His sharp eyes that seem to cut through me, as if he has somehow bypassed my permission and gained access to the truth hidden in my memories. He has the same accent as the boy who begged for his life in that alley.

"Who are you?" I ask cautiously.

This time, he does smile. And it doesn't vanish as quickly as before. "My name is Luca Vittore; I am the underboss of the Italian mafia. An enemy of the Stepanov name. And older brother of Mario Vittore, the boy you saw in that alley six months ago."

The boy I saw get shot in his head.

I ran away because I didn't think the police could keep me safe. I ran because I thought it was only a matter of time before that boy's killers caught up to me and killed me so I couldn't testify in court. But I was wrong. I'd been hunted down by a different force. A man who wanted vengeance.

I can see that vengeance burning in his gaze. Two brown eyes ablaze with rage so strong, they look like tongues of fire in his face. The anger he feels is alive. All-consuming.

I'd wondered how I managed to live with so much frustration and fear all those months, but I can't imagine the burden of living with such rage. Which is worse? Rage or fear. That feels like a trick question, because I feel like you can't have one without the other.

So that makes me wonder. What does Luca Vittore fear?

When he steps forward and cups my chin, I think I have a hint. "I've finally found you," he says in a murmur.

He's afraid of losing me. The only chance he has at seeing his brother's killer brought to justice.

"Tell me about that night," he says softly.

The command catches me off guard. For some reason, I expected him to already know what happened. He managed to track me down, after all. But as I look into his syrupy eyes, I see the pain behind the rage. He isn't asking because he doesn't know, he's asking because he doesn't want to forget.

Anything he knows about his brother's murder would have come from a written testimony or a taped interview. Hearing it directly from me would make it fresh. Real.

"Tell me," he says, and his voice is almost strained.

I wonder what the pain does for him. If he's torturing himself or building his resilience. Using the pain to fuel his determination.

I swallow and slowly nod. "Okay, I'll tell you everything."

The story leaks from my mouth like dirty water sucking down a drain. The details feel gross and make my head spin as they summon vivid flashes of memories from that night. Luca stands and listens intently, still cupping my chin, staring into my eyes and hanging on to each word. He catches every syllable, each one like a spark threatening to ignite the furnace I see building behind his eyes.

He has heard this story on the news a million times, replayed it in his mind even more. But hearing it now is like opening a fresh wound, the details like acid running over raw, bloody skin. He closes his eyes when I tell him how Mario cried out when the gun went off. And when I clamp my mouth shut, I feel his fingers tighten on my jaw, still cupping my chin.

"The men who killed him," Luca says in a raspy, strained voice, "describe them to me."

Their faces are a blur. I've described them to the police countless times, but it was evening, and it was rainy. I never got a good look at anyone.

"Any detail will help," he says.

I exhale slowly, racking my brain. One thing stands out in my memory—not a facial feature, or even the sounds of their sharp accents.

"One of them had a tattoo," I whisper. I saw it when the gun went off because I'd screamed and caught their attention, crouching in the alley from the rain. I'd turned and taken off as soon as their heads jerked in my direction, but there was a moment of pure silence that'd hung in the air, like time had slowed down to take a breath. And in that moment, where my brain interpreted everything in slow-motion, I saw a black blur crawling up the neck of one of the men.

In my head, it'd been a bug because that's what bugs do. Crawl. But as the memory swells in my head now, the image clears up and realization pops the cloud of mystery like a pregnant bubble.

"A scorpion," I say, almost to myself. "He had a scorpion tattooed onto his neck.

I tilt my chin up to see a wicked grin dancing across Luca's face. I don't know if I should be afraid or not. The sight is scary enough that I try to take a step back, but I'm already leaning against the glass doors. There's nowhere for me to go.

He kidnapped me because I'm the key to his brother's justice. The key to his vengeance. I don't think he wants to hurt me. I have to remind myself of this as I watch the madness glow behind his eyes.

I am looking at a man consumed by grief, a grief that has turned pitch black and spoiled. Now it sits rotten in the back of his mind, poisoning his every thought. Using his pain against him. He is beyond mourning, now he is hunting. And I've just given him his prey.

"Are you going to kill me?" I ask again. Just to be sure.

He shakes his head. "It took me six months to find you. *Six months* just to track you to some seedy motel in the middle of a rundown town two hours away from Benton." He chuckles like he can't believe where he found me. "I need you alive," he says. "That means I'm never letting you go."

4

Luca

When I tell Effervescent that she will never escape from me again, I expect her to get angry or defiant, maybe even try to yank open those balcony doors again. She'd greeted me with a surprise attack and had fought hard enough that I honestly respected her for it. So I am absolutely caught off guard when her shoulders slump and her eyes roll to the back of her head.

She lets out a little whimper as the last of her will peters away. And then she crumples. It happens so fast that I reach out to catch her without even thinking. Now, I'm holding a small woman in my arms as I stand in the middle of my bedroom.

Yes, this room is mine. It was not wise to lock a suspicious prisoner inside my own bedroom, but this is the safest place for her to be right now. I don't trust anyone except my sister. And Serena has no reason to be in here, so it seemed like a good idea.

I lift Effervescent so I can carry her to my bed like a bride.

It's the middle of the afternoon now. Putting her back in bed will ruin her sleep schedule, but it's not like I can do anything else. She's passed out. Besides, I've already got the information I wanted.

A Russian Bratva with a scorpion tattoo on his neck. That might sound like a drop in the bucket, but Benton has more Italians than Russians—there's even a tiny French mafia growing in the shadows. The point is, I'll be able to narrow down the suspects with that information. It's only a matter of time.

I look down at Effervescent, gingerly setting her on my blankets. She does not deserve such gentle handling. She attacked me, hard. And had every intention of killing me. I don't blame her. She was kidnapped and locked in my room against her will; I had expected hostility. But if she believes in the God of the Bible, she'd better thank Him when she wakes. Any other man would have reacted by drawing his weapon.

My eyes narrow as I stare at this wild woman. I didn't expect any of this to be easy. I just wish that it was.

For the last year, my family has been slowly falling apart. My father got sick, which inspired my mother to start dragging him to church—a mafia queen as a Christian is not a good idea—my little brother died, and now my little sister is one step away from being sold to some middle-aged fart who wants her for her money.

All of that ... and here I am, somehow surviving in the middle. My mother thinks she can atone for the sins of our family all by herself, my father thinks it's more important for us to get married than to find my brother's killer, and Serena is too busy running from suitors to stand by my side.

The only sense of peace I have in my life right now is this woman who lies unconscious before me. She is the key to it all. And she tried to take that from me. She ran away and took with her the one chance I had at seeing my brother's murderer get what he deserves.

How dare she….

If she would have had her way, she'd still be living on the streets. And the trial would have come and gone, and we would have had no eye-witness, and the killer would have walked free. All so she could run around the city like a street rat.

What a selfish woman.

I stare at her, wondering how easy it would be to kill her now. To wrap my fingers around her slender neck and squeeze. I want to do it. I want to release every ounce of rage I feel coursing through me every day. But I need her alive. No matter how much her cowardice pisses me off, I cannot kill her, and I cannot allow anyone else to harm her. She is my responsibility now.

I've taken the time to look into this woman. There's a detective on my payroll who passes me information, he was more than willing to hand over everything he had on his star witness when she went missing. I learned that she's an orphan who was never adopted by any of her foster parents. I learned that her name is Effervescent Storm, one of the ugliest names I've ever heard. Mercifully, she goes by Effy most of the time. Except now.

After she escaped from witness protection, she changed her name to Morgan Blank which is only marginally better than her real name. And she lived in conditions that were only relatively better than where we found her. It seems she's always been a lost cause, living hand-to-mouth, hopping from place to place. Never really belonging anywhere at all.

I didn't need to look into her file to see how lost and alone she is. The look in her eyes as she fought me, screamed at me, tried to claw my eyes out. That wasn't just survival instinct, it was anger. The same burning anger I feel every day. But our fuel is different.

Behind the curtain of Effy's rage is something wild and mysterious, a part of herself she likely doesn't even understand. She is untamed. I am the exact opposite. Years of this life has sharpened my rage, smoothing the jagged knife's edge into a razor blade. My anger has cut out my heart, replaced it with something dark. Something with fangs and poison.

The look in Effy's eyes is something I see in my own mirror every day. But there's something else there that isn't in my eyes. Something bright. Something innocent. Something that could ensnare me if I look too closely.

Beyond that, I also see loneliness. And I imagine that deep-seated loneliness is what drove her to make the mistake of confessing her messy secrets to her trashcan boyfriend. He ratted her out in a heartbeat. Called up one of my guys with info on a girl running from a murder he'd heard about on the news.

He sold us her location for five grand in cash. It was more

than what the police were offering for tips, so I can't really blame him. But still… I can't stop thinking of how different this would be if he hadn't gone to one of my men. And then I think of the fact that we wouldn't be here at all if Effy hadn't run away in the first place. Now I don't know who to be angry at, but Effy's right here, so I guess it's her.

When I place her head against the pillows, I get a good look at this small woman. She's an inch over five feet tall, tiny compared to my 6'1. She can't weigh more than 110 pounds, which isn't surprising considering the nasty motel my men tracked her to. She's probably half-starved and feral.

Outside, the wind blows and the curtains flap over the window, letting in a sliver of sunlight to cut through the darkness of the room. In that moment, I see her face very clearly. She's young, even younger than Serena, with a round nose and full lips. But there's something else I see that makes me frown.

There's a bruise on her face.

I couldn't see it at first because her skin is brown and her afro hair is so thick and puffy it covers part of her face. I reach forward and brush some of it away so I can see her better.

The bruise looks bad. Like she's been kicked in the face. The sight ignites a furnace within me, a careful anger that could storm into an inferno or burn out like the flicker of a dying candle.

I never hit Effy. We'd scuffled on the floor, and I'd grabbed her by her hair when she'd first attacked me, but I'd never hit her. Not a single time. All that wrestling we did was her attacking and me trying to hold her down. So I know this bruise isn't my doing.

Then again, it could be from anything. Her useless boyfriend who ratted her out could have put his hands on her before we found her. She could've had a scuffle with a dissatisfied customer at her awful dead-end job. Or one of my men could have done this.

I gave them specific instructions not to hurt her. I told them to be discreet and careful. She is our captive, but she isn't our enemy. We kidnapped her to keep her safe, not to *break* her.

With a huff, I turn and storm out of my room, not at all surprised to see my assistant Lorenzo standing in the hall. He's a short man with glasses and a well-trimmed beard. Lorenzo has worked for my family since I was a child, he was my father's assistant but when Vincent's illness prevented him from working as much, I took Lorenzo under my wing instead. He follows my orders just as easily as he followed my father's. And he's a lot less distracting than my last assistant, whom I slept with. She taught me the awful downside of mixing work with pleasure. By the time Lorenzo came to me about needing work, I was happy to let that woman go.

Now, I run my hand through my hair as I march down the hall, not even glancing back as I say, "Talk to me."

He clears his throat. "Miss Serena is currently with your father—"

"I know that."

Of course, she's with him. When she interrupted our

meeting, she told him there was news about Mario's case but that was for me. When she got him out of that room, she probably made up something silly to keep him distracted while I handled the serious stuff.

The truth is that our father has no idea we've tracked down the star witness of this case and are currently holding her hostage in our family manor. He can't know because if he finds out, he will get angry enough to give himself an ulcer.

My father wants us to trust the justice system. Ironic for the don of the Italia mafia, right?

Since the diagnosis, he's been trying to turn his life around, as much as a mafia boss can. That means he's refused to give the order to bring hell to the Stepanov's doorsteps.

"Mario wouldn't want more bloodshed," is what he keeps telling me.

My father is willing to bet everything on the testimony of a street rat.

I don't have as much faith in our justice system as he does. That's why I have half the Benton police on my payroll. To make sure crap like this doesn't happen to our family. But it *did* happen. Which means something isn't right. Someone got to the prince of the Vittore family, and no one has died for it.

My father has gotten weak. He can blame that on his illness, he can even blame it on his newfound faith as he begs God to forgive him for the lifetime of nightmares he breathed into this city. But I am neither ill nor pious. I will not sit by and let Mario's killers walk around as I wait for *justice* to prevail.

I will *be* that justice. I will make the Stepanovs pay. And that woman in my bedroom is the key to getting that done. She saw their faces. She knows exactly who was there that night. The police managed to take the gunman into custody, but there were four others present. I've read Effy's written statement. I know every gritty detail of my brother's death. And now I've heard them firsthand. Five people put Mario in an early grave, but the cops have only made one arrest. I'll give them that one. Because I'd have to tear down the prison doors to get to him. But the other four are mine.

"Any other news?" I grunt to Lorenzo.

He clears his throat again. "Your cousin is in your office."

I stop walking. Lorenzo walks into my back.

"Sorry, sir," he mumbles, adjusting his circular glasses. Lorenzo looks like a mafioso from a 1920s Hollywood movie. He's almost adorable as his cheeks tint and he straightens his bowtie.

"I'll be in my office for the next hour," I grunt. "Round up the men who brought in the woman. I want to see them as soon as possible."

When I look down, Lorenzo is blinking at me in confusion, but he knows his place is to obey, not to question, so he simply nods and says loyally, "I'll find them, sir."

5

Luca

As expected, my cousin Louis Valentino is waiting in my office when I walk through the cherrywood door. He does not smile when he sees me, but I'm not surprised. He's not here for fun.

"Cousin," I say with a nod.

His mouth twists in anger, he has to unscrew his jaw before he can speak. "You're the son of Vincent Vittore. Out of respect for your rank within our organization, I'll say this as kindly as possible."

I roll my eyes, crossing my office to pour myself a drink at the display. "Spit it out, Little Louie." That's his childhood nickname, though he outgrew it around age 10 when he hit 6'0. Thankfully, he hasn't grown much since then, but he certainly threw his weight around when we were kids, using his height to his advantage whenever we played sports together. Everyone wanted Little Louie on their team.

Louis narrows his eyes at me, his voice is a growl as he says, "What the heck is going on, Luca? I'm getting calls about a kidnapping!"

I nod. Check my watch. We picked up the woman last night, and Louis has made his way to my family estate by the next afternoon. Not bad timing, honestly. Perhaps the police force isn't full of incompetent fools after all. That'd be a lot easier to believe if Effy hadn't gotten away in the first place, of course.

"There has been a kidnapping," I admit.

Louis takes the gun off his belt and sits it on my desk. "I'm going to take this off because I'm very tempted to use it right now."

He wouldn't dare, but his cute little temper is enough to make me chuckle.

"You're being dramatic," I tell my cousin.

"You need to return the girl. She belongs in police custody. Witness protection."

"She escaped from witness protection. Who's to say she won't escape again? And who's to say *my* men will be the ones who find her when she does?"

I don't need to remind him of how awful things would be if Bratva men had found her instead.

"You found her; I'll give you credit for that. But she's still a witness to a murder. You have to give her back," Louis says, pointing his finger at me.

I narrow my gaze over the rim of my glass. Suddenly, the whiskey in my cup burns more than it had a moment ago.

"Careful where you point that," I warn.

Louis retracts his finger, but his voice still sounds angry

when he says, "I have been loyal to you."

"As you should be. We *are* family, Louis."

"I'm still a *cop*, Luca!" he practically yells. "I've got a job to do! What do you think the rest of the force will say when they find out the person responsible for kidnapping a star witness is my own cousin!"

I shrug. "You're the one who insisted on joining the force. You grew up in the mafia. And after everything you learned about those pigs—about what they think of men like us—you still decided to join them."

Louis shakes his head.

"My father allowed you to join the force on one condition."

"That was years—"

"What was the condition, Louis?" I cut him off.

He sighs. Sets his hands on his hips and looks at me seriously. He's calmer now. Knows he should choose his words wisely.

"What was the condition you were given when joining the police force?" I repeat.

Louis licks his lips. "That I remain loyal to the family."

"Which means reporting *to* us instead of reporting *on* us."

Louis pinches the bridge of his nose. "I still have a job to do, Luca. I have a wife and a kid. That means I can't lose my job." His voice begins to rise. "Which means you cannot make things difficult by sticking your mafia nose into my case!"

I calmly set my tumbler onto my desk and walk over to my cousin, but before I can address his tone, a knock rings out at my door.

"I've got the men from the assignment earlier," Lorenzo says from the other side.

I smile. "Bring them in."

Three burly Italians darken my doorway, marching in to stand before my desk like obedient little grunts. I recognize them as typical guards, but they are not men I would have picked for this job myself. Obviously, I would've picked guys who understand the rules I set are not for fun. They're meant to be followed.

"When I sent you out to retrieve the girl, I told you not to hurt her," I say to the guards.

The one in the middle looks nervous all of a sudden. He doesn't even look me in the eye when I stare at him, instead his gaze slides to the man on his right, and I immediately know who broke the rules.

I walk over to the man on his *left*. He does not expect me to hit him, so the howl he lets out when his nose cracks under my fist is filled with both pain and shock.

I hear Louis curse behind me, but I ignore him as I walk over to the guy on the right now. The rule breaker. He *does* expect me to punch him, so he throws his hands up in defense, but I have no plans for that. When his hands go up, I grab his pinky finger.

It's amazing how much control you can have over someone by twisting one of the smallest parts of their body.

The cry he lets out is a high-pitched shriek. He stands on his tiptoes and his back arches as he tries to comprehend the pain he's in.

I nod at the man in the middle. The snitch. "There's a bat in my coat closet. Get it."

He blinks but quickly follows orders.

"A bat?" Louis echoes somewhere in the background.

The snitch brings me the bat, but I don't take it. I nod at the rule breaker, squirming as I twist his pinky finger. "Break his foot with it," I order.

Now everyone goes silent, even the pinky man has stopped screaming, letting out little whimpers as I hold his finger.

The snitch blinks. "S-Sir?"

"Break his foot," I repeat. "Now."

"Wait! Mr. Vittore!" the pinky man wails. "We didn't mean to hurt her! Sh-She *fought* us! We had no choice."

"You had no choice but to stomp on a five-foot-tall woman who weighs less than a hundred twenty pounds?"

No one responds. Because they know they're full of crap.

"Break his foot or I break his finger and then break your nose just like I broke the other idiot's," I say one last time.

"*Jesus*, Luca," Louis tries to cut in, but I snap my fingers at him when he starts to step toward the door.

"Don't you dare leave!" I holler.

Now he gets it. All the color drains from Louis's face as he gulps and nods. This is his lesson too. A demonstration of what happens when my orders are disobeyed. I don't care that Louis is a cop. I don't care that he has a job to do. His loyalty is to this family first. He needs to know he can't let his work come before his duty as my cousin.

Effy escaped on his watch. I'm the one who brought her back. Instead of thanking me for that, he showed up at my office with an attitude and the audacity to think it's justified. He's about to learn who's in charge here.

The snitch has tears in his eyes now, but he lowers his head and grips the bat. "I'm sorry," he mutters. I have no idea who he's talking to. Me, the guy whose foot he's about to break, or maybe even God. Either way, he lifts the bat and gets the job done.

6

Effy

I've been locked in this room for almost three days now. I feel like I shouldn't complain because this one room is nicer than any place I've stayed in the last six months. There's also a woman who brings me meals three times a day and a change of clothes. I pick around the food, still unsure if I trust it isn't poisoned, and I refuse to wear the clothes.

My rebellion is petty, but it's all I've got. This is the only way I can fight back. Even though I'm not even sure if I *should* be fighting. Luca isn't really my enemy, but it's hard to see him as a hero when he's keeping me locked up like this. I'm going insane. For someone who's spent most of their life constantly moving, being kept away like this is torture I cannot describe.

I guess I'm safer than I would be on the streets, but at least on the streets I wasn't being held hostage. A prisoner in luxury is still a prisoner.

My back stiffens when I hear footsteps approaching my bedroom door. I've already come to recognize the dainty click-clack of Isabella's steps, so I know it's her before she even knocks.

"Breakfast, Effy," she says in a sweet Italian accent.

I sigh. "Come in."

Isabella cracks open the door and then pauses. "I'm sorry, am I interrupting?"

"No, no, I was just finishing my morning prayers." I stand and lean against the bed. I hadn't really been praying much, but I still get on my knees every morning and try. Even here. I have no idea what to say to God right now. I'm being held hostage by the mafia because they want to … save me? *Is this a good thing, God? Should I be afraid?*

I feel like I can't hear Him. So I don't even want to try. But I know that's not the way I should respond, it's just that I have no idea what the *right* response is right now. I guess all I can do is keep trying, every chance I get.

Isabella gives me a nervous smile as she sets a tray of hot food down on the little table in the corner of the room. She has a wardrobe bag as well and hangs that in the closet before she checks the bin of dirty clothes from the previous day. It's empty because I haven't showered or changed since I woke up here.

Despite my attitude and childish rebellion, Isabella has been kind to me. I watch her check the bin and then press her lips together before she turns to look at me. Her smile is diplomatic, a gesture she offers because there's nothing else to say. At least she doesn't tell me I stink. I know I do.

"Are you in the Vittore family?" I ask in the awkward

silence.

She pauses. "No. I'm not a Vittore. I just work for them."

"So, is your family mafia?"

"My family has worked for the Vittores for many generations. My grandfather was good friends with Sergio Vittore, that's Luca's grandfather."

Luca's name makes my stomach clench. I'd managed to block out our encounter these last few days, but now his name summons the memory like a storm and my body ignores my fear and skips straight to the warm allure I felt rolling off his shoulders and nearly drowning me. I mean, we rolled around on the bedroom floor the other day. We were fighting to kill each other but still, I've never been that close with a man before. If things were different, I might've liked the wild action. But they're not different, so instead of being turned on, I feel intensely ashamed of myself for even entertaining those dark parts of my mind.

Perhaps I should spend my morning praying for my thoughts instead of praying for escape. I'm clearly messed up in the head.

Still … Luca Vittore is someone I equally fear and admire. He is strong. Powerful. And he made it clear he wants to protect me, but he also made it clear that he's seeking vengeance. Even if he isn't fully aware yet. There is a hunger inside him waiting to break loose. I just hope it's never aimed at me.

"Where is Luca?" I ask.

Isabella's face changes; it's slight, her jaw clenches just a little before she forces a smile and says, "Mr. Vittore is very busy—"

"Is he here?"

"I'm sure he's working."

I start walking toward the door. "Let's go find him."

Isabella practically runs across the room to block my exit. "You cannot leave without permission!"

Her reaction is quite dramatic. The door is locked. I know because I've tried to leave before and was met with a door that wouldn't budge. Even the balcony is still locked. But I do notice the key hanging around Isabella's neck as she wedges herself between me and the door. It's a pointless gesture since I can't get out without her key, but I don't comment on this.

Instead, I say, "Whose permission do I need to leave?"

"Ms. Storm—"

"Effy."

She takes a breath. "*Effy*, please do not make this difficult."

"What's difficult about walking around?"

She chews her lip like she's contemplating something. Then she sighs and reaches into the back pocket of her jeans to retrieve a cellphone.

"You can use this."

It's not the same as leaving this room, but it's more than I've gotten in almost three days. I snatch the phone from her hand and cradle it like its gold.

"Don't bother calling the police. Mr. Vittore has many officers on his payroll, he will find out if you try to contact law enforcement."

I frown. I honestly hadn't thought of calling for help. What would I even tell them? Help… Some gangsters are serving me breakfast and trying to keep me safe? Somehow, I don't think I'd be taken seriously.

"I'll come back for the phone after breakfast," Isabella says. "Please don't make me regret this."

I clutch the phone to my chest. "I won't."

My breakfast is a slightly sweet porridge with toast, fluffy eggs, and two strips of bacon. I don't eat any of it. I pour myself a cup of tea from the pot on the tray and sip from that as I search the internet for any news about myself. I Google my name, the case, even the name of that kid who was killed, but nothing new comes up. There aren't even any articles from when I escaped witness protection six months ago.

It's like I've never existed. Luca could kill me today and the world would keep going on like I was never alive in the first place.

For some reason, it's this knowledge that shatters me. Not the fact that I'm being held hostage by one of the most powerful men in the city. Not the fact that I saw a child get shot in the head. Not the fact that this child's killers want me dead before I can testify in court. I am shattered by the realization that if anything truly terrible happened to me, no one would care.

I have never felt more like Morgan Blank than I do in this moment, and it's terrifying. But instead of sobbing into my white fluffy pillows, I climb into my big bed and dial the only number I have memorized.

He answers on the second ring. "Hello?"

"Travis, it's me."

He pauses, then inhales sharply. "Morgan! I'm so happy you're okay!"

He doesn't sound happy at all. He sounds surprised.

"That's interesting," I say, "were you expecting me to *not* be okay?"

Another pause, this one longer than before.

As far as Travis knows, I never showed up for our lasagna dinner. He should be wondering what happened, asking why I stood him up. But instead, he's announcing he's happy I'm okay. Like he knows something bad happened to me.

"Morgan—"

"What happened that night, Travis?"

I walked into my apartment, and someone attacked me. I now know those people were men who work for Luca Vittore, but how did they find me? How did they know that I'm not really Morgan Blank?

There's only one person I've told my story to.

"You ratted me out," I say, more to myself than to Travis, but he hears it anyway.

"Morgan, you—you lied to me, okay? I thought you were just another girl, and then you told me you witnessed a murder and that some crazy guys want to kill you for it. You ran away from witness protection!" His voice goes up a notch. It's very feminine sounding. And gross. "How was I *supposed* to react to that?" Travis practically squeals.

All this time I thought he was a pathetic church boy. I thought the worst he'd ever done was slide his hand up my shirt when I let him kiss me in his car. But that was only the beginning.

"You ratted me out," I repeat. "I shared something personal with you and you used it against me."

"I…" he takes a breath, "they said they wouldn't hurt you."

"So you knew you were giving me up to men in the *mafia*?" I hiss into the phone.

How does he even *know* men in the mafia?? Who did he contact when he ratted me out?

I shake my head. I honestly don't want to know. It's obvious I didn't know Travis as well as I thought I did. But as far as I'm concerned, I'm done with him now. There's no reason for us to ever speak again.

"Morgan, listen—"

I hang up the phone without another word. What's the point in saying goodbye to a guy like him? He didn't even say goodbye to me when he wasn't sure if I'd be alive after he turned on me. They could have killed me. Luca can do whatever he wants with me, and Travis would be the one to blame. I doubt that keeps him up at night.

Someone knocks on my door; the sound makes me angry. What's the point in knocking when they can just unlock it and enter whether I say come in or not?

After a moment of silence, I hear Isabella's voice on the

other side, "Ms. Effy? May I come in?"

"Yeah," I grunt.

She walks in and her eyes immediately land on the phone in my hand. "You have used the phone?"

"Yes."

She holds out her hand. "You have to return it now."

Without even thinking, I walk over and yank the bedside table drawer open. The Bible inside slides around.

"I think I'll keep this phone."

Isabella's eyes pop. "You cannot—"

"If I can't leave, then I'm keeping the phone."

"That is my work phone, Ms. Effy. I'll get into trouble if you do not return it."

I shrug. "Maybe you should tell Luca, then. I'll give it back if he comes to get it."

"I don't understand." She shakes her head.

"I want to speak to Luca Vittore. I demand to speak to him."

Her face withers into anger. "You cannot *demand* to speak to the underboss. Who do you think you are?"

"Tell him I want to speak or else I won't testify."

The room goes silent. For a moment, I wonder if Isabella will turn and run out of the open door behind her. I even contemplate charging her. But her next words bring me back to reality.

"It is unwise to make demands of the underboss," she says slowly.

"Unwise indeed."

Both of us freeze at the sound of that deep voice. I don't want to look up when his tall figure darkens my doorway, but my eyes betray me.

Luca Vittore stands with his head tilted to the side, wearing an expression that falls somewhere between angry and amused. I have no idea what to make of him right now. But I know he overheard our conversation. And I know he likely isn't pleased by what I said.

But he's here now. This is what I wanted.

"I-I want to talk," I say bravely.

Luca doesn't even look at me, his gaze drifts down to Isabella who is nearly shaking as she looks up at him. They stare at each other until Luca fires off something in Italian. Isabella answers in a shaky voice, and he replies, but his voice is clipped. Angry.

He glances up at me, and then storms past both of us to the bedside table. When he yanks open the drawer, he shakes his head and walks back over in three strides.

Isabella takes a step back.

"I'm sorry, Mr. Vit—" she says quickly, but he snaps his fingers, and she cuts herself off.

"Who did you call?"

It takes me a moment to realize that question is aimed at me. When I glance up, I see Luca's sharp mahogany eyes burning a hole in my forehead. They peek out from beneath the wisps of brown hair that have fallen into his face, not quite bangs but still enough for me to notice. They look as if he ran one of his large hands over his head and forgot to smooth his hair back down. He blinks, as if to clear the strands from his eyes, lashes fanning like a hundred little butterflies.

At this point, I realize I've been staring, and I feel my cheeks burn as I reply, "I called m-my ex-boyfriend."

A dark chuckle fills the room, making me feel even more embarrassed. Luca tosses the phone to Isabella and jerks his head at the door. She leaves without a word, shutting it behind her.

I gulp. "Isabella said I could use it—"

"She shouldn't have. And I'll deal with her about that later."

What does that mean? I want to ask, but I'm too afraid of the answer. Isabella's worked for this family for years. Her grandfather was *friends* with Luca's grandfather. Yet, that means nothing to him now. He's still going to *deal* with her.

So what will he do to me if I make him angry?

He takes a step toward me.

I take a step back, bumping into the table behind me. The teapot shifts, I hear the tepid liquid sloshing around inside its porcelain cage, much like my frantic thoughts bumbling through my head.

"Y-You said you wouldn't hurt me," I remind Luca.

He scoffs. "Yes. But there are rules you must obey while you're here, Effy."

It's strange, in this moment, I see every unimportant thing in the room. I notice the sunlight glinting off Luca's shiny shoes. I notice the crispness in his dress shirt and how it stretches and molds to the lines of his structured body as he moves. When he reaches out, I notice the thick veins in the top of his hand—and I can't stop myself from cowering.

I snap back to attention and back away from him, swiftly stepping around the table until my back hits the big wooden door. I am trapped between a locked door and a 6-foot stack of angry muscles.

Luca takes another step, hand extended.

I close my eyes, but it's unnecessary. His touch is surprisingly gentle. I had convinced myself that he was going to hit me, or even choke me. But instead, he wipes one of my unruly curls from my face. Tucks it behind my ear. Cups my chin.

"Do not cause me any trouble," he says firmly.

I nod.

"That means you don't leave this room."

"But—"

His hand slides from my chin. To my neck. His grip is firm but loose enough so that I can still breathe. He doesn't need to squeeze to make me feel afraid. I already know how much power he has. What I don't know is how much he's willing to use.

"You are mine now, Effy."

Those words shove off the confusing embarrassment and fear I felt earlier, replacing it with a sudden storm of anger.

I grit my teeth. "I don't belong to you." Then, in a shock to both of us, I add, "I don't belong to anyone."

I have no idea where those words come from, but I can't stop them from tumbling out of my mouth. They fill the stale air in the room, prodding at the tension between us until it chips away, and we're left standing in awkward silence. Blinking at each other.

I drop my gaze to the floor, but it's immediately brought back to Luca's face when he murmurs, "Do you want to?"

My eyes snap to his. He's looking right at me, almost looking *through* me. But he isn't angry like before or threatening, either. He looks … sad.

"Do you want to belong?" he repeats softly.

I can't speak. That's a question I've been wondering almost my entire life. I'm an orphan who was never adopted. Someone who never found anyone to love them, until I was introduced to a God who said He loved me for no reason except that I existed. It was overwhelming, and in a way, I didn't fully believe it. What's loveable about me anyway? And if Jesus loved me so much, why'd He let me get kidnapped by the likes of Luca Vittore?

I squeeze my eyes shut. Of course, I want to belong to someone, but if I can't even believe that I belong to God, then who could I possibly trust in this world?

Somehow … the look in Luca's eyes tells me I can trust him. It's the same distant look I've seen in my own eyes, staring blankly into the dirty mirror of my mold infested bathroom. Luca might be the underboss of the Italian mafia with a family who loves him and people he can trust, but I know brokenness when I see it. I know emptiness when it's looking right at me.

Luca is just as lost as I am. I can see it all over his face, in the downward curve of his perfect lips. In the subtle droop of his wide shoulders. I can see it in the pain he keeps hidden inside, masked behind a curtain of rage.

For the first time, I wonder if maybe I'm not the only one who's been plucked from one life and tossed into another.

Luca shifts. I've been silent for too long, but it's too late to answer now. I see the moment he walks away. It starts in his heart before it reaches his mind, then it commands his legs to move, and he takes a step back. Moving further away from me.

My silence has shattered whatever semblance of peace he'd just offered. That open vulnerability is gone. The shutters have slammed shut, closing off that gentle part of him he'd allowed to surface for just a moment. He's back to being the Italian underboss, but I reach into that darkness, groping for the softer side of him anyway.

"I won't leave," I say in a whisper.

He stares at me, teetering between underboss and brokenhearted. He clears his throat and lets the underboss win. "Good."

"Luca—"

"You wanted to talk," he says, cutting me off.

I had wanted to speak, but not to this hardened closed off man. I want to speak to the Luca I saw a moment ago, the one who asked me if I wanted to belong. The one who left off the last two words of his own question.

Do you want to belong *to me*?

I shake my head. Defeated. "I don't want to talk."

"Well, I wanted to talk," Luca admits.

"Talk about what?"

"That night."

We've already talked about that night. My thoughts must be written on my face because Luca drops his gaze.

"I have one more question," he says. The way he stares at his shoes is unnerving. This is not the dangerous, confident man who just had his hand around my throat. This odd creature before me now is subdued … almost embarrassed.

No, I realize, *he's afraid.*

"What is it?"

He clears his throat. "Mario… Did he have any last words?"

My mouth feels like it's been stuffed with cotton. When I swallow, my spit tastes sour. My eyes start to burn. This is what Luca fears. More pain. His *brother's* pain. Pain he couldn't stop or prevent.

Will my answer to his question alleviate that pain—or make it worse?

I lick my lips. "He did."

Luca's eyes snap to mine and emotion crackles through the room like a strike of lightning. The air heats between us, fire bursting to life from his gaze alone. It's a sudden crash I wasn't ready for. If I wasn't already against the door, I would've stepped back from him again. But I'm pinned. Trapped.

"What were his last words?" he whispers.

I hesitate. Not because I don't want to tell him, it's because the thought of his words have awakened the memories. I can see Mario on his knees again, in his high school uniform. A kid with tears in his eyes, his hair disheveled. He looks like a younger version of Luca, but more innocent. Not as closed off. Or broken.

The gunman presses a pistol to his forehead. I blink rapidly as the memory continues, even though I wish it wouldn't. I'd give anything to forget these horrid details.

"Any last words, Vittore?" the Russian gunman asks.

Mario lowers his head. A sob rolls from his bleeding mouth. "I … I wasn't enough."

There's a weighty pause. And then the gun goes off.

When I blink back from the memory, Luca's face is frozen in horror. He doesn't even look like himself. His eyes are wide open, his mouth has formed a perfect O. I watch his Adam's apple bob as he swallows.

"I wasn't enough," he whispers.

Oh God… I'd said the words aloud without even realizing it. The memory had been so vivid. The images so real. I didn't know I'd spoken. But now the words are out there. Now Luca knows the truth—and it's shattering him right in front of me.

I have no idea what to do. We're not familiar enough that he would accept any sort of comfort from me. And the look of absolute horror on his face tells me he is beyond comfort. Right now, I don't even think he's here anymore. His eyes are not filled with that familiar rage I've seen before. They're no longer confident. They aren't even smug or snarky like when he'd first entered the room today.

They're vacant. Empty.

"Thank you," he says in a flat voice, then he nudges me aside and walks out of my room like a zombie.

7

Effy

The sound of a key clicking into place snatches me from my slumber. Isabella has been my sole companion since this isolation began. I live my life mostly in disturbing silence now, so I've become outrageously attuned to the slightest sound.

I'm sitting upright in bed when the door opens and a tall, beautiful woman steps into my room. She has long hair so dark it looks black until she strolls across my room and opens the curtains. Then I realize her hair is a shiny, brilliant mocha brown. It looks heavy, bouncing against her hips as she walks and stands before my bed. She's wearing a tight nude colored dress that's just a shade lighter than her tan skin, the carpet is thick enough to muffle her steps, but I can tell she's wearing high heels—the sort of woman who wears blood red lipstick this early in the morning must match them with equally daring shoes. It's a crime if she doesn't.

"Morning, sleepyhead," she says. Her accent is lighter than Luca's. I've only interacted with three people in this house so far (Luca, Isabella, and now this woman), by far, she's the easiest to understand. Luca's accent is so strong, sometimes I have to replay his sentences in my head. But the more we communicate, the easier it is for me to make out the dips and patterns of his speech.

"Good morning," I say in a hoarse morning voice.

She sniffs the air, and I suddenly feel awful for how I've refused to take care of myself. I still haven't eaten much or bothered to shower. Now, with the way this woman openly fans the air, I realize the only person being punished by this childish rebellion is me.

"Um, can I have a minute to clean myself up?" I ask.

The woman laughs, it sounds charming. "Of course. Change into something nice once you've showered, I'm taking you out for breakfast."

My face lights up, then quickly drops.

"Luca said I couldn't leave this room."

"Luca says a lot of things." The woman winks. "I'll be back in an hour."

I watch her walk out in awe. This world I've been dumped into isn't pretty at all. Every corner, every crevice is covered in darkness. But I've just decided that I want to be exactly like this woman when I grow up. I want to be the sort of woman who laughs at powerful men like Luca Vittore. The sort of woman who is amused by dangerous things, not the sort who cowers and runs away.

I toss my covers back and slide down to my knees. No matter how crazy my life gets, I will not skip my prayers. I'm positive they're the only thing keeping me sane, even though I'm not even sure if God is listening anymore. Technically, He already knows what I'm about to say. He's just waiting for me to speak the words. Add my faith and breathe life into my request.

I have no idea what I should request. No idea what to ask for. Safety? Protection? I've got that while I'm here. But I don't have any clarity on what comes next.

"God," I whisper, "please don't let me lose myself."

As beautiful and inspiring as that mysterious woman is, I know that if I end up like her then I won't be myself anymore. Women like that lady don't wake up that way. That comes from years of this life. Years of living and experiencing crime, deceit, and misery. There is beauty in the ashes of this world, but even that is a lie. And I'd be a fool to want any part of it. So even though these people have vowed to protect me for Luca's sake—for justice—I will not allow myself to be dazzled by the luxuries I've been given.

What is it to gain the world and lose my soul?

I finish my prayer, "Keep me safe. Remind me of who I am. In Jesus' Name I pray, amen." Then I stand and run to the shower.

That woman said she'd be back in an hour, so all I'm able to do is scrub myself down with the expensive smelling bodywash and then wrestle my hair into a bouncy puff on the top of my head. I would have *loved* to wash my hair too, but afro curls simply cannot be tamed in less than 60 minutes. If I had washed my hair, I'd have to reschedule this breakfast outing for tomorrow.

It also doesn't help that everyone around here is Italian. That means the bathroom isn't stocked with hair products for my type of curls. It isn't stocked with products for *women* either. I hadn't noticed before because I'd never showered until now, but I certainly pick up the masculine fragrance of the soap and bodywash. The razors are all for men, and the deodorant is too. Even the design of the bathroom is masculine. Dark brown, like the tinted color of rustic cherrywood.

There's an impressive set of lights above the mirror which I might attribute to a woman's touch, if she cared about putting makeup on like a movie star, but there isn't any makeup anywhere in the cabinets or drawers. All I find are more razors, a bottle of aftershave, and a set of clippers for *down there.*

I have never seen such a creation in my life, but I appreciate the idea, so I stash those away exactly as I found them—wash my hands—and then run to the closet to pick out a dress.

By the time my bedroom door swings open, I'm wearing a comfortable sweater dress and a pair of low heels. There were some higher ones in the closet, courtesy of Isabella, but I'm more comfortable in these. In case I've got to run.

The beautiful woman from before strolls in in a burst of lavender perfume and smiles at me. Her face falters after a second.

"Luca didn't leave any makeup in the bathroom, did he?"

I shake my head. "It's fine. I don't mind going out without it."

She clicks her tongue. "You might not be one of us, but if you're living with us, you've got to look like us, sweetheart."

I don't stop her as she takes my hand and leads me back into the bathroom. Like a big sister, she turns me toward her and fishes out a silver tube of lipstick from her purse. The color is crimson, but when she rolls it across my full lips and turns me toward the mirror for a look, it looks darker on me. Almost the color of wine.

I'd say it's because my skin is medium brown while hers is summer tan, but it doesn't matter. The color is gorgeous on me. If I'd had the money for makeup, I would've worn more of it before. But I was making crap money at a crap job, paying weekly for a crappy motel room. Lipstick wasn't high on my shopping list.

The woman sees the stars in my eyes and grins behind me in the mirror. "You can have it," she says, thrusting the tube into my hands. "That color was made for you."

I accept the gift with a nod and then stand there awkwardly. "Um, I don't—"

"Change of plans," she says suddenly, "we're going shopping. Because you need makeup and a purse to put it in."

There are so many other things I should be concerned about right now, but my mind has been in overdrive for the last six months. It will feel good to sit back and pretend I'm a normal girl going shopping with a friend. Just this once.

I step aside and motion to the door. "Lead the way."

Her name is Serena Vittore and she's Luca's younger sister—the only daughter of the Vittore head family. She's 24 and runs a small portion of her father's organization all by herself, which is apparently rare for a woman.

Serena tells me all of this as she drives us to a cute strip in the city and steals a parking spot in front of a glamourous-looking boutique. This part of town is foreign to me. Every part of it screams luxury and money; the only cars on the street are BMWs and Volkswagens. Serena drives a Cadillac truck that rocks smoothly over every bump she hits and looks like a black diamond parked on the street. I know I'm out of place, but I don't let any of that bother me as I follow Serena into the shop she's picked out.

The boutique is entirely empty except for four mannequins in the center of the floor. But as soon as we cross the threshold, a dainty woman rushes from behind a curtain near the back and gives us the red-carpet treatment.

We're actually served hors d'oeuvres and sparkling water while two stylists bring out clothes for us to pick out and try on. While I stuff myself with macaroons, Serena prattles on about her life as a mafia princess.

She tells me her family moved to America when she was just 4 years old. Luca was 13. I do the mental math and realize he's 33 now. The info makes me gulp because I'm only 19—but I have no idea why I'm thinking of my age in comparison to his.

Apparently, the thought runs deeper than I want to acknowledge because Serena stops talking and leans over the little table between us to touch my hand. The contact makes me jump.

She laughs. "You've been staring into space for a while."

"Sorry," I say with a weak laugh. "I was distracted."

"By what?"

"I didn't realize Luca's age."

A sly smile crawls across her face, she looks like a feminine, mischievous version of Luca. It's weird.

"You know, my parents are thirteen years apart."

"Okay," I say slowly. I've no idea why she's telling me this. Okay, I *do*, but I don't want to talk about this right now. I thank God my cheeks are too brown to turn pink, though I feel them heat with embarrassment.

"I don't blame you for noticing my brother. He's a ladies' man. Lots of women notice him and he notices lots of women."

My cheeks cool down. "Sounds like fun," I mumble.

Serena presses her lips together. Her hand is still on mine, I feel her brush her fingers back and forth over my knuckles. The gesture is soothing, almost sympathetic.

"It's not as bad as you think. When you grow up in this world, you come to expect it." She shrugs. "I know my father has had other women, but if it ever bothered my mother, she didn't show it."

She says this so casually, I can't help but nod in return, even though every part of my soul hates what she's just told me.

Serena senses my mood and pulls away from my hand. I

can hear her defenses clicking into place as she says, "It's not something you'll have to worry about anyway."

She's right. I'm her brother's hostage, not his fiancé. So I let her comment roll down my back and reply, "Will you have to worry about it?"

Silence for a moment.

"I don't want to get married. But women rarely get what we want in this world."

"Not even a woman like you?"

She laughs. It's sharp and dry.

"I'm a rare case, Effy. But it seems my time in the spotlight is coming to a close. If my father gets his way, I'll be married within a month."

I feel awful for her. I don't know much about the mafia, except what I've seen in movies and dirty books. If any of those things are even remotely true, then Serena likely doesn't have a choice in getting married.

The way she sighs tells me I'm not entirely wrong about this.

"This world is pretty on the outside," she says, reaching for her glass of sparkling water. She motions around the room with it, glancing at the stylists who are tripping over themselves to pack up all the clothes Serena has decided to purchase for me. "We live in luxury—richer than any celebrity in the country. And we live above the law. But it's all a façade. The public is obsessed with the mafia; they make movies and write steamy books about us. But those are fantasies." She sips her water. "The truth is so much darker. The beauty you see is nothing but a lie."

"You don't have to live this lie," I say softly.

She seems to snap to her senses, setting her glass down and looking at me seriously. "What else am I going to do? You can't run from everything."

I glance away.

"I'm going to be honest with you," she offers, "I'm not your friend, Effy. But I can be. I took you out today because my brother isn't handling this the way he should. You don't have to be locked away for him to protect you."

I nod. She's not wrong about that at all.

"But my friendship isn't free."

Then is it really a friendship? I wisely decide to keep that thought to myself. I don't need Serena to be my friend, I just need her to like me enough to unlock my door sometimes. She's the only person besides Isabella that I've seen in days. And every time I see Luca, we end up almost murdering each other.

"What do you want?" I say slowly.

Serena wipes a smudge of lipstick from the corner of her mouth. "I want the truth."

"I've never lied about what I saw in that alley."

"I believe you."

"Then what are you talking about?"

Serena leans over the table, her movement is so quick, it rocks under her weight. Our food shifts slightly, the bottle of sparkling water wobbles but doesn't tip.

"My brother needs you. But not just for the case."

"I don't understand—"

"Protecting you is personal for him. Why do you think he chose to keep you in his own bedroom?"

I frown. I had no idea I've been staying in Luca Vittore's *bedroom* all this time. That would explain why everything is so masculine. But that doesn't make it easier to swallow. I've been using his toilet. Sleeping in his bed. Wrapped up in his blankets. I bet I smell like him after using his bodywash and deodorant.

I can't stop myself from blushing now, but Serena's next statement chases all my butterflies away.

"It's personal because he couldn't protect Mario."

Her words slice through my heart. Luca isn't just guarding my life; he's guarding his own conscience.

I can hear the crack of emotion in Serena's voice as she goes on. I worry it will shatter her, but she bats away the storm of sorrow with her long lashes and looks me dead in the eye.

"Luca is the type of person who carries everyone else's weight. When our father got sick, he immediately placed the crown of don on his own head. That means he made this organization—this family—his own responsibility. Without anyone asking him to." Her chin quivers as she exhales. "He's taken care of this family. But he couldn't save Mario. When it mattered most, he wasn't enough. He hasn't been enough for *anyone*. Our father is still sick, our mother is grieving, I'm going to be sold to some old man soon."

I glance away, embarrassed by how wrongly I'd judged Luca. I had pegged him as some power hungry mafioso, keeping me locked away just because he could. I thought my confines had been a demonstration of his power over me. But in some lost, twisted way, it was all he could do to keep me safe. It doesn't make any of his decisions right, but it does make it easier to understand. He truly isn't my enemy. He just doesn't know how to be my friend.

Serena says, "You can help us honor Mario's death. If Luca can keep you safe, it'll be like keeping Mario safe all over again."

It's a heartbreaking truth that strips away the hard exterior of the man I'd fought in my room. It lays him bare and makes me see him as a person with a heart and soul.

I'm not surprised when tears gather in my eyes. Because at this point, all I can see is the look of fear on Mario's face right before that man pulled the trigger. His eyes are so large, still so innocent, but instead of the childish naivety you see on the faces of smiling children, he is crying. The last thing he saw on this earth was the barrel of a gun. And the last thought on his mind was that he wasn't enough. That his older brother, the underboss of the Vittore mafia, hadn't been enough to keep him safe from the monsters of this world.

I sniffle as I reach up to swipe away a tear that burns my cheek. I thought I'd had it rough living as an unloved orphan on the streets. But is it worse to be alone and never know the pain of loss, or to enjoy a family and have them snatched away?

Luca is broken. But is it fair to expect me to play along while he fixes himself?

"Tell me the truth," Serena says, dragging me from my thoughts, "can you protect my brother the way he's protecting you?"

I immediately shake my head, but she cuts me off.

"Not his body. Can you protect his *heart*? Can you protect him from himself?"

This isn't fair. I can't be his personal redemption. I can't make up for the loss of his brother. I can't be the answer to his failure six months ago. The weight of that responsibility is too great.

"How am I supposed to do that?" I ask.

Serena gives me a rueful smile. "You'll know when the time comes."

8

Luca

"Tell me about Italy," Mario says. "Tell me about grandma's farm."

Mario was born in the States. He never had the chance to visit our motherland because our father doesn't trust anyone to fly his family home, but he's never had the time to fly himself. I haven't been back to Italy since my early twenties.

In my memory, I look at Mario as he leans against the passenger door, head tilted upward. He's staring up at the clouds outside. The weather is warm, almost muggy. It leaves an uncomfortable warmth settling over everything. Even with the A/C on in the car, Mario's dark bangs stick to his forehead. He brushes them away as he sits up and glances at me.

"Tell me about home," he says with a shy smile.

Home. It's strange for him to think of Italy as home when he's never been there.

"It's a nice place."

Lackluster words for a place I considered my personal slice

of heaven for 13 years. The farm was rich, lush with green grass and deep black soil. It always smelled of citrus from the grapes, big fat clusters that seemed massive to my adolescent eyes. During the harvest, they were so ripe I couldn't stand it. I'd risk my grandmother's wrath to steal a handful. The skin burst beneath my teeth with a crisp pop, sweet juices spilling over my tongue, staining my mouth purple. That's what always got me caught. But it was worth the whack to the back of my head I'd get from my grandmother's wooden spoon. She was always cooking something, whenever she wasn't tasting, fertilizing, or nurturing grapes.

Italy was my home. A place with cobblestone roads and mouthwatering smells rising from food stands in the city. I spent most of my time in the countryside, where I rode horses and chopped wood and watched my grandmother make gnocchi from scratch. I was homeschooled, so I didn't spend much time with other kids my age. It was a lonely life. But it was rich.

I had my family, and I had my childish naivety. I thought we were honest-to-God farmers selling our fruit to local markets. I thought the guards on our property were protecting our *grapes*. And I thought the meetings my father held with all those men in suits was to discuss how he would divide his harvest.

Ignorance is bliss.

I would give anything for that ignorance again. To be happy with my family. Living in an unrealistic bubble of security where all the dangers in our world lie beyond the farm.

Like the picket fence was the only guard we needed. And maybe it was. Because Mario didn't die in Italy.

"If you aren't going to tell me," Mario says, pulling me from my thoughts, "then I'll just head inside. I'm sure my friends are waiting for me."

He unbuckles his seatbelt and grabs his acid yellow backpack before he steps out. When he closes the door, he leans into the window like he always does.

"I'll take you to Italy," I blurt. "So you can see it for yourself."

That makes him smile. "I thought you didn't want to talk about it because it was secretly awful."

Quite the opposite. Italy was the only place I'd ever experienced peace or happiness. And not because it was *Italy*. I think it was because Italy was home to the deception. I learned the truth over here in America. But Italy was the beautiful lie. The dream of what could have been.

Would Mario still be alive if we never left the farm? If we remained on that isolated land, sheltered from the real world my father lived in.

I'll never know. I never got to take him.

"Thanks for the ride, Luca," Mario says, waving. He let's go of a very self-conscious chuckle, trying hard to make himself sound more serious. More mature. But his laugh is still goofy as all get out and he can't help but snort at the end of it. It makes me chuckle too.

Mario grins, swiping at his unruly bangs again. He gives me one more wave and a wink before he turns toward the school. "See you later."

I blink from the memory with his last words ringing in my ears.

See you later. See you later. See you later.

"Sir?"

I stir, snapping my head to the side. Lorenzo is looking at me, his thick eyebrows pressed together like one big brow in the middle of his forehead.

I glance around the room, realizing where I am. Remembering what I was doing.

There's blood everywhere. Puddled on the floors, sprayed onto the walls, my shirt has a smear of blood across the chest. My knuckles are raw and red.

When I look down, I see a man on his knees, and everything clicks into place.

"Oh, right," I say casually.

I was torturing someone.

The man is Russian. Big guy, at least 6'8, with arms the size of oak branches and fists big as hams. It took three guys and four tasers to bring him down. Fought like a rottweiler. But once we subdued him, the real battle began. A war of wills. A test of his loyalty and my determination.

I stare at the scorpion tattooed onto his neck as I retrieve my gun from my waistband. We're in a secure warehouse, a place my father constructed for this very purpose. These kinds of things get messy. Imagine cleaning this blood out of my bedroom carpets.

And out here, no one can hear him scream.

He's done a lot of that. Snippets of the last few hours snap back into place in my blotchy memory. Giving him a beating. Issuing threats. Asking questions—getting no answers. We started breaking bones after that. He squealed and gave us the name of one of the other three men.

Tough guy. One name in exchange for four broken fingers.

I started *taking* fingers after that. They're scattered around the room 'cause I got a little dramatic and started flinging them when they popped off. Took six fingers to get the second name. But only three teeth to secure the last one.

Well, that explains the blood, I think, cocking my gun. The Russian sobs, a string of bloody saliva drips from his mouth all the way down to the floor. He's muttering in his own language, so I have no idea what he's saying, but I've done enough executions to recognize prayer when I hear it.

We all answer to Him someday.

Respectfully, I give the guy a moment to plead the only case that really matters.

Where do murderers go when they die? I don't intend to find out for a very long time. But this guy will learn in about 30 seconds.

I'm not killing him because of what he did to Mario. That's only part of it. I'm going to pull the trigger because he's useless to me now. I've got the names I wanted, but no information.

After Mario's body was found, we started making calls and learned he'd never made it to school. That means he was taken in the morning. Yet, Effy didn't witness his murder until the evening.

What were they doing with my brother all that time? Why did they *kill* my brother?

See you later. See you later. SEE YOU LATER.

I squeeze my eyes shut, shoving his voice from my mind. The gun shakes as I press it against the Russian's temple. He lets out a warbled sob. I have no sympathy.

He could save himself by talking, but I know better. Any man who endures broken bones, the loss of six fingers, and three pulled teeth isn't withholding information. He truly doesn't know. Either Scorpion Man wasn't high enough ranked to know, or the information was kept close. That could only mean whatever happened involves the Bratva boss himself.

No one in the mafia except another boss would dare lay a hand on a fellow boss's child.

I should've known this from the start, but I kept those thoughts at bay. Because we weren't at war with the Bratva when Mario was killed. We weren't enemies. But they took him anyway, knowing this would make us enemies.

That could only mean they believe their reasons were justified. That could only mean Mario had done something. He'd committed some unforgiveable sin against the Bratva. But how? What could a fifteen-year-old kid have done that deserved a death sentence with no explanation?

Whatever it was, this guy clearly doesn't know. So I pull the trigger.

It's raining when I leave the warehouse, using one of Loren's handkerchiefs to wipe the blood spray from my chin. My car is already waiting out front; when no one steps out to open my door, I realize who's come to pick me up.

"How was your shopping trip?" I say, sliding into the passenger seat. The creamy leather melts beneath me, warm and smooth, much like the smile Serena gives me as she tilts her head to the side. She's wearing a new black dress that's tight and makes me wonder if I'll make it through this drive without her accidentally flashing me. My sister has never been a modest woman, but her attire has been exceptionally rebellious ever since my father announced her wedding plans.

Serena turns on the windshield wipers. "It was nice. Effy's a nice girl. You should really give her a chance instead of just locking her door and ignoring her all day."

"Keeping her at home is what's keeping her alive," I say with a sigh, leaning my head back against the rest. She has no idea that I want to do so much more with Effy.

It started with my hand around her throat, a desire to kill the woman who ran away with my vengeance tucked into her ratty back pockets. But that anger fizzled into something more carnal when I beat up three of my own men for hurting her.

Protecting Effy isn't just a duty anymore. I meant what I said to her. She is mine. She is Mario's secret replacement, my new chance to correct my wrongs. To finally *be enough* for someone. But that's our little secret. You and me.

Can I trust you?

No one else needs to know that I almost slipped when I had her pinned against the bedroom door. No one needs to know how the look in her eye tore down my defenses and left me with a whimpering question.

Do you want to belong?

I felt so pathetic afterward, I could have shot Lorenzo. But the sting of Mario's last words sobered me. Reminded me of what I'm truly doing here. What all of this is for.

Effy is a beautiful woman, but her burning eyes are not my priority. I must remember that she is a mission. A means to an end. Protect her to honor my little brother. Get the job done and move on.

"You shouldn't have taken her out," I tell my sister. "Anyone could have seen you. Anyone could have tracked you."

"I know what I'm doing." Her tone is sharp, a little sharper than it should be when speaking to her underboss and older brother, but I let it slide. Serena's always pushed her limits. And she's also telling the truth. She does know what she's doing.

It was Serena's men who tracked down Scorpion Man. All I did was pass her the description Effy gave me and the next day, I had a wonderful gift waiting for me in our warehouse. I have no idea how she managed to track him down, but that's part of our life. When you live in the shadows, you become a master at navigating darkness.

Serena didn't grow up on our cozy farm, she was raised with her eyes wide open, exposed to the brutal truth of our world as a toddler. To this day, I wonder why our father kept me so sheltered for so long, especially as his heir. I suspect that was, in part, my mother and grandmother's doing. But their lies only served to hurt me when the walls came tumbling down.

If I had known the truth from the start, like Serena, I'm sure I'd be as strong as she is. I'm sure I wouldn't have foolishly believed I could've ever kept Mario safe from all this. That was, perhaps, my greatest failure in this life. Thinking that I could ever save anyone from the consequences of our sins.

That's the thing about the mafia, no one is ever safe. When you play with the devil, it's only a matter of time before demons join in on the fun. And they never play by the rules. Because in darkness, there are no rules. You couldn't see well enough to read them if there were.

"I don't want you taking her out again," I say firmly.

Serena glares at me but doesn't talk back.

"I just tortured and killed a Russian informant. I've instructed Lorenzo to make arrangements for his body to be delivered to the Stepanov mansion."

My sister's glare becomes a wide-eyed stare. She blinks, willing herself not to panic, but I notice the way her hands grip the steering wheel, long, black acrylic nails curling into the leather. She knows what this means.

"You've just started a war," she whispers.

I grunt, feeling anger swell inside me. My words roll out like a smelly burp, fouling the air around me. They're as dirty as my bloody clothes. "They started it first."

9

Luca

Serena drives us to her favorite place for a drink. Even though my white dress shirt is still speckled with red, I don't turn down the chance to get away from everything for a little while. The only thing waiting for me at home is my sick father, delusional mother, and a woman who hates me. I'd much rather spend the evening trading jokes with my little sister as we share a bottle of whiskey.

The bar is called *Qui*, which means *here* in Italian. I have no idea what the inspiration was behind that, but the drinks are good, and the women are pretty, so I shrug off my prickly dissatisfaction and relax into the leather seat of my booth.

We're in the VIP section on the second floor. From my perch in our balcony view, I can see Serena at the bar, ordering our drinks. As the Vittore princess, she shouldn't be seen at the bar, it's beneath her. But she's been carrying on a fling she thinks I don't know about with the owner, so she makes it a point to go down there herself with her order.

I watch as she bends over the glass counter, her body swaying toward the manager. He's playing bartender tonight, showing his face to his customers. It's a good face. The hardened skin of someone in his fifties with tattoos on his muscular forearms and a piercing in his right ear. He's the type of handsome you'd see in a motorcycle club, but with a thick Italian accent and a penchant for younger women.

He smiles when Serena laughs at something he said, then he slides her drinks over to her and leans close to whisper in her ear. The whole exchange makes me sweat. I don't like seeing my sister with this old man any more than I enjoy the thought of her being with Antonio Caruso. But at least this guy is her choice. Her own mistake.

I can live with Serena's poor decisions, as long as they're hers. But being forced into a marriage with a man like Antonio is nearly unfathomable. Even though we were raised for this. I don't expect to choose my bride any more than Serena can choose her husband. Our marriages aren't for love. They are business arrangements complete with contracts and even promises of heirs.

My grandmother's contract promised *five* sons to my grandfather, Sergio. She had eleven kids before it was fulfilled. Six girls and five boys. The very last boy killed her. She died bringing him into this world and my grandfather was known to have said in response, *But at least I got my last boy. It's done now.*

That baby boy grew up to become Vincent Vittore, my own father.

My mother's agreement with my father wasn't as

demanding. Just two sons. Serena was an unexpected bonus. Now, we realize she was absolutely necessary because Mario isn't here anymore, and I can't keep things together alone. Regardless of what happened in the unforeseen future, my mother's marital contract was fulfilled the moment Mario was born.

I was there when my father wrote a check to her parents to close the contract. Like most women in our dark world, she'd been purchased like a mule for breeding. But she knew that going in, and she cried tears of joy when Mario came screaming into this world and the doctor announced he was a healthy boy. I know because I was there for that too.

I was a teenager, and I watched my mother give birth. That might sound disgusting to upstanding westerners, but it's standard protocol in our organization. Serena was there too. And two other high-ranking members of our mafia—one man and one woman—who signed statements to confirm they'd witnessed the natural birth of the last male heir owed to my father. It wasn't about staring up my mother's skirt. It was about fulfilling a contract.

When I think of that day, I can still feel my father's hand on my shoulder when he realized it was a boy too. He'd squeezed hard, and nodded his approval, his firm grip the only evidence of his joy. Then he turned and poured two fingers of whiskey into two glasses. To my shock, he passed one to me.

"It's done now," he'd said, echoing the words of my grandfather. Then he tilted his glass, and I mimicked his actions.

That was the very first time I had a drink with my father. To celebrate Mario's birth, all while my mother closed her legs and cried in the background.

I used to wonder why she didn't have as many children as my grandmother had. I used to ask her why she waited so long between each kid. It wasn't until Mario's birth that I understood. Children had never been a choice or a joy for my mother.

I was born exactly nine months to the day of their wedding. My father never used protection with her, he'd wanted his heir as quickly as possible. But my mother sneakily put her foot down and used whatever means necessary to prevent (*not* terminate) a second pregnancy until *she* was ready. My aunt would sneak her birth control, sometimes she would get my father so drunk he had no idea whether they'd had sex or not when he woke in the morning. Other nights, she would finish him in ways she never shared with me nor Serena. But I didn't need to know. I'm a man of 33 whose had enough women to learn on my own by now.

Witnessing Mario's birth and my father's callous reaction to the whole thing wasn't as traumatizing as you might think. I feel like our society tosses that word around a little too frequently these days. It wasn't healthy and it did impact me, but not in a bad way.

You have to understand that I was a teenager by then. I was a teenager who was well aware of who my father was and what our family did. But I still hadn't fully grasped my mother's role in all of this.

She stood by my father's side at fancy dinners. She smiled when expected. She spoke when spoken to. But she was neither a wife nor a mother. It was clear she didn't love my father and in the back of my teenage head, I knew she didn't really love me either. Any of us. I just never knew why not.

So, Mario's birth wasn't traumatic at all. It was eye-opening. It made me understand my mother better. Made me realize why she'd always been so distant toward us. Nothing like the loving, sweet mothers I'd seen on television. That day, with whiskey dripping into my system and my father's hand on my shoulder, I finally understood.

My mother didn't hate us, but she also never wanted us.

I cannot imagine Serena succumbing to the same fate. I cannot imagine her walking down the aisle in a white dress or giving Antonio three children. But it must be done. The contract we've written requests two sons and a third child of either gender for fulfillment. Serena will also be required to breastfeed and take no alcohol until each child is weened. There will be eight witnesses present for each birth—this is overkill and is likely a demand added by Antonio to shame Serena. But we've agreed to it anyway. I will be one of the witnesses, as well as my mother, one of Serena's close friends, Antonio, his brother, and three witnesses of his choosing.

I've already signed my copy of the contract. Serena's name is the last one waiting to be scribbled down. But instead of reading over her thirty-two-page agreement with her future prince charming, she's in a bar flirting with a man who's almost old enough to be her father.

When she gets her drinks, she turns and looks up—directly at me. I smile and then nod. It's a small gesture, but she knows what it means. I've seen her little boyfriend, and I approve. I bet Bartender Dude won't demand babies from her, and if they have kids, he won't make a group of people stare between her legs during the delivery. He won't shame her. He won't make demands of her. He won't care if his child is a son or a daughter. And he won't treat her like she's his personal slave.

I hope Serena hires her tattooed boyfriend to kill Antonio. No one would miss him.

My sister passes me my drink and then sits on the very edge of her seat. Crosses her legs. I'm honestly surprised she can do that with how tight the dress is. I'm not sure which is more offensive, the length of her dress or the fact that it's strapless. Her toned arms are bare so I can see both sleeves of her tattoos. She's got more than me.

A mafia princess is not supposed to look like Serena. They're supposed to be innocent virgins who look like pretty little dolls until their husband's eyes are finally drawn to another woman.

I was eleven the first time I walked in on my father with someone else. I told my mother in a fit of tears, snot running over the curve of my upper lip. She had wiped my tears and instructed me to never mention it again. I did as I was told, confused but obedient. When I saw Vincent with another woman two months later, I did as I was told again. Looked the other way.

In her tight dress, bloody red lips, and extravagant tattoos,

Serena looks like all the women I've caught our father with. Like the lady who struts over in a G-string and steps onto the platform of our table to dance on the pole in the middle right now.

I watch her for a moment, then glance at my sister again. She's staring at Bartender Dude. It's a miracle any man in this business wants to marry Serena. My father was far too liberal with her. She's an embarrassment to the head family, but only in appearance. The business she does on my father's behalf is exemplary. Her ten percent of the organization brings in fourteen percent of our entire revenue. She's better at her job than I am at mine. So no one complains about her tats or her tight clothes or the fact that everyone knows she isn't a virgin anymore.

"How long has this been going on?" I ask my sister. I already know the answer, I'm just testing her to see if she'll be honest.

Her eyes slide over to me, and she studies my face for a moment. Thinking.

"Six months."

Huh. That's the truth.

"So it wasn't him, then?"

Her jaw clenches for a second before she shakes her head. Stares into her drink. "No. It wasn't him."

That's the one secret between us, the name of the man she let taint her. She was 22 years old, a record for most women today, but society's standards don't apply to our world. Serena is a mafia princess; she's supposed to remain pure until she's married. No matter how long it takes. But now that she *is* engaged, I don't blame her for ruining herself. Antonio doesn't deserve to be any woman's first experience.

"Is it serious?" I ask.

Serena's smile is genuine over the rim of her glass. When she pulls her tumbler away, there's a crimson kiss left on her cup. *I wonder if Effy wears red lipstick.*

My mind freezes, blinking around the bar. Where the heck did that thought come from?

I know I care about that woman more than I should. I can admit that. In fact, I anticipated this happening. Because protecting Effy is like protecting Mario all over again. Shielding that spark of innocence that exists nowhere else in my life. But Mario was my teenaged brother. Effy is a beautiful young woman. Protecting her is entirely different.

With a grunt, I shut down that part of my mind. The part that wonders about her lipstick. There is no point in indulging those thoughts. Effy might be a new spark of innocence—one I long for, and even need—but she comes from a different world and will return to that world once all this is over. There is no point in wondering anything about Effervescent Storm.

"I don't know if it's serious," Serena says, yanking my focus back toward her.

I'm not even sure what we were discussing. I mumble something noncommittal and stare at the dancer on our pole. She's flipped upside down now. I smile.

"He knows about Antonio, and he doesn't care."

I quirk an eyebrow.

"He thinks we should try for a baby."

That makes me squeeze my glass. I toss back the rest and motion to a passing server to bring me another. Then I settle my searing gaze on my stupid little sister.

"So, you've been sleeping with him."

"I don't have to answer that."

"When our father dies, I will be the official don of the Italian mafia. If you haven't married Antonio by then, you'll be under my control."

"What are you saying?"

I lean forward, glaring past the dancer's legs as she twirls. "I'm saying it's better you answer to me than to Vincent. You've ruined yourself once, do not make a second mistake, Serena."

"If I get pregnant, Antonio won't want to marry me—"

"And then you'll have a bastard to raise. Alone."

She doesn't speak because she knows I'm right. In our world, the only thing worse than a broken woman is an illegitimate child. They are the product of affairs and relationships that never should've happened. They are a threat to carefully written contracts. They are problems from the moment of conception.

Serena knows this. But she's so desperate to get out of this marriage that she's willing to try it anyway. She's willing to take her chances at being disowned by our father.

"Serena—" the server returns with my second drink; I knock it back and motion for a third. "Serena, don't be stupid."

"I have no other choice."

"I can help you."

She shakes her head, but I'm on my third whiskey now. I feel my confidence rising, feel the words leaking from my mouth before I can stop the flow.

"I can take care of this. I'm your brother. I'll deal with it. I'll deal with our father. I'll handle everything, Serena. Trust me."

She wipes her nose and finally meets my gaze, tears in her eyes. "You can't fix everything, Luca."

I sit back into the leather booth, staring through my dark bangs. Serena doesn't look away, which solidifies everything I'm suspecting. Her words … *You can't fix everything*. She's not just talking about her engagement.

SEE YOU LA—

I shove to my feet. "I'm going home," I grunt, ignoring the way Serena stares after me.

I'm a little too tipsy to drive, so I call Lorenzo when I make it outside. It takes him fifteen minutes to find me stomping down the street two blocks from the bar. He doesn't ask any questions, just pulls over and opens my door. Neither of us speaks on the drive home. I have no words and it isn't Loren's place to say anything. What would he say anyway?

Sorry your father is dying and your sister is getting sold and your brother is dead. And I'm sorry you keep trying to fix everything but it's just not going to happen.

I'm sorry you're not enough.

Lorenzo opens my door when we get home. I can see the stress on his face, wondering if he should acknowledge that

I'm drunk and offer help or just pretend not to notice anything. I make the decision for him and ignore him entirely as I step from the car and wobble up the front steps of my family's estate. It's a massive manor with more than enough space to house every member of the family, plus our staff and a few guards.

As I walk through the house on heavy legs, it feels far too large, and I feel far too tired and sluggish to go any further. I've been staying in a guest bedroom since Effy arrived, but in my slightly drunken state, I get an uncontrollable urge to sleep in my own bed instead of on the stale mattress of one of the other rooms.

That's not it, I laugh at myself, at the excuse I've just made up. *I want to see Effy*. I want to see my hidden spark of innocence. The only breath of life to enter this dark world in a very long time. I saw that innocence in her eyes when I held her by the throat. The fear in them. She's a tough girl, I'll give her that, but she isn't as strong as she thinks she is. She isn't strong enough to protect herself.

She needs me.

And in my own twisted way, I need her. I need something bright and pure. I need something that isn't marred by this awful world. Mario had been that something. He'd been a smiling, innocent kid whose goofy laugh made my day a little easier. He'd been an inspiration to be a better person. He'd been a reminder that not everyone on this dark side of the world is evil.

And yet, he died a brutal death. And I died right with him.

Because there is no room for anything good or pure or innocent in the world I live in. It's better to kill that ideal when it's young, before it ever takes root inside. That's how I've lived for the last six months since I watched them lower my brother's coffin into his grave. Every part of me that was good died when Mario died. Every part of me that believed in hope and love was buried with his lifeless body.

And then Effy stumbled along. She was an accident, a woman whose path never should have crossed my own. She was walking home from *Bible study* when she witnessed Mario's murder. It doesn't get much more innocent than that.

I need that innocence. I need that light. I crave it like a drug.

I thought I could bury my hopes with Mario, but Effy has reignited them. With her here, I have a purpose and a connection to Mario again. I have a chance to fix things, in some small way.

Visiting her like this may be the stupidest decision of my life, but I'm allowed a mistake or two. What's Effy going to do? Fight me? We've done that already, and if I remember correctly, it ended with me on top. So if she wants to roll around on the floor again, I'm here for it.

I almost chuckle. Not even an hour ago, I had shut down the part of myself that thought of Effy in ways I shouldn't. I'd closed the door to whatever musings had lingered in my head about her. Yet, here I am, stumbling down the hallway with my key in hand. Opening her door without a moment's hesitation.

10

Effy

My eyes pop open when I hear the familiar click of the lock on my door. I'm hypersensitive to that stupid lock—that happens when you're trapped in a house with a bunch of gangsters who don't like to knock.

At first, I expect Isabella to rush inside with some sort of bad news. Maybe Luca's changed his mind. Maybe he's giving me back to the cops. Then I think it might be Serena. She could have news far worse than Isabella. Maybe Luca is dead. Killed by the Russians who killed his brother and want to kill me. Maybe he went after them with the intel I told him, and they proved more formidable than he'd assumed.

My stomach clenches as the door swings open. It seems to happen in slow motion yet too fast at the same time. I almost feel sick.

A panicky voice in my head tells me to hide, like the whisper of a child, convinced there is safety hidden beneath the blankets.

I listen to that voice, rolling over and yanking my covers over my head. I know it's futile, but I'm not ready for whatever's going to happen next. I need a few more days—a few more minutes to cope with the fact that my life is about to drastically change yet again.

"Please, God," I whisper, squeezing my eyes shut. "Please—"

The rest of my prayer is cut short when the mattress sinks. It dips far lower than it would from Isabella's thin frame. Even though Serena is sky-high tall, I doubt she'd weigh this much either.

Don't move, I stupidly tell myself. Then I feel something grab my arm and I flail, letting out a pathetic little yelp.

A deep voice grunts and my heart stops. It's Luca.

For some reason, that makes me fight a little harder. I lash my arm in the direction I've been grabbed, but it's caught in a sweaty fist and then the covers are snatched away entirely. I shout in surprise as the cold assaults my skin, raising pebbles and bumps along my arms and legs.

"What the heck!" I yell, shivering from the sudden cold.

Luca chuckles, holding up my blankets. "Calm down. It's just me."

Just me? He says that like I should feel safe with the Italian underboss strolling into my bedroom after midnight. I've read dark romance. I have a very good idea about what's supposed to happen next. The thought makes me keenly aware of the fact that I'm sleeping in one of *his* large t-shirts with no bra underneath.

I reflexively cross my arms over my chest. Luca scoffs. It's the single most insulting thing I've ever heard, and he didn't even use words. He just wrinkled his nose and let out an ugly noise.

"Calm down, princess. You're not my type."

He's saying that with his mouth, but the look in his eyes tells a different story. I don't miss the flash of Luca's eyes. A split second where he drops his gaze down my body. Just as quickly, he's looking at my face again the next instant. His eyes are darker than normal, rich chocolate compared to his usual syrupy brown. But the color doesn't matter. It's the expression on his face, the heat in his gaze, that makes my heart double thump.

Luca drops the blankets on the floor, then shuffles awkwardly. When he presses a knee onto the mattress, I realize he's removed his shoes.

"What are you doing?" I ask angrily.

"Move over."

I don't move.

Luca shoves me aside and rolls into the bed to lay on his back.

"What are you *doing*?" I demand, shoving him back. It's the most futile thing I've ever done. Luca is like a rock lying beside me. My foot actually *hurts* when I kick his thigh—it's like stomping on a stone. I shouldn't be surprised. Staying fit is probably mandatory in this life; it makes it easier to beat up other criminals or run from the police.

Luca exhales slowly, totally unfazed by my anger or the

shove I gave him. He stares at the ceiling, gaping upward in this sea of inky darkness. I can just make out his facial features in the ashen moonlight. It trickles into the room from the slanted curtains, pooling on the far side of the bed, like a pale spotlight hanging over him.

"Luca?" I say, looking at him closely. His brows are drawn together, his jaw is clenched. But when I call his name again, he closes his eyes in a flutter of lashes, his lips part gently.

No words come out.

"What's going on?" I whisper.

"Tell me again."

I frown. "Tell you what?"

"Tell me how my brother died."

His words choke me. Why does he want to hear this right now? Or at all… Did he really stumble into my room half-drunk to listen to the gruesome story of how his brother was beaten and murdered? This isn't some innocent bedtime story. The life of a child was taken. A child he loved.

I swallow thickly. It feels like quicksand is clogging my throat. Maybe that's why he wants to hear it. Sometimes confronting the pain is the only way to make it stop or go away. Who am I to judge how he copes?

I roll onto my back and stare at the ceiling too. My voice comes out shakily, but I manage to get through the details, ignoring the icy burn of a hot tear that slips from the corner of my eye. This is torture for me too, remembering how it happened, seeing it play out in my head all over again. I can't cope any better than Luca can. And he wasn't even related to me. He was a nameless boy. But he *was* a boy. A human being who was alive. And now he's not.

I turn my head to look at Luca. He's lying flat on his back, his face unreadable in the dark. I can still make out the way his eyebrows furrow together, but the rest of his visage is hidden in the shadows.

"Effervescent," Luca says slowly, like he's tasting the word. "It means vibrant. Like a light."

I know what my name means, but I get the feeling he's not really looking for a response. So I don't say anything. I just lie there beside him, blinking at the ceiling too.

"You are a light," he whispers. "My light now."

I flinch when I feel something touch my hand. It's Luca, reaching for me.

I take his hand, fingers interlocking on their own.

I'm not a light at all. But if I say that now, I know he'll slip away, even though I'm holding on to him. That's how fragile this hard, muscular mafioso is. He's nothing but a shell filled with cotton. All soft and puffy on the inside. I know because I'm the same way.

"There's a greater light," I say softly, treading unknown territory.

Luca doesn't speak.

"I can only shine so brightly. But Jesus … He—He's the Light of the *world*."

He still doesn't speak. But I don't let his silence stop me.

"If you let Him in, Luca, He can heal whatever pain you're feeling. He can—"

Luca grunts, cutting me off. "I don't believe that."

"I know you're hurting right now—"

"It isn't *right now*," he snarls. His hand clenches mine tightly. I take a slow breath, biting down on my lower lip to stop the sharp pain. I don't think he's even aware that he's hurting me. "It isn't right now," he repeats. "I hurt all the time. I hurt every day. I hurt nonstop."

Luca rolls over suddenly, so he's on top of me, pinning me to the mattress. I stare into his dark, angry eyes, but what I see doesn't scare me. The rage that used to fill me with fear only serves to break my heart tonight. It's hard to hate a man like Luca when he's so much like me. That would be like hating myself.

"I'm hurt, Effy," he whispers. "Can your God make that stop?"

"Of course He can. He *wants* to."

His face curdles, anger taking over. "You're a fool if you believe that."

"You're a fool too," I say softly. "I know you believe, Luca. There wouldn't be a Bible in your bedside table if you didn't."

That breaks him. He buries his face into the crook of my neck. The noise he lets out is a painful groan, something that comes from deep within. The cries of his soul. I can't imagine what he's feeling right now. The raw agony of his brother's death, or the aching pain of his failure to protect him.

In my head, I replay Mario's last words, and I wonder what they mean. I wonder if they haunt Luca as much as they haunt me.

I wasn't enough…

The song of a nightmare.

Did Luca try to bury that nightmare in the Word of God? Did he flip through the pages in a desperate search for relief? I would have. I *have* done that. Sitting on the back pews of the church with tears streaming down my face. I've felt that sharp, cutting pain. I've felt desperate enough to believe there's a Man in the sky who loves me just because I'm me. I've accepted that. And I haven't looked back. Even though I've witnessed a gruesome murder, even though I've been stabbed in the back by a guy I thought I could trust, even though I've been kidnapped by a dangerous man who's nothing more than a grieving older brother. I still believe.

Without thinking, I reach up and thread my hands through Luca's hair, tangling my fingers in his dark wavy locks. He inhales slowly, and I feel his breath on my shoulder, I feel his lashes tickling my neck as he blinks.

"It's okay," I whisper. "No matter how angry you are at God, He still loves you. Even when you feel this awful pain."

Luca leans away to look me in the eye. "How would you know anything about what I feel?"

"Because I feel the same."

He glares like he hates me. "You're an orphan who's never been loved. You have no idea what it's like to lose your family."

I could let that break my heart, but then there'd be nothing left of me to care for him. It isn't fair that I'm his emotional punching bag. It isn't fair that he's kept me locked up as his personal stress reliever—his light. But pushing him away will serve nothing. So instead of letting his words tear into my heart, I exhale the pain and look him in the eye.

"I'm lonely because I've never had anyone close. But you're lonely because you're losing everyone close to you. Our pain comes from different places, but it's pain all the same. Loneliness is loneliness. Heartbreak is heartbreak."

Luca blinks at me, and I don't understand the look on his face now.

"We're both in pain," I whisper, "but we don't have to face that pain alone."

"We don't," he agrees in a murmur, his eyes flicking down to my lips.

"God is here for us," I say.

He groans. "Shut up about God, Effy. I'm trying to kiss you."

It's hesitant at first, like he's afraid to do it. Little butterfly kisses spark between us, his soft lips pressing against mine. And then he dips his head to kiss my neck, and his name slips from my mouth.

His head snaps back up, eyes wide as he blinks down at me. I've shocked us both, but Luca recovers first. He kisses me again, with his eyes closed, and a groan pouring from his mouth to mine. It buzzes between us, a throaty vibration against my lips. The sensation tickles, and I lean back to laugh, but that just gives him entry.

Luca deepens the kiss, his passion fervent, quick, almost overwhelming. I place one hand against his chest, trying to stop the flow, trying to stymy the desire rushing through the room. But that only makes him more desperate. His touch growing needy.

I can feel it in the way his kisses burn, his mouth hot and filled with fire as he sets me ablaze. I cannot cool him down. I stumble into an inferno with him, dragged by the hem of his own t-shirt as he slips a calloused hand underneath.

"Stop," I whisper, grabbing his hand.

He catches my wrist and pins it above my head.

"Luca," I say, but he doesn't listen, dipping his head to kiss me again. I tug a fistful of his hair, and he hisses, biting my lip.

I bite him back, and I don't let go until I taste blood.

Luca grunts, jerking upward so he's leaning away from me. He blinks, eyes wild with shock and desire. "You bit me."

"You wouldn't listen."

"I thought you were teasing me. I thought this was what you wanted."

I glance away, staring at the bundled-up blanket on the floor. It is what I want. But I know this isn't what God wants, and if I don't stop it now, it'll reach a place it can't come back from.

I don't know how to explain this to Luca. I don't know how to tell him that God wants me to honor my body. To treat it like a temple. He's already angry at God. He already told me to shut up about Him. How will he react if I tell him it's because of my love for God that we've got to stop?

Suddenly, I realize I'm pinned to the bed with his hand up my nightgown. Luca could take what he wants from me. With or without my permission. But I know he's not that sort of man.

"I'm not ready for this," I whisper, hoping that's enough to get him off of me.

Luca remains on top of me for another long moment, staring like he's searching for the truth. Like he doesn't quite believe me.

Just when I think I'll have to repeat myself, he rolls off me and lays on his back again. I try very hard not to stare at the tent in his pants. He doesn't even try to hide it. Shameless jerk.

With the heat dying down between us, I feel a sudden chill in the room. My arms break out in gooseflesh, and I roll to the side so I can grab the blanket from the floor, but Luca wraps his arms around my waist and yanks me back from the edge of the bed.

I yelp as I'm held against his body. "What are you doing!" I squeak.

"Spooning you."

"Luca—" I'm breathy and lost for words, but Luca seems perfectly at home. He snuggles me closer and exhales in a tired groan.

"Go to sleep. I promise I won't do anything more than this." He pauses. "Unless you want me to."

"I want to grab the blanket. I'm cold."

He doesn't speak.

"Luca!" I say.

"Go to bed." Somehow, he pulls me even closer, until I'm totally wrapped up in his arms. "This is warm enough."

I will never admit this to him, but he's right. Lying together like this, so close I can feel his breath on the back of my neck, it is warm. It's so warm, I feel myself relax despite the anger that'd swelled within me a moment ago. It dissipates as I listen to Luca's heavy breathing. It lulls into a calm peace when I feel his heartbeat against my back. We're so close we might as well be one person now.

In a way, we are one person. A copy of the same messed up nightmare stumbling through this dark world. Luca calls me his light, but I'm trying to follow the Light of Christ. My footing isn't stable in the least, but if I keep running toward it, I know I'll get there. And as long as Luca is following, he'll make it too.

So I close my eyes and relax in his arms. *This feels like a dream…* those are my last thoughts before I succumb to a deep slumber. But those thoughts of fancy dreams become a worrisome nightmare when I wake to an empty bed.

Every part of my body aches, my muscles tight with tension from shivering all night. I sit up and glance around, blinking at the harsh morning light. The other side of the bed is empty, like no one was ever there. But I know there *was* someone there. There was a tall man holding me against him all night. But he's gone now. Like a cheap hookup that lasted too long.

Luca left me while I slept. And he didn't even cover me with the blankets.

11

Luca

This one doesn't cry. He looks me dead in my eye as I pull the trigger, going out like a man. I am not impressed. The only reason he didn't cry is because we didn't torture him. It was pointless to do so. The motive behind my brother's death lies in the hand of the *pahkan*. The Russian don. It is meaningless to torture the lower ranked men because they know nothing. I could do it for vengeance. Bloodlust. Or just because. But I'm not one for unnecessary bloodshed. I pull the trigger and walk away. There isn't a need for any more than that.

Lorenzo is standing by the door when I turn around, tucking my gun back into my waistband. He looks nervous but waits for my orders before he speaks.

"Get rid of the body," I say.

"We're not sending it home?"

"No. The Russians know we're behind the murders by now. If you try to return the body, they'll kill you. Just get rid of it."

Lorenzo nods and adjusts his bowtie. It's already crisp and perfect so I know the gesture is something he's doing out of nervousness. The sight makes me sigh in irritation.

"Spit it out, Loren," I growl.

He gulps audibly and trots behind me as I shove through the first set of doors in our warehouse. "Sir, I don't know how he found our location—"

My heart stops.

"But Louis is waiting in the parking lot."

Annnd it starts back up again.

"Louis? What the heck, Loren." I stop walking to glare down at him.

He blinks, confused. "Sir, I'm sorry?"

His words sound like a question. Like he isn't sure if he screwed up or not. It just annoys me.

"I don't care about Louis. I thought someone *important* showed up."

"Good to know I'm not important," Louis says from down the hall.

My eyes narrow. "How did he get in?"

Loren clears his throat. "I—well, I let him in."

"Lorenzo."

"He is your cousin."

"I am your cousin." Louis grins. He's standing with his feet wide apart, hands in his pockets, as I approach. I can see his gun and his badge clipped to his belt, it peeks out from the edge of his brown leather jacket. He must be on duty right now.

"Do not tell me you came here in a *cruiser*," I hiss.

His grin drops into a frown. "I'm not stupid, Luca."

"Yes, you are." I shoulder check him as I walk out the door, snapping at Lorenzo over my shoulder, "Get rid of the body and get home. I don't need you for the rest of the day."

"Body?" Louis says, but I ignore him and keep stomping down the steps of the warehouse, going toward my car. Lorenzo can walk home.

"Luca, hold on." My cousin grabs me by the shoulder.

I whirl and snatch his wrist, twisting it until he yelps. "Don't *touch* me," I hiss.

"Would you calm down and talk to me!" He's shouting now, voice high and irritated because he's in pain, rubbing his wrist.

He's right. I should calm down. I've been snapping ever since I crawled out of bed with Effy. I spent the night with her wrapped up in my arms, sleeping until sunrise without a single nightmare for the first time since Mario's death. I didn't need to get drunk or high or bang a hooker to fall asleep. With Effy, sleep was instantaneous. It was peaceful.

She truly is my light. I don't care what she says. I don't need her God. I need *her*.

But she won't have me. She stopped me last night—she told me she didn't want me. I'm so pissed off I could shoot Louis. And then Lorenzo too. I don't know what to do with myself. I feel like I'm unraveling all because I got told no. It's not like I've never had to sleep off a stiffy before. It sucked, but it wasn't unpleasant enough to put me in this sort of mood.

It's a miracle I *didn't* end up torturing that guy in there. Taking out my bottlenecked frustration on a lowlife who deserved it.

But I know better than that. I need to channel this anger, not let it explode on everyone everywhere I go. So I take a deep breath and nod at Louis's arm. "Sorry," I say.

He stares at me. "What body, Luca? Who's in the warehouse?"

"A dead Russian."

He turns away from me, running a hand over his head. "*Luca*," he says, then he starts cursing in Italian. I would translate it, but you can fill in the blanks. "This isn't even your warehouse!" my cousin shouts.

He's right, which is why I don't punch him in the throat for taking that tone with me. We're standing outside of a warehouse that belongs to the Carusos. I don't know if it's owned by Antonio specifically, but that doesn't matter. The message is clear enough no matter who owns it.

"I know you and Serena are close," Louis says, running a hand through his hair. With his light brown locks pulled away from his face, I can see the lines around his eyes, and the little bit of fuzz at the edges of his hairline. He's balding prematurely. I wonder if it's from the stress of the mafia or the stress of being a cop on the mafia's payroll.

I don't really care either way. He chose to join the force. I hope the stress gives him an ulcer.

"I know you hate that *Zio* is setting her up with Antonio, but you cannot antagonize them!" He stares at me, gently tugging the fistful of hair he's holding. It's a nervous habit he's had since we were kids.

"Zio," I repeat the word. It means *uncle* in Italian. I've always found it interesting that Louis never called my father don Vincent, like everyone else. Even I use the proper title when in public. But not Little Louie. To my dear cousin, it's always Zio. His favorite uncle.

Ultimately, it doesn't matter what Louis calls my father. The fact is that he's right, yet again. Killing that Russian inside a Caruso warehouse wasn't smart, but it was deliberate. It could drag them into this war and cause unnecessary bloodshed. Or it could go nowhere entirely.

If Lorenzo gets rid of the body quickly enough, the Carusos will never know who was killed here. They'll only see the blood stain and be left with a million questions. It won't hurt them, but it'll definitely give them a headache, which is enough to make me smile.

Sometimes pettiness is more satisfying than outright revenge.

Luca curses again and then smooths his hair back down. "This is so bad," he mutters.

"You're being dramatic, cousin."

He glares at me. "Luca, you've made me an accessary to murder."

"I didn't tell you to drop by the warehouse unannounced."

"I got a call about gunshots in the neighborhood! You should have known someone would come sniffing, and you should be thankful it's me!"

I roll my eyes, stepping toward my car again.

Luca follows right behind me. I hear the jingle of his belt, but I don't realize what he's doing until he says, "You've got to let me take you in. At least for questioning."

I whirl around to find him holding out his handcuffs.

How dare he?

The punch I throw hits him in the jaw. Louis stumbles backwards, dropping the cuffs to cradle his chin.

"Luca!" he shouts, but it sounds weird because he's holding his face. There's blood leaking from the corner of his mouth. I may have loosened a tooth.

"Do you honestly think I'm going to let you handcuff the underboss of the Vittore organization?" I ask, massaging my knuckles.

He doesn't reply. Wise decision.

"I'm going home, Louis. I'll do you a favor and forget you ever said that to me."

I climb into my car and buckle my seatbelt. By the time I've finished, Louis is at my window, motioning for me to roll it down.

"Luca, you're acting on impulse," he says, wiping blood from his mouth. It smears along his chin. "Don't be a loose cannon."

I roll my window back up and speed off, hating that my cousin is absolutely right for the third time today. For the third time in *ten minutes*. He knows me better than I'll give him credit for, but you don't need to be my *bestie* to notice my awful mood. I've been spiraling since I woke up this morning, slowly falling into a dark void where nothing matters, and everything sucks.

I've been to that place before. I lived in that hole for six months after Mario died. Now that I think about it, I don't think I ever left that hole. I just got used to it. And now I've felt something similar to what I had before, a tiny flicker of a candle lighting up the black space around me. It's small, but it's hot and burning. And it's ignited something inside of me. Something I can't explain or put into words.

But I feel it. And it isn't warm and fuzzy. It doesn't make me want to run to a church and cry out to God with tears streaking my cheeks. It pisses me off and makes me want to destroy everything in sight.

I shouldn't be surprised. Humans call the Word of God a work of beauty. Something that brings joy and comfort. But have you ever noticed what God calls His Word?

A weapon. A *sword.*

Humans say Jesus came to show us His love. But when He spoke to His disciples in **Luke 12:51**, He said He came to divide.

That's what I feel inside. The sharp pain of confusion that makes my palms sweat. Something inside me is rebelling against everything I know. The very division of my soul. Like I'm fighting a battle against myself.

I want to destroy everything, but I also desperately want to fix it. I want to go home and run Effy through the bed, but I also want to cherish every part of her that she's given me. I want to murder every person responsible for Mario's death.

And I will do just that.

Effy's words last night might have taken root, but I will not let them grow. I will choke them out so I can survive. So I can be the man I need to be to exact my vengeance on this city. I've already taken down two men on my list. Just two more to go, and then I'll be free. I can handle that. I can keep my head straight for that.

Just two more, Luca, I tell myself, gripping the steering wheel for dear life. *Just two more.*

That's the mantra I repeat as I speed home and storm into the house. Two more names. Two more bodies. Two more bullets. The song is loud in my head, screaming over my own thoughts. I hardly hear Serena calling for me when I pass through the open foyer. If she weren't close enough to grab me by the elbow, I would've walked right by her.

I jerk to a halt with her grip on my arm. My eyes flicker down to stare at her slender fingers, sharp pointed acrylic nails painted matte black. They're pretty. I like them. Especially the white rose decorating the middle finger of her left hand. I stare at the flower as I say, "What is it?"

"Papa was looking for you," she says. "I covered for you, but I won't be able to do it again."

"What was it?"

"Another dinner."

I groan. Dinners with our father usually mean some sort of marital discussion. He probably invited some young virgin to the house, expecting me to salivate and sign the stupid papers. But my father is mistaken. He takes me for some abstinent gentleman, but in reality, I've had more than enough women to be thoroughly unimpressed and uninterested in a young virgin. If I were 25 again and half drunk on our own wine, I might've raised an eyebrow and skimmed the contract. But as it stands, I've got better things to do than plan a wedding. Not even my own.

Serena moves her clawed hand from my arm to my face, touching my cheek. "You look awful."

"Thanks."

"Was it bad this time?"

She's talking about the Russian. Once again, my baby sister came through for me, hunting down the men responsible for Mario's death. She delivered this guy personally but said I should be the one to pull the trigger. So while I was busy transporting him to a Caruso warehouse and digging up dirt on the rest of the Bratva, Serena was here dealing with our ailing father. I owe her more than I can pay.

"It was bad," I say. This is a lie, but Serena doesn't need to know that I'm truly messed up because a certain Christian princess wouldn't give me a lap dance last night. I have half a mind to go to her room and strip her down just because I can. She belongs to me. This is my house. I own her. How dare she tell me no. How dare she *preach* to me instead of giving me what I wanted?

And why on earth did I just lie there and *let* it happen?

I've never forced myself onto a woman before. I have tortured and maimed and kidnapped and murdered. But rape is where I draw the line. Rape is unforgiveable. Because no one deserves to have their body violated. I mean, yeah, my knife might have violated someone's eye socket before, but that's different. If I need to torture a woman, I'm not going to use my junk to do it. Plain and simple.

With that said, I have no idea what else I was supposed to do except back off when Effy said no. I wasn't going to hold her down and take it from her. That wouldn't have been worth it at all. But I didn't know what else to do. I've never been told no before. And maybe that's the real reason why I've never resorted to using force. I can't remember a single woman ever refusing me. Until last night.

And she didn't even do it because she doesn't want me. She did it because God said so.

What-the-ever-loving-heck does that even mean?

I want to rip my hair out.

"Maybe you should take the rest of the day off," my sister suggests.

I absolutely agree.

"Send Isabella to my room," my voice comes out gruffly, strained.

Serena doesn't question my orders, just nods and steps back so I don't bump her as I leave. She's well aware of my relationship with Isabella. Everyone in this house is, we just don't speak of it.

It's been going on for a few years now, ever since her 18th birthday when I became her first. And I've been her *only* since then. Isabella is a woman I reserve for times like this, when burning pain can only be edged by raw ecstasy. It's a shameful thing I'm doing, using a girl to bury my troubles, but let's be honest, it could be worse.

In my defense, I never planned for this to happen. I'd attended her birthday party out of duty as the underboss. Presenting her with a gift was a show of respect for her family and their longstanding friendship with my own. Dancing with her was a sweet gesture meant to make her young girlfriends giggle. Sleeping with her was a mistake.

She woke up the next morning in tears, screaming that I'd ruined her. At that point, I couldn't cover up the incident—I was just happy she didn't cry rape. Isabella isn't high-ranking by any means; the only reason anyone even knows her family name is because our grandfathers were friends. But that's it. The Romanos have never done anything except exist.

But still, I'd ruined an eligible woman in the organization. I couldn't marry her because of her low rank, but I had to do *something*. So I took her in and promised to take care of her for as long as I had to.

I thought she would eventually grow up and develop her own dreams and desires. I thought she'd want to go to college or travel the world or even start her own business. Women are doing that these days. I was ready and willing to foot the bill on any venture she pursued. But none of that happened.

Isabella has remained here since the day after her 18th birthday. I tried to inspire her a little by making her my personal assistant but that was an awful mistake. After just a few months, I fired her, gave her an apron, and called it a day. Now, her only duties are to answer when I call and change the sheets when I'm finished with her. She's had three years and a blank check to pursue more—to do anything she wanted. But this is all it's come to. A few cheap nights a week and a prayer that I didn't get her pregnant. If that's all she wants for herself, who am I to judge?

12

Luca

Isabella arrives in my room wearing a nightie that I probably paid for. I've got three fingers of whiskey in my glass that burns my throat raw as I watch her take it off and then stroll to my bed and lie down. She knows the drill. There's no need for words, but she opens her mouth anyway.

"You look like you've had a rough day."

She doesn't know the half of it.

"Let me help you relax."

I throw back the rest of my drink and walk to my bed, swaying a little. I probably smell like alcohol, but if it bothers Isabella, she doesn't comment. She gets busy removing my suit jacket, loosening my tie, undoing the first few buttons of my dress shirt. Her hands feel like two slices of heaven as she massages my shoulders. I hiss through my teeth at the pleasure, muscles tensing and relaxing beneath her touch.

"You're stressed," she whispers before kissing my neck. Then she says something in Italian but I'm not listening anymore, all I can hear is the rustle of the blankets as she drops to her knees in front of me, the jingle of my belt buckle, the clicking of my zipper. My head sags back as I sigh in relief, blinking at the ceiling in blurry-eyed ticks.

"Um…" Bella sounds confused.

I glance down to find her staring at my crotch.

"Where is it?" she says. "I thought you wanted this."

Huh. I thought I did too. I guess my body says otherwise.

Isabella reaches for me, but I slap her hands away. "Leave it."

"I can help you—"

"I said leave it."

She looks hurt as I stand and tuck myself away, zip my pants again. "Believe me, I'm as surprised as you are. But you can't force it, Bella. If it's not happening, then it's just not happening."

"Where is it?" she says again. Like my penis is missing. "It's that stupid girl. You've let a street rat get to you—"

Her voice is cut off when her head is yanked backwards. Her eyes bulge. Her hands fly to her hair, where my fist is knotted.

"What girl," I challenge. "What *street rat* girl is getting to me, Bella?"

"Y-You're hurting me," she whispers.

I shove her away and her hands slap the floor as she reaches out to catch herself.

"Get out," I say flatly.

Bella obeys, standing on shaky legs so she can retrieve her

nightie from the bed, but I stop her with a command. "Leave it."

She stares at me. "But… I'll be naked."

"I don't care." I walk over and snatch the nightie from her hands, they tremble now that there's nothing for her to hold.

I step back and motion to the door. "Get out."

"Luca, please—"

"Do not make me say it again."

She drops her head, letting out an ugly, wet sob that doesn't move me. I watch as she wobbles to the door, grasps the knob.

"Bella," I say behind her. She stops but doesn't turn around. "If you ever insult Effy again, I will make you crawl to your room."

She doesn't reply, just walks out the door and begins to sob hysterically. I can still hear her shrieks echoing through the halls when I walk out a few moments later, heading in the opposite direction.

Curse that girl. I didn't send her away naked to punish her for insulting Effy, I sent her away to punish her for bringing Effy up in the first place. I'd just forgotten about her. I'd just buried my anger, drowned myself in the pleasure that would serve as a distraction at least until the morning. Everything would have been perfectly fine if Isabella had kept her silly mouth shut. But she couldn't help herself because she's jealous of any woman I have besides her.

Isabella is not my wife, nor will she ever be, but I have to admit she is the only woman I've had for this long. My personal little toy who takes all my trouble with a smile and a groan and a see you next time. There have been other women, but they were all fleeting. As insignificant as Bella herself, but it's hard for her to understand her unimportance when she's been the only woman around for so long. The only woman I've taken care of like a little housewife for the last three years.

Things have got to change. I've got to put my foot down with her or it'll just get worse. I confirm my plans with a nod as I stop outside Effy's door. Now that she's on my mind, I won't be able to rest until I've seen her.

I flatten my palm against her door, staring at the wood. I know I'm not going to get anything but a sermon and an attitude if I enter this room, but I'd rather hear Effy talk about the Bible than listen to Isabella's whining about a limp stick. Like that's all *my* fault.

I take a breath and then pull the key to her room from my pocket and open the door.

Effy is already asleep. She's bundled up on the far side of the bed, near the window. The last time I came in here, she was on the near side facing the door. I can't help but interpret her change in position as a subconscious effort to get away from me. Like sleeping on the furthest edge of the bed will somehow make me go away.

It doesn't.

I tuck my key away and walk over to the bed, climbing inside with a groan. Effy wakes up immediately, I feel her small feet kick me beneath the blankets, but it doesn't hurt.

"I'm not leaving, so you're wasting your time," I say.

She kicks me again, harder this time.

"Get out!"

"No."

I feel the covers shift when she extends her leg for yet another attack—this time, I catch her foot and press my thumb into the sensitive area right beside her ankle. She gasps and her foot spasms as I hit the nerve there.

"Kick me again and I will break every one of your toes," I say.

She nods mutely, and I release her foot.

In the dark, I can see the scowl on Effy's face. She isn't happy, but neither am I. Join the party.

"What do you want?" Effy asks in a fearful voice. The sound of it almost makes me hate myself. I hadn't meant to scare her. Then again, what else did I expect when she lives under lock and key?

"Relax," I say, as if that's possible for her. I should know better than anyone that she's afraid. Effy and I come from two different worlds with two different sets of beliefs, but we are more alike than we'll ever admit to each other.

While she has her crazy Christian values, I have my mafia code. She doesn't believe in sex before marriage, we consider it a grave insult when one of our women is deflowered before walking down the aisle. I should know. I've spent three years trying to make things right with one woman. It doesn't matter that she's low-ranking or not. Women are both cherished and overlooked in the mafia, much like the church.

Half the congregation views them as precious gemstones.

Gifts to husbands who've spent a lifetime on their knees begging God for a life partner. The other half gets their partner and treats her like a secondhand maid.

Cook. Clean. Take care of the kids. Work a nine-to-five and give me a lap dance before bed. Rinse and repeat without a single complaint. Because that's your job. That's what you were born for. And if you don't serve, submit, and obey, you'll be labeled as a wayward woman who doesn't deserve such a wonderful *king*.

The mafia is only slightly different. We pretty much treat our women the same way, we just don't use the Bible to justify it. We are animals who treat our women like maids, personal sex slaves, or whatever we want because it's what we want. At least I'm man enough to admit that. I don't need to twist sacred Scripture to understand I've got issues.

So when you look at it that way, who's the bigger monster? A mafia boss or the pretty church boy who sits beside you on Sunday morning?

"Relax," I say again to Effy. "I'm not here to try anything. No kisses or cuddling tonight."

She's silent for a while. I don't mind it at all.

"Then … what did you want?" she asks.

Peace. A good night of sleep. And one more thing…

"Tell me about my brother again," I whisper.

Effy inhales sharply, the sound seems to cut through the night. Outside, there are crickets chirping, there's a bird singing a mournful tune. And then there is Effy, gasping and then sighing, disrupting the natural sound of the night.

"Luca, you've heard the details already—"

"I know."

"This isn't healthy."

"I didn't ask you that."

"How many times—"

"As many as it takes!" I snap.

SEE YOU LATER. SEE YOU LATER. SEE YOU—

"*Please*," I mutter, squeezing my eyes shut.

In my head, I can see Mario's grin as he waves and heads into school. I can see my father's grief when the news of his death reaches him. Then I see a bottle of whiskey. I see the room swaying in my drunken stupor. I see red-hot rage as I torture that first Russian. And I see his red blood spilling onto the floor. The last thing I see is Isabella, naked and crying. And I realize none of it is enough. None of it will ever be enough.

The whiskey didn't stop the pain. Killing that Russian didn't stop the pain. Isabella didn't stop the pain.

Only Effy. Somehow.

But she can't give me the relief I want. She isn't like Bella; she won't strip down at my command and make this night all about me. Effy loves God more than she fears me. It's a fact I both hate and admire. The best thing I can do is settle. Sleep beside her fully clothed instead of tearing her nightgown from her body. Listen to the sound of her soft snoring instead of making her scream for me. Have a normal conversation, instead of telling her everything I want to do to her right now.

This is a strange connection we have. It's the first connection I've *ever* had. And I don't know how I feel about it.

We are perfect strangers. Yet we are completely intimate with one another. I didn't even know Effy existed until recently. And we haven't spent much time together. I can acknowledge that. I can admit there isn't much ground for the strong emotions I know we both feel. But that doesn't erase them. Because you don't need much ground when the thing that connects you is stronger than casual conversation and flirty first dates.

We didn't need a year of passion to establish this strange relationship. We needed one night of terror and a dead kid.

Effy and I are connected by the same thing that tore our lives apart. Mario is a ghost that has haunted us both. I was there for his last ride to school, his last serious conversation, his last silent plea for help. And Effy was there for his last breath. We share the same pain, like two halves of one nightmare.

Now I am the only one who can seek vengeance for Mario while Effy is the only one with the knowledge to set it all in motion. We are meant to be together.

I will never have a stronger connection to another person besides the woman lying next to me. But Effy either doesn't see it that way or she won't admit to seeing it that way. I can't just bury my troubles with her. I can't drown my sorrows in her desire or our passion. With Effy, I've got to confront everything head on. I've got to be a man about this.

Isn't that what the best women are for? Making you into the man they knew you could be all along. Tired husbands call that nagging, but I call it elevation. Only a bum sees progression as a chore. Only a bum is satisfied with being the same person he was on prom night twenty years later.

I am not that man. I will confront the pain I feel, but I'll do it my own way. Even though it makes Effy shift away from me on the bed. Even though I know it makes her question my sanity. I'm not going to back down. I need to hear this again, more than she'll ever know.

Just two more… I remind myself, clenching my jaw.

Effy takes a breath and goes through the details again. I listen in agony as I envision the entire thing like a nightmare on repeat. It's the worst thing I've ever heard but I need this. I won't be able to function without it. So I force myself to stay there, in mind and body, to listen to each word, hold them captive in my heart. And I force myself to remember that this will all be over soon.

Just two more…

When Effy is finished, she falls silent. I half expect her to be asleep when I say, "What would your God say about all this?"

"That's the funny thing about God," she replies, "He doesn't say much."

I blink at the ceiling.

"In the Book of First Samuel, the Bible says the word of the Lord was rare. That means it'd been quite a while since God had spoken to anyone, even though there were priests and prophets dedicated to worshipping His Name."

"I don't understand," I say honestly.

"Sometimes we focus on the wrong things. As Christians,

we desperately want to hear God's Voice because He's God. When He speaks, mountains fall down. Our problems run away."

I hear Effy adjust on the bed before she starts talking again, when she does, her voice is closer. Like she's inched toward me.

"But the amazing thing about God isn't that He talks to us. It's that He listens."

I suck in a breath.

"Most of the time, God doesn't speak because we already know the answer to our problems. He doesn't need to tell you, yet again, that you shouldn't use foul language. That you shouldn't hang out with people who are leading you astray. That you shouldn't be drinking. We already know this. We already know right from wrong. But we do wrong anyway and then beg God to talk to us because we feel guilty about it."

Effy laughs in the darkness. It's almost haunting.

"We know better. And God knows we know better, so He doesn't speak because there's nothing to say. He's already spoken enough in His Word. Too bad we don't read it as much as we should."

"Well don't you sound perfect," I say in a clipped voice.

Effy ignores my sore anger. "I'm not perfect at all. I'm not a preacher—I don't even go to church as often as I should. But I am honest with myself. I know I *should* go to church; I just choose not to. So I don't throw a child's tantrum when God goes silent. How could I expect Him to trust me with His words and revelations when He can't even trust me to get to church once a week?"

For some reason, that makes me chuckle, and I instantly feel the tension in the room lighten up a little.

Effy sighs. "You shouldn't ask what God would say to you, Luca. You should be asking yourself what you want to say to God."

I have no idea what I want to say to God. I have no idea where to even begin.

I must have said some part of this aloud because Effy scooches even closer to me and says, "You could start by saying sorry. You could ask Jesus Christ to forgive you for your sins and invite Him into your life as your Lord and Savior."

I chuckle. "You trying to convert me?"

"Is it working?"

I fall silent. "I … I can't do this right now, Effy."

It isn't because I don't believe. Honestly, I hesitate because I *do* believe God is real. And I know choosing to live for Him would change me. It would take away all the dark parts of me that I need to keep going. The dark parts that help me stay focused. The dark parts that will get the job done and move on.

Just two more…

Giving my life to Christ would release those two from my wrath. I'm halfway through this job. I will not give up now.

To my surprise, Effy isn't bothered by my hesitancy. She snuggles closer to me and rests her head on my shoulder. Her voice is a whisper in the room, dancing to the tune of the crickets and the bird's mournful song.

"You can't do this…" she repeats my words. "Maybe not right now, but soon."

13

Effy

I wake up alone. In fact, I've been waking up alone every day for the last week. That's how long it's been since I've seen Luca.

I'm confused because I used to dread his visits. Just the very thought of him nearby made the hairs on the back of my neck stand on end. But then I got to know a deeper part of him. Luca surprised me by opening up. He bared his heart and confusion in a way that I could sympathize with because I felt the same sharp pain. Deep wounds that gutted me each night.

In a way, his presence was as calming as it was alarming. And just when I'd convinced myself that he was no longer my enemy—that he truly was my protector—he vanished.

He did it once before, and I stupidly chose to overlook it because he came right back. But this time feels different. I don't know what happened. Was it something I said? Was it all the stuff we discussed about God and the Bible? Did I push him away?

I shake my head as I pick out a dress for the day. Luca's absence might hurt now, but I will never allow myself to feel guilty for sharing the Gospel. If talking about Christ pushes someone away, then they were never meant to be in my life in the first place. The Word says bad company corrupts good character; the way I see it, if I mention Jesus and someone runs for the hills because of it, then I dodged a bullet.

But that doesn't mean it doesn't hurt.

I made the mistake of letting my guard down. I let Luca in as much as he let me in. And now he's gone. The silence in my room twists my heart into another shape. How could I be so foolish?

Was it the way he kissed me? Was it his gentlemanly promise not to touch me? Or was it his shocking vulnerability? The way his heart fractured when he spoke of Mario and how he never tried to hide the cracking in his voice.

The man who lay beside me in bed, that wasn't the underboss of the Vittore organization. That was simply Luca. I wonder how many others have seen that side of him. I wonder how many others he trusts with all those emotions.

"It doesn't matter," I tell myself, grunting as I zip the back of my dress. It's a beautiful dress that stops just above the knee, navy blue and made of thick material so I only need to pair it with a light cardigan.

That's one of the only good things about Luca's absence. He's given me free range of the estate. My bedroom is no longer locked. I can come and go as I please, explore any room, even walk through the gardens outside. That's where I'm headed now, so I step into a comfortable pair of nude heels, check my makeup, and then I leave my room filled with a confidence I don't actually have.

Every part of this massive house makes me nervous. There are servants and guards posted on each floor, there are stone statues standing sentinel as ancient decorations at the ends of some of the halls. The main corridor has a massive portrait of the entire Vittore family hanging above a fireplace that looks as if it were built for a king. There are far more people in the painting than I've seen in the house—at least fifty people. Maybe more. I'm going to take a wild guess and say it's a portrait of everyone. Cousins, grandparents, aunts and uncles. Anyone with the Vittore—or the Valentino—name.

Luca and his family are front and center. There are no smiles on their faces. Honestly, their deadpan expressions make the painting feel accurate. In the few weeks I've been here, I've never seen Luca or Serena smile with genuine happiness.

I walk past this painting now, feeling my skin prickle with nerves. I swear they're all watching me. Staring. I have that same paranoid feeling wherever I go on the property. The staff members are all polite, happily offering me food or promising to change my sheets while I'm gone. The security guards offer stiff nods and continue staring ahead. No one bothers me. But still, I can't shake that feeling. The same feeling I had when I was living in that awful motel, constantly looking over my shoulder. The feeling that kept me safe for months. A feeling that reminded me that someone was watching me. Someone wanted to harm me.

I have that feeling here. I just haven't figured out who's responsible for it.

As I walk down the front steps of the house, I'm immediately reminded of all the luxuries a life of crime can give you. It sickens me that the massive mansion behind me was likely purchased on drug money or whatever illegal business the Vittores conduct, but that doesn't make the place any less gorgeous.

The estate sits on over fifty acres of property entirely gated off by a massive black wrought iron fence and finished with hedging on the forward-facing section of the estate. The Vittores like their privacy. I don't have to guess why.

There's a stone fountain out front with statues of men I don't recognize. They're dressed like farmers holding clusters of grapes in their hands. There are grapes all over the property, in the paintings on the walls, in the fixtures of the architecture of the house—vines wrapped around doorknobs, carved into the hearth above the fireplace, grape-shaped crystals that dangle from the chandelier of the dining room.

If I had to guess … I'd say this property may have been purchased with wine money, not drug money. Which I guess isn't so bad? I mean, wine is legal.

Considering their obsession with grapes, I'm not surprised the Vittores have a lavish garden that's little more than a decorative vineyard with exotic flowers lining the pathway for guests to stroll through. It's the end of October now, so most of the grapes have been harvested, but the leafy green vines still look beautiful dangling from the trellises outside.

I smile as I think of the simple yet luxurious feel of the Vittore Garden. I'm about halfway there when I begin to hear voices coming from that area. The sound of my heels goes from click-clacking to muffled when the gravel walkway ends, and the garden grass begins. Now that I'm closer, I can see tents set up on the lawn and smell food on the grill, I can even hear classical music being played on a stereo. The voices that chatter become more distinct, and I'm able to pick out specific ones when the owners come into view.

There's a party in the garden.

A very elegant luncheon is going on that I had absolutely no news of. I can see smart suits and beautiful dresses, each one paired with a lightweight jacket or a cashmere sweater to fight the autumn chill. There are oxfords and high heels and diamond rings and Rolexes. Everyone here is a walking stack of money.

I have no idea why I feel a stab of resentment as I spot Serena standing with a skewer, a laugh filling the air like a pop of happiness bursting from her mouth. She tilts her head back and points the skewer at someone I don't recognize.

I thought we were friends. I thought she would tell me about this.

I don't even know what *this* even is. I'm living in a house full of gangsters, this could very well be some sort of twisted assassination party. Maybe they'll drag out one of those Russians and execute him on a stage somewhere later on. Or maybe they're all here to do business. Secretly making arrangements for shipments of illegal products. I have no idea. So maybe it's good that I wasn't invited. Maybe this is another one of the weird ways that Luca is protecting me. Shielding me from the darkness of the world he lives in.

Or maybe that's not it at all. Maybe Luca is protecting me from the truth.

I realize this truth as my gaze skitters through the crowd and I find Luca. He's standing beside two old couples, which isn't out of the ordinary. It's the young woman on his arm that makes my heart clench in my chest.

She's beautiful. Pale skin so smooth and milky she is literally the color *blush pink*. Her hands are manicured and dainty, I notice a single pearl on her finger when she covers her mouth as a giggle tumbles from her perfect lips. Her lashes flutter when she looks at Luca, gazing like he's the only man here. She is already in love with him. I don't know why this surprises me, I haven't known him long and I feel a lover's sense of heart wrenching betrayal as I observe this exchange.

But maybe this woman *has* known him a while. I keep forgetting … I'm the stranger here. *I'm* the one who stumbled into *their* lives. I'm the intruder.

No. Not an intruder—I'm a *captive*. I didn't stumble into Luca's life; I was dragged into it. Unconscious. He kidnapped me and held me here. Then he announced he would protect me from the dangers of this world, but he never told me the most dangerous person here was himself.

He came to my room every night. He kissed me. He slept beside me. He shared things with me I'm sure he's shared with no one else, just as I've done with him. And then he rolled out of bed and went on with his life like none of that mattered. He put on a suit and found this woman and decided I no longer exist.

The mystery woman has long hair swept up in a loose bun, so a few tendrils hang loose. She swipes one away as Luca passes her an hors d'oeuvre. He leans over to say something as she takes the food and the woman giggles again, leaning even closer to him. He doesn't seem to mind her proximity. He doesn't even blink when she takes a bite and then offers the rest to him. I watch in horror as he eats from her manicured fingers, but that horror twists into wretched betrayal when the woman reaches up and swipes a bit of sauce from the corner of his mouth.

They're so familiar. They're so … perfect. And I'm just here, watching from the sidelines as confusion stabs me like a jagged knife.

I take a step back, feeling coldness wash over me. That's when Luca glances up, as if my movement or my mood alerted him to my presence. His eyes snap to mine immediately, and I gasp aloud.

To his credit, Luca looks shocked to see me. He even looks embarrassed, quickly glancing at the woman at his side. She doesn't seem to notice his sudden discomfort as she touches his arm, gently tugging him toward the display of food nearby. She probably wants to feed him more snacks. Luca lets her pull him away, finally breaking eye contact.

I take that as my cue to leave. I'm clearly not wanted here, or else Luca or Serena would have said something. But they didn't. And now I see why.

I thought Serena understood my complicated feelings. She's the one who asked me to be there for Luca. But I guess I was only supposed to be there until he was strong enough to stand on his own. Until he didn't need me anymore.

And Luca… He yanked his own heart out of his chest a week ago and gave it to me still hot and bloody, pumping strongly in his palm. Then I woke up alone and haven't seen him since.

When it mattered, Luca cast me aside for someone else. Someone from his world.

I'm surprised by the tears that burn my eyes as I turn and immediately begin marching back toward the house. I didn't know how much this would hurt. I didn't expect the pangs of betrayal to be so brutal. But I guess I never realized exactly how I felt toward Luca.

I'd tried to fight it because of who he is and how we met, but the truth is that I've never felt safer than I have here with Luca. I've never felt more understood. I've never felt like I belonged anywhere but here. By his side.

I'd finally found someone to share the pain and the loneliness with and he tossed it away.

That's alright, I tell myself when I make it to my bedroom. I use my key to lock it from the inside and then I kick off my shoes and climb into bed. I crawl across the blankets and open the bedside table, smiling through teary eyes at the Holy Bible that's waiting for me.

I never should've allowed myself to feel anything for Luca. We're from two different worlds. And that couldn't be more obvious. He's a mafia boss and I'm a Christian woman. We have no business being so close in the first place.

Still…

"I've already let him in, God," I sob, tears plopping onto the leather cover. "I know it was wrong. I know we're unequally yoked. But I messed up, and now it hurts."

I open the Bible and mindlessly flip through the pages. I'm not even looking for anything specific. I just want to be close to the Lord right now. Because even though I walked into this heartbreak myself, I know God is kind enough to fix it. He loves me enough to put me back together, even when I'm the one who tore myself apart.

"Please make it stop," I whisper, clutching the Bible. "Please make the pain go away, Jesus."

I don't hear an answer. But I wasn't expecting one. So, instead of giving up, I clutch the Bible to my chest and lie on my side so I can cry myself to sleep.

14

Luca

Her name is Belén Moreno. I'm sure you've already heard all about her. Beautiful girl, barely nineteen and meticulously groomed in mind and body. She is the princess of the Spanish mafia, and she's ripe for marriage. A pretty face, mild manners, and a body illuminating with the glow of youth. Wide set hips for carrying babies, a slender neck meant for kissing. When she looked at me, all I saw was a curtain of lashes that batted like the wings of butterflies, fluttering and pretty and difficult to look away from.

Belén is mafia perfection, especially because her father kept her so close to home. She is thoroughly obedient, raised for the very purpose of fulfilling contracts with powerful men like me. She rarely spoke without first being spoken to. She came off as wary, barely holding eye contact for more than a few moments. To an observer, this would be interpreted as innocent shyness, but those of us inside know that it's disrespectful for an unmarried woman to maintain eye contact with someone of my ranking for so long. It could be interpreted as a challenge—or worse, distasteful flirtation.

I am aware the world around me has abandoned our severely outdated standards for men and women. But the mafia has never been part of the normal world. We have always existed on the outskirts of reality, creating our own world and our own rules to live by. They aren't great rules, but I promise I'm just as unhappy as any woman I've ever met in this business. If that makes a difference.

Eventually, Belén did loosen up at the garden party. I could tell it was her first time at such a social gathering, which meant her father had dragged her along for one purpose only. To put her on display for me.

It almost worked. Belén is a beautiful girl and despite her nerves, she carried herself well. I could see the other men around me salivating as she strolled by on my arm, the prettiest decoration I've ever seen. My father knew what he was doing when he invited Emilio Moreno to our gathering. That's the head of the Spanish mafia, all the way from New York City. And king of his very own snow fortress.

By snow, I mean cocaine.

Emilio is one of the richest men in the world, taking advantage of the defunding of police in NYC and openly distributing his cocaine throughout the city that never sleeps. Now, he's decided to expand his business so an alliance with my family would benefit us both. The Morenos are one of a handful of people in this business who could easily afford our rates for adding their cargo to our wine shipments. Working with them would make us very rich.

But it's deeper than that.

Emilio would be able to distribute his snow in other countries, and he would finally cross over into more upstanding business. Cocaine is lucrative, and it's earned Emilio a lot of money. But it's also dirty and has earned him an ugly reputation. No one is surprised. When most of your customers are junkies, hookers, and gap-toothed pimps it's hard to imagine the seller being much better.

That's where we come in. Wine is beautiful. Elegant. And attracts an entirely different crowd of buyers, whether we're working legally or not. Adding cocaine to our shipments won't sully our hands too much and it'll allow Emilio to shake off some of the dirt stuck to his own hands. All I've got to do to make that happen is marry pretty little Belén and put a kid in her by next year.

But I don't want to marry Belén Moreno. I hadn't even wanted to meet her—didn't even know I was going to meet her that day in the garden. We were having our annual harvest party, a celebration of the last of our grapes being plucked and the soil turned for the next season. It's something we've been doing since I lived in Italy on my aunt's farm. Except, back then we only did it with close family and a few select friends.

Here in Benton, it's become a business meeting of sorts. My father invites prospective investors and other business partners to schmooze and impress. He also does some observation of his own, carefully watching which men decide to discuss work and which men merely enjoy the free food.

Business deals are conducted in hushed whispers, contracts are laid out with a handshake and a toast, and women are strutted around for show so all the unmarried men can have their pick.

I didn't get to pick. This year, I was *chosen* for Belén. The contract is all but set in stone. I know because this business deal is too big for my father to let slip away. He will drag me down the aisle by my hair if he has to, wheeling his oxygen tank along with him.

Old man Vincent managed to make it through the party without an issue, but he slept for two days afterward. A shocking revelation of just how close we are to losing him. Which is why I haven't found it in me to completely turn down the contract.

My father wants to see me married before he dies. He'd love to see a grandchild, but I think we all know that's too far out to hope for. The least I could do is walk down the stupid aisle before he croaks. Belén isn't even a bad deal. She's beautiful and over ten years younger than me. I'm not a pervert looking for a young girl, it's just the way our world works. Women are married off as soon as possible, starting at eighteen and wearing a white gown by twenty. Some of them sign contracts as young as age ten and consummate the marriage the day after their eighteenth birthday.

It isn't my fault I didn't start looking for a wife until my thirties. But it's better than waiting for as long as Antonio Caruso did. He's in his mid-*forties*. If my sister didn't have a contract with him, he could very well turn his rheumy eyes toward little Belén. And she'd be expected to marry him without a single complaint. Just like I was expected to entertain her at the garden party without a complaint.

It was awful of my father to throw her onto me like that. I had been expecting to handle business while I was there. I thought, if there was time for socializing, it'd be between myself and Serena. But my father blindsided me, calling up Emilio behind my back and then practically shoving his daughter into my arms. I couldn't just ignore her. Not in front of so many important figures from our organization. I had to spend time with her. I had to smile. I had to entertain her. Anything less than open flirtation would have been seen as a sign of disrespect toward her father and disinterest in an alliance.

I just wish Effy hadn't been there to see that. She walked in on that whole thing with no context and no chance for me to explain. She saw another woman in my arms and immediately jumped to conclusions that I don't blame her for.

She shouldn't have been there…

I'd given her freedom of the estate, but I never expected her to stroll into the middle of the garden party. What were the odds… And now everything is so messed up. My father found out about her presence here at the estate but, mercifully, he's been too tired and too distracted by the deal with the Morenos to care much.

My issue is entirely personal. I'm stuck in an engagement that's a written contract, leaving no room for emotions. Meanwhile, Effy holds my broken heart, but our circumstances complicate everything.

Not only does she come from the normal world, but Effy arrived in *this* dark world as my hostage. Our relationship started off twisted and demented. It could only end the same messed up way. If not now, then soon. Perhaps when her holy God revealed how much of a monster I am. Perhaps when He rumbled the heavens and forbid her from even looking at a sinner like me.

We're just too different. Too far apart. It's better this way.

That's what I tell myself as I keep up this distance for the next three days. Ignoring the sobs I hear from her quarters. Pretending I don't notice her quickly passing through the foyer when my back is turned. She is avoiding me as much as I'm avoiding her, and that's a good thing. We only need to make it to the trial, then I'll release her and never see her again.

The thought of letting Effy go makes me grind my teeth as I leave the estate and hop into the backseat of my car. By the time Lorenzo drives me to our warehouse, I have a headache from clenching my jaw so tightly. But I exhale the throbbing pain in my temple and use it as fuel to help me through what I need to do next.

"Is he in there?" I ask Loren.

He nods, watching me through the rearview mirror. "Yes, sir. Miss Serena dropped him off an hour ago."

"And did her men handle him?"

He pauses. Glances away. "Somewhat, sir."

That means she tortured him before I even got here. He must have pissed her off, and how could he not? Serena hunted down the third Russian on our list. Just the *thought* of him pisses me off. He beat up my brother. He watched him die. And now he's about to pay for it.

The man is younger than I expect him to be, though it's difficult to really tell from his swollen eyes and busted lips. He looks awful, and I don't feel bad at all.

Just one more after this…

I don't waste any words; I just press my gun to his temple, and he obediently bows his head. I give him a moment to get right with God, then I begin to squeeze the trigger—but my finger stops when he says aloud, "I didn't know who he was until afterward."

"That doesn't matter," I rasp, glaring down at him. "That just means you beat up an innocent kid without having a clue why."

He coughs—or at least I think it's a cough. It takes me a moment to realize the noise he's making are words coming from his mouth. "She was a kid too."

That makes me pause. This is the closest I've come to getting a reason for why my brother was murdered.

The gun shakes in my hand. "Who was a kid? Who is *she*?"

The Russian doesn't speak. He stares blankly ahead, out of pride or ignorance, I'm not sure. All I see is red.

There's a crack that fills the air when I ram the butt of the gun into his face. I have no idea what I've broken, and I also don't care. I hit him again and he falls backwards, flat on his back, and stays there. He's still alive, his breaths coming out slowly. They sound wet, like he's breathing through a sponge.

I stand over him. Cock my gun. "Who is she?"

He doesn't speak. To his credit, he does try. I can see his jaw moving, but it looks broken so he can't get the words out.

My shoulders tremble in rage. "Why did they kill my brother!?" I scream.

The man's eyes roll to the back of his head and a bloodcurdling wail fills the room. I don't realize the sound has come from myself until my eyes go blurry and I feel the tears racing down my cheeks. They're so hot they burn my face. I shudder as a sob rocks through me and I lift the gun … and press it to my own head.

"Mario…" I whisper.

I can see his face in my mind. I can hear his last words. But louder than the song of my nightmares is Lorenzo's voice, screaming my name.

"Mr. Vittore!" he shouts, and I feel his hand slap mine away.

The gun falls and skitters across the floor. At the same time, I drop to my knees. Blinking wildly. I can't believe that weapon was just pressed to my own head. I can't believe what I was about to do.

What is wrong with me?

I tremble as I stare at the Russian's dead body. I was *this* close to being as lifeless as him. Joining him on the concrete floor, blood trickling from my nose. What drove me to that point?

Was it Mario? Was it Effy's absence? Was it the

bloodshed?

"I don't know," I whisper. "I don't know…"

Lorenzo is dragging me to my feet. He's asking if I'm all right, and he thinks my words are for him. I don't correct him. He doesn't need to know how confused I am. How lost I feel. I'm the underboss of the Vittore mafia and I just lost myself in a moment of madness. This world will do that to anyone, but it's not allowed to happen to me.

There's too much at stake. Too much I could lose. Too many people depending on me. What would my father do if I killed myself? What would Serena do? She's the only one in my life who truly loves me now that Mario is gone. I won't fool myself into thinking Vincent loves me. I never have.

I love you.

The Voice is warm and comforting. And it scares the living daylights out of me. I almost scream when I hear it in my head—not my head—in my *soul.* Like someone is speaking directly into my spirit. That's when I know I've truly lost it.

I squeeze my eyes shut as Lorenzo leads me back to my car, and I remain that way during the drive home. My head presses into the rest, my eyes close, my body melts into the leather seats. I'm doing everything I can to drown out the thoughts in my head. To distract myself from that Voice.

I don't want to hear it again. Because if He speaks, I'll eventually have to answer.

So when Lorenzo pulls up to the house, I make him vow he will remain silent. No one needs to know how much I've unraveled. No one needs to worry over me. I can keep it together.

Just one more, I tell myself, marching through the house to my room. I instructed Loren to send for Isabella when we arrived, so I have my tie loosened and the first few buttons of my shirt undone when I make it to my room.

She doesn't arrive right away. I have enough time to pour myself a drink and take off the rest of my clothes. When the door opens, Isabella slowly steps inside, blinking into the darkness like a mouse searching for a hungry cat. She is cautious because of our last encounter. I haven't seen her since I sent her away naked. I haven't needed her.

Her apprehension is warranted, but I have no intention of sending her away the way I did before. Not unless she provokes me. Tonight, I want her here. Tonight, I need to forget.

Isabella's eyes widen when she sees me standing naked at the drink display. I can see the bob of her slender throat as she swallows, even from across the room. My eyes never leave hers as I toss back the rest of my bourbon. I watch her over the rim of my glass, standing by the door in a black nightie, her hands clasped in front of her. I love that she always acts so innocent but comes dressed for the show. Like a virgin prostitute.

My throat burns. I cough.

"You called for me," Bella says softly.

I jerk my head at the bed. "Take off your clothes."

The best thing about Isabella is that she knows how this works. When I bring a woman home from a bar or a club, things are always awkward. Once the fun is over, I have to sit through idle pillow talk or coldly ask the woman to leave. I could hire a dedicated girl, but paying for it isn't nearly as fun as picking up a stranger. Flirting, touching, whispering into her ear as we ride to my home. Stumbling through the house because I'm too drunk to stand up straight and she's wearing heels too high to keep up with me.

Hiring a woman just isn't as exciting. The chase is thrilling. But even that has a downside. A woman from a bar doesn't know what I like or how I like it. She doesn't know what I want or need. And she doesn't know this encounter will lead to nothing.

Isabella is perfect because she knows how this works and has no expectations. She's obedient. Quiet. And takes my frustration like a pro. It never surprises her when I don't hold back. She can tell what I need from my mood. And she can handle everything I give her. That's one of the things I enjoy about her most. I don't have to restrain myself—so I don't.

Isabella is a drug and I take every piece of her. The dose is nearly lethal for us both. She scratches ribbons down my back, I can't tell if it's from pain or pleasure. I don't ask. I don't care. And I don't stop until I'm satisfied. Until I can't feel the pain of failure anymore. Or the blinding fear of the Truth weighing heavy on my conscience.

My chest rises and falls as I heave for breath. I collapse on top of Bella, drained. Exhausted. We're so sweaty we stick together. She doesn't try to move for a few moments until my weight becomes too much for her. Then she shifts uncomfortably, and I roll off with a sigh.

"I needed you today," I say, voice raspy.

She doesn't respond.

"Tell me you love me."

There's a weighty pause. It's not a request I haven't issued before. I've explored a lot of things with Bella that she keeps between us. This is one of them. Wondering what it's like to actually make love, not just have sex. Pretending we're a real couple with real feelings for each other. Isabella has always indulged my fantasies, wearing whatever I've requested, staying as long as I need her, saying the words I tell her to say. She has never denied me anything.

Today, she hesitates, but she says it eventually. Her voice small. Shaky. "I love you."

It doesn't sound anything like the Voice from before.

Isabella shifts, sitting up and swinging her legs over the edge of the bed. "May I leave?"

It's the first time she's ever asked to leave. Usually, I send her away on my own or keep her until morning. I squint at her bare back, chocolatey tresses plastered to her dewy skin. I'm tempted to wrap my hand into her locks and pull her back for more. But I exhale a sigh and shake away the thoughts.

"Sure. Go ahead."

"Goodnight, Luca," she whispers, grabbing her clothes. She slips on the nightie she'd been wearing when she arrived, and then pads barefoot into the hallway. I stare after her until the door closes.

15

Effy

There is a fat burger on my plate, the cheese is perfectly melted and oozing down the side of my greasy beef patty. A pile of French fries sits on a platter in the middle of the table, Serena snatches one with a dainty finger and grins as she takes a bite.

"This is one of my favorite places to eat. It isn't fancy, but sometimes I get tired of Italian food and expensive restaurants. You know?"

I don't know, but I nod anyway. We're sitting in a bar I've never been to, the curtains drawn back to let in the daylight. As I glance around, I wonder how different this place looks after 10pm. If they still serve greasy burgers, or just beer and shots of tequila. From my place in our little booth, I can see stripper poles in the lounge on the second floor. There aren't any dancers on them, but I'm positive there will be after sunset.

This is Serena's favorite place. In the time I've known her, it's become clear she isn't your typical mafia princess. In her short sleeves, I can see all of her tattoos, and I've noticed she doesn't travel with security. She even drives herself around, which is apparently a luxury for women in this business. Most of them have drivers who take them wherever they want—in my world, *that* is a luxury. But Serena says it's just another way to keep the women in line. Without a license or a car, you can't go anywhere without your husband knowing. And you can't get away from your husband if your driver refuses to help you.

But Serena gets to go wherever she wants. Whenever she wants. And that freedom is exactly how she discovered her favorite place to get a burger. Though, from the way she keeps stealing glances at the man behind the bar, I doubt it's the burgers that keeps her coming back.

He's an older man, tatted up and handsome. Exactly the sort of guy I'd imagine running a bar frequented by the mafia. Serena seems enamored, not even trying to hide her grin when he smiles at her and winks.

I grab my burger and take a bite, chewing loudly enough that she frowns at my smacking. "It's good," I say with a shrug.

Her eyes narrow. "Something's bothering you."

"Why'd you take me out to lunch today?" I haven't seen her since the garden.

"We've hung out before," she says.

"But why now?"

"Ask what you really want to ask, Effy."

I sigh. Push my plate away. "Why didn't you tell me about that other woman?"

She glances away which makes me angry. She knows I'm upset over Luca. She knows I've found out something that was supposed to be a secret. I feel like such an idiot.

"You told me to be there for him," I remind her. "But you knew there was someone else all along."

Serena brushes salt from her fingers and sits up straighter. "Things are more complicated than you think. There are some things you won't understand."

"How can I when no one ever tells me anything?"

"We don't owe you an explanation for everything, Effy. You're only here because my baby brother is dead. Not because we want you here."

"I don't want to be here any more than you want me here," I snap. "I was kidnapped, remember? I've never had a choice. And the moment I thought I could choose something for myself, it was taken away from me."

Serena blinks at me, her face full of pity. She extends her hand like she's going to take my own but thinks better of it and grabs a fry instead. She doesn't eat it, just holds it and shakes the salt off.

"I didn't expect you to develop feelings for him," she says softly. "I'm so sorry."

I glance away. I don't want to talk about this anymore. I don't want to eat. I don't want to be here.

"If it's worth anything," Serena continues, "he feels it too."

I can't stop the dry laugh that claws its way up from my throat, it nearly chokes me, like a stone tumbling out of my mouth. It's hard and hurts more than it helps.

"Ha!" I feel my eyes burn with angry tears. Luca feels it

too. A wonderful joke.

Serena looks confused. "It's true. I know my brother, Effy. Whatever happened between you two, it was mutual, okay?"

"*Was*," I emphasize.

"You're not the only one who's hurt. He's doing bad. Worse than I've ever seen him." She pulls her arms in so she's hugging herself, looking weak and fragile for the first time since I've met her. This powerful mafia woman. "He has this list he's going through … he's almost done, but…" she shakes her head. "The cost is too high. It's breaking him."

"List?" I whisper.

Serena seems to snap back into focus. She clears her throat and stops hugging herself to grab another fry. This time, she stuffs it into her mouth and then takes a big gulp of her soda.

"What list?" I ask.

"It's complicated."

"I deserve to know more—"

"He's getting married," Serena blurts, and I don't know if it's to change the subject, to shut me up, or if it really seemed like the right moment to lay that on me.

I have no reaction except a slow blink. My eyes feel dry, even though they were burning with tears a few moments earlier.

"What?" I say dumbly, like I hadn't heard.

"The woman in the garden," Serena says, "she's Luca's fiancé. He's going to marry her. Next week."

This can't be happening. He was just in bed with me. He'd just kissed me. It happened nearly two weeks ago, but still. It's quite a leap to go from cuddling with one woman and marrying another.

My throat feels sticky when I swallow, and as I start to speak, my upper lip sticks to my front teeth. I clear my throat. Lick my lips. "Why are you telling me this?"

"Because you deserve to know." Serena gives me another pitiful look. "And because you're invited to the wedding."

I reel back in my chair, clutching the side of the table. I don't know if I'm angry or hurt. But I can barely think straight.

"It's more of a security thing," she says quickly. "We need our best guys at the venue for Luca and his bride's sake. But you're a high priority too. So it's best if you come along." She shrugs. "Two birds. One stone."

"You want me to watch him get married."

"Effy, come on. At least this wasn't thrown on you—"

"It wasn't?"

"Not like the garden party."

"Was that an engagement party?"

She takes another sip of her soda. "Not really. That was a harvest party for investors. But Luca and his fiancé met there. The arrangements were made there."

They met that day. That beautiful woman is going to marry a man she met less than 14 days ago. From the way they'd behaved at the party, I would've assumed they were in a serious relationship, deeply in love. But now I see that's just another one of the façades of this world. Another beautiful lie. Happy, loving couple on the outside, complete strangers behind closed doors.

It dawns on me now, as I watch Serena pick at her burger. "Did Luca put you up to this?"

She stares at me.

"Did he tell you to take me out and break this news to me?"

"No," she says, and I'm not sure I believe her. "I volunteered to do it. After he told me about you walking in on the party."

"I see."

She leans forward, dropping her voice to a conspiratorial whisper. "You don't have to end things," she says, holding eye contact. "The marriage is just a contract. He'll have to make an heir and hold up appearances at events, but you can still be there. Behind the scenes. If you want."

I blink at her, the offer finally clicking into place.

Anger burns inside me like acid in my chest. "I am not going to become Luca's mistress."

Serena backs off. Her dark hair is tied back in a tight ponytail, it sways as she nods and leans away from me, adjusting in her seat. "I just thought you should know. He'll likely have a mistress anyway—most men in this world have a few—it might as well be someone he actually likes for once. Someone who understands him."

"I am not a side piece."

"It's not as bad as you think. He'll take care of you just like he would his own wife."

"What would you do?" I challenge. "Since it's such a great offer."

"Honestly? I would take this as my chance to walk away. No strings attached."

I blink. That was not the answer I was expecting.

"Effy, you're not from this world," Serena says seriously. "You were dragged into it against your will. And I know you've gotten used to some things, and even attached to some things, but there's no reason for you to stay here any longer than you need to. It isn't a pretty world. It isn't a world I would choose to live in. If I *had* a choice." That last part comes out bitterly, spitting each word. It makes me wonder just how powerful this mafia princess really is. Or maybe her tattoos and her driving and her secret bartender boyfriend are just another façade. A lie that screams power and freedom but only hides a shackle I simply cannot see.

Serena is as trapped as I am. But I won't be trapped forever. Once the trial is over, and I've given my testimony, Luca will release me, and I'll likely never see these people again. I'll be free. And if Luca is any good, he'll give me severance to make up for holding me hostage and as a reward for helping lock his brother's murderer away for good.

I could walk away from this a very rich woman. That should make me happy. Luca's engagement should make me happy. I knew from the beginning that we were unequally yoked, but I let myself fall for him anyway. I'd prayed and asked God to protect me from myself. Keep me from getting attached and lured in by the fake luxuries of this world. Maybe this is His answer. Maybe this is God's way of snatching me away from sin when I'm too weak to walk away on my own.

Every heartbreak hurts, but not every heartbreak is bad for you. Sometimes, it's the best thing that could've happened to you. I have to accept that if I ever want to move on from this. I have to believe that God is still on the throne. Still in charge. And if this isn't what He wants for me, He will correct it.

"Okay," I say with a sigh. "Maybe you're right. Maybe I should just walk away."

Serena gives me a cautious smile. "You're stronger than you think, Effy."

She's entirely wrong. I'm weak and I know it, but that's okay. Because when I am weak, God is strong. His power is made perfect in weakness. That's **II Corinthians 12:9**, a scripture I keep close to my heart because of all the times I've been so weak and pathetic. Weak enough to fall for a crime boss and pathetic enough to be heartbroken when he moves on.

That scripture is the only way I've been able to hold my head high sometimes. Which is funny because the world will shame you in your weakness, but Jesus says His grace is sufficient for you. Your weakness is when His goodness overflows and He is glorified as your Rescuer. In a way, its good to be weak, because it gives God a chance to show us just how strong He is. And how much stronger we can become by placing our faith in Him. Letting Him fight our battles.

So I sit back and promise myself I won't intervene in God's plans. As Serena drives us home, I repeat that Scripture in my head, and I pray to God for His strength. For His comfort. For His forgiveness because I knew better from the start.

After praying, I'm able to walk into that estate with my head held high. With a renewed vigor and confidence I've never felt before.

And then my joy pops like a bubble when I turn down the hall to head to my room. Serena stops me with a gentle hand on my shoulder. "Actually, your room is this way," she says, glancing down the hall in the opposite direction.

I frown. "But I thought—"

"You have a new room," she says, cutting me off, then she turns and walks away before I can ask any questions.

I follow her in silence, trying to control my emotions as everything becomes clear. Serena didn't just take me out to break the bad news to me, she also got me out of the house so Luca could move my things out of his bedroom while I was gone. He packed me up and sent me away like a cheap hooker who wouldn't leave.

I don't just feel betrayed, I feel dirty and used. This is insane because I never actually slept with the guy. We've had the most innocent exchanges of my life—even Travis got to slide his hand up my shirt once. But Luca and I didn't have a sexual or physical bond. Despite the kiss we shared, everything between us was emotional. Even spiritual. That's why it hurts so badly.

When Christians love, they love hard. Because we know our love transcends time and space. It isn't just for right now or even just this lifetime. Our love is eternal because we know we'll be reunited in Heaven. And it's overwhelming because all of it is reserved for just one person. The spouse God has given us.

When you look at marriage biblically, as an equal partnership ordained by God, built to last eternity and to be shared with one person only, it's almost too much to comprehend. It's strange to think there could be enough love between two people to last infinity. But it's possible because we are spiritual beings. We don't love the person; we love their *spirit.*

It's the reason Christians who are full of righteousness can still be reduced to this heartbroken mess over a sinful mafia boss. Because I love the person Luca can become. The man I know God created him to be. Not the man he is right now.

It's like we're all stuck in eternity. Loving people for the perfection they can become in Christ rather than the mess they are right now.

When you think of it that way, Christianity doesn't sound so appealing, does it? But that's because you're thinking in the flesh. Just as I've acted in the flesh.

Because our love is so powerful, we are instructed to be careful in our relationships. Not just romantically, the people in your circle of friends can harm your spirit too. You can be unequally yoked with *anyone*, not just a lover. Your best friend. Your sibling. Your coworkers. If you aren't careful, anyone can drag you off the path of righteousness. The Bible says as much in **I Corinthians 15:33; Do not be misled, bad company corrupts good character**. And for the last few weeks, I've been *surrounded* by bad company.

But soon, I'll be set free.

So even though this hurts, I let Serena lead me to my new room and I thank her with a smile and close my door as politely as possible. Then I wait a full minute to make sure she's gone before I collapse to the floor in tears.

16

Effy

The Vittores are throwing a dinner party. It's to celebrate Luca's engagement and also double as a rehearsal dinner for the wedding itself. I know because I've been dragged out of my room to attend this awful event.

Serena arrived at my door with a new dress and a box of apology chocolates this afternoon. I cooperated for the white chocolate fudge dipped truffles. Not for her pouting lips or the Jimmy Choos that came with the dress. Though they were a welcome bonus.

My nails are manicured, my eyebrows plucked, every hair on my body strip waxed until I screamed. When I asked the point of being bald as a baby, Serena asked why on earth I'd ever willingly stuff a woolly mammoth into my panties. I had shut my mouth after that because I did *not* have a woolly mammoth down there. I swear.

Now I'm wearing an expensive perfume I can't name and carrying a handbag that cost more than three months of rent at the best complex I've ever lived in. My makeup is professional, and my hair has been washed and silk pressed. Normally, my afro curls rest on my shoulders, but straightened like this, they tumble halfway down my back in a curtain of black glossy locks.

Even *I* think I look different when I pass a mirror hanging on the wall in the back of the dining room. The Vittores rented out a hotel for the event, so the 'dining room' is technically a grand hall, but it's been sectioned off by hanging drapes and decorated to look like an elegant dining room from a family home. A home large enough to house over 300 ridiculously rich gangsters.

I thought I saw suits and ties at the garden party, but this is entirely different. Diamonds, pearls, and shoes shined brightly enough to see my reflection in them. The hall is filled with people wealthy enough to purchase this very building in cash. Twice. And they're all as dangerous as the Russians who would've killed me.

A shiver runs down my spine as I shuffle to the back of the room. I'm not uncomfortable because of how rich and powerful these people are, I feel weird because they're all staring at me. But not in a way that makes me feel beautiful. They look like they hate me.

The women openly shake their heads at me. The men leer like I'm a new doll on a shelf for them to buy. I don't know what's going on but it's clear my presence is causing a stir. I thought these people would welcome me. Considering I'm the one helping them get justice for the Vittore prince. But right now, it seems like my endeavors mean nothing to them. It seems like I've somehow become their enemy.

I tuck my chin and keep walking toward the back. My feet practically glide over the carpet in my ridiculously comfortable heels. I pass a display of seafood on ice which sits beside a table of hors d'oeuvres. There's caviar with crispy crostini—but also caponata and a rustic-looking dip topped with baked goat cheese. I see Caprese flatbread, stuffed dates, and melon bites wrapped in prosciutto.

My nose is assaulted by at least a dozen different kinds of cheese, which I suppose I can pair with anything from the antipasto display. A waitress passes me with a platter of nothing but marinated olives and peppers in oil. And then there's the wine table. SO. MUCH. WINE. I can barely take it all in. Deep reds, earthy Pinot noir, sparkling white wines—even a bold blackberry wine called *Her Tears.*

I have never seen so much Italian food in my life—then again, the extent of my exposure to the Italian cuisine is, like, *Olive Garden* and the pizza place up the street from my motel.

Every part of this party is richly cultural and vibrant. From the décor to the food, even the grapes lining the wine table. They spill over the tablecloth and onto the floor where kids run over and scoop them up. Angry mothers shout in Italian, scolding them for their behavior, but the children only giggle and run away. This event is for everyone, business partners, young ladies, and even children.

It's strange to picture children in this world. When I think of the mafia, I only see those Russians who tried to kill me.

And Luca, who kidnapped me and locked me up in his bedroom. But even people like Luca were children once. He was a kid who giggled and ran and played just like these kids here. He was innocent once. Before the darkness ruined him.

The thought of a young and innocent Luca almost makes me smile, especially as I pass a kid with dark hair just like him and burning amber eyes. He's so young, yet he's here at this gathering with hundreds of other mafiosi. Murderers, drug dealers, adulterers, and liars. Everyone has come out to congratulate the Italian underboss on his upcoming wedding.

And then there's me.

I don't feel like I belong here. But I certainly look like I do. Serena had whistled when I stepped out of my room wearing the dress she'd given me. A dramatic red gown that hugs every inch of me, revealing curves I didn't even know I had. It has a plunging neckline that almost makes me blush, but Serena's gawking gave me confidence. I have never dressed this daringly in my life. Mostly because I could never afford to.

"You're going to turn heads," Serena had told me as we'd climbed into her truck. "You might even outshine Belén."

I assume *Belén* is the bride-to-be. I've only just gotten here but, so far, I haven't seen her. I'm certain she's here somewhere. Probably hanging on Luca's arm like she was in the garden. If that's the case, I hope I never see her. I don't know how I would react. And I certainly don't know how I would react to seeing Luca.

It suddenly occurs to me that maybe he's the reason Serena dressed me up so well. Is this some sort of twisted joke on me?

Or is she trying to help me get his attention? It's so hard to tell with Serena. One minute she's telling me to be there for him, then she's saying he's getting married and they don't owe me any explanation for it. Then she's offering me the chance to become his mistress but also telling me I should hightail it out of this world as soon as I can.

I don't know what she wants. I don't know what *I* want.

God, help me, I pray as I scan the room for a corner to hide in. There are so many people here, enough for me to get lost in the crowd, but I stand out in this red dress. And also because I'm the only Black woman in this entire building. Serena left me as soon as we arrived. She said she's a Vittore, so she's expected to be with the family. I understand. I'm not even a *friend* of the family, so I doubt I'll get any special treatment. That much is evident. I'm only here because it's easier to drag me around rather than leave half the security force with me to keep the angry Russians away.

Still searching for a place to disappear, I turn almost in a circle, trying to decide if I should mosey by the ice sculpture or hide in the crowd of men gathered by the wine table. That would seem a little desperate. I choose the ice sculpture, but I never make it there.

"You look like you need this," says a voice behind me.

I spin, almost too quickly, and find a smiling man holding out a flute of white wine. He looks so charming and … normal. It throws me off for a second. Because he also looks familiar.

I wrack my brain as I hold up a hand, refusing the drink. "I don't drink alcohol."

"So you really are a good Christian girl," he says, retracting his hand and tipping the glass at his own lips.

I watch him drink, frowning. "Do we know each other?"

"We have a mutual friend."

"Luca Vittore," I say flatly.

My tone earns a wide smile that takes up half his face. "I could have been talking about Serena. Interesting that you immediately assumed I was referring to him."

My cheeks burn, but realization chases away the shame. This man does know me—or at least he knows a lot about me. I mean, why would he insinuate Serena could be our mutual friend unless he knows how much time we've spent together?

I shouldn't be surprised. Most people in the Vittore family probably know about me. But there is something about this man that just feels off.

He steps closer to me, close enough that I can smell the fruity wine on his breath. When I tilt my chin up, I can see the scruffy hairs on his cheeks, like he skipped the razor this morning. He looks so ordinary. So blue collar—I almost gasp.

He *is* blue collar. Like literal *blue* collar. This man … he's a cop.

I remember him from the case, when I was first brought in for questioning over Mario's death. He was there. He was in charge. And now he's here at Luca's dinner party. Smelling of wine and mints and smirking like he's got a big fat secret.

"I bet you've gotten to know Luca well lately," he's saying when I interrupt him.

"I doubt I know him as well as I know you."

He leans back, squinting like he isn't sure if I mean to insult him or not.

"You're a cop," I say bluntly. "The cop who questioned me about Mario Vittore."

That grin is back. "A detective, actually. And yes, I did question you. You have a good memory."

"It's difficult to forget everything I've been through."

"I can imagine."

"What do you want with me, *Detective*?" I demand.

He holds up both hands. "Just Louis. And I don't want anything. You just looked lonely, and I thought I'd try to make you more comfortable."

"Shouldn't you be making arrests?" I gesture around the room. "This place is full of criminals."

He presses his lips together, and I suddenly see his resemblance to Luca. Despite their difference in stature, this man is very clearly related to the Vittores. Which means I am very clearly trapped here in this world. No matter what. Louis isn't a cop who's been bought or threatened. He *is* mafia.

I bet he's their eyes and ears inside the force. I bet he helped Luca hunt me down—which was better than the Russians hunting me down, but all that means is this man will not help me if something goes wrong. He works for Luca, not law enforcement.

"My role here is complicated," he says.

"I am so tired of everyone telling me how complicated things are."

He chuckles. "This is the mafia. Nothing about who we

are or what we do is simple. Only our goals are straightforward."

"And what is the goal of a dirty cop?"

His eyes narrow into slits. "Careful. You're cute. But not that cute."

"I'm not here because I'm cute."

"You're right. You're here because you're useful. But you'll stay because you're cute. Right?" He looks sideways at me, like we're sharing a private joke. The expression on his face makes my hand itch to slap him.

"I don't know what you're insinuating—"

"Yes, you do," he says casually. "You're his whore. We all see it."

My eyes bulge, but he cuts me off before I can respond to the accusation.

"Luca wants to protect you, I know that. We all know that. But there's only one reason for him to dress you up and parade you around like this." Louis looks me up and down, his tongue dashing out to wet his lips. "How old are you?" he asks.

I turn and walk away.

Now I get it. The reason everyone's been looking at me like they hate me.

It's because they think I'm Luca's mistress. They think I showed up here in this stupid dress to cause trouble and stir up drama with his future wife. I can't help but wonder if Serena did this on purpose. If this is a cruel joke on me or just her having fun.

Why? I ask, refusing to feel sorry for myself. The only thing

I feel right now is burning anger. I'm not wondering why Serena did this. I'm wondering why I so blindly fell for it. I can't trust these people. Not a single one. Serena isn't my friend any more than Luca is my lover. I am alone here.

I am with you…

I jerk to a halt, but not because of God's message. I've stopped walking because someone has grabbed my arm.

I turn to find Louis giving me a sympathetic face. "Don't leave," he says. "I didn't mean to push you away."

I twist my arm free. "I'm ready to go. It's clear I don't belong here."

"Listen—"

"*Please*," I say. The pleading in my voice makes me cringe, but I just want to go. I'm tired of this.

Louis shows me a small bit of mercy, nodding and stepping back to shove his hands into his pockets. "I can have a car pull around the back for you."

The back. It makes me feel even worse. I have to leave through the back door like an unwanted guest. It makes sense. Without Serena by my side to protect me, I'm just another woman Luca is sleeping with.

"I'll meet you out back," I say to Louis.

17

Luca

I want a drink. But all we have is wine. One of the worst things about our organization is that there's never anything strong enough for my tastes. My father used to say wine was a woman's drink. As a kid sneaking away any alcohol I could get my hands on, I'd strongly disagreed. As a man who's itching for something dark, strong, and burning, I have to say my father may have been on to something.

I throw away my dignity and order a servant to pour me a glass of our signature blackberry bottle. It's a specialty line we released some years ago, and it's been a hit ever since. Stronger than your average red with a dark undertone, when paired with savory foods it almost tastes sour. I thought everyone would hate it, but it's gotten quite popular. Serena calls it a fruity beer; I call it *Her Tears*.

The name is an homage to my poor grandmother who planted the first seeds to our blackberry bushes. It's taken my father's and my own entire lifetime to produce a suitable bottle.

The first batch was tested when my father was a teenager—it was a total failure. So they let the bushes turn, tried two seasons later, and got a suitable flavor. From there, the aging process was tested. For twenty years. By the time I turned fifteen, we had a room in our cellar full of legacy bottles with my aunt's stamp of approval. When my father asked what we should name it, a week out from release, mind you, I offered the name, *Her Tears.*

I was twenty years old, not even old enough to drink in the US yet. But my suggestion earned a unanimous vote, and the bottle was premiered at our next harvest party. We charged nearly five grand per glass, just to make it look extra bougie. It was a hit.

Since then, we've begun the process of adding pomegranate, cherry, and blueberry wine to our collection. Next year, we expect to unveil a long-awaited plum wine. I'm looking forward to it.

The blackberry wine slides down easily enough. It doesn't burn but after another glass, I feel the shackles on my shoulders fall away and I shake off my nerves. This wedding party was not my idea. The wedding was not my idea, but my father was insistent and as long as he's focused on me, he isn't pressuring Serena. She's the reason I'm here. Because even if I end up marrying a woman I'll never love, I can always have a fling or two that will be overlooked. But Serena will never be able to escape her husband.

Life is different for men and women in this world. It's shocking to find a loyal man. But women have been killed for insulting their husbands with infidelity. It isn't fair, but nothing in this life ever is. That's why I've set everything aside for this wedding. It's why I can suck it up and marry a woman I hardly even know because my worst-case scenario will always be better than whatever Serena will face.

I failed to protect my little brother, but I don't have to fail my little sister too. Marrying Belén will keep my father off Serena's back for just a little while longer. It may even butter him up enough to forget about her arrangements altogether. She still hasn't signed her contract. We can get out of it if we really want to.

If all else fails, I can do my best with Belén during our short honeymoon. My father has already scheduled a weeklong visit back to the family farm to introduce her to our extended family. If we make it back home with a positive pregnancy test, it just might be enough to save Serena altogether. Because the one thing my father wants more than seeing us married is seeing his legacy live on. He wants an heir. A young son to replace the one he lost. He's obviously too old and frail to produce one on his own, a grandson is the best he can hope for.

I can give that to him. Belén is young and fertile and if I want her every night, she will give herself to me. A woman of her status won't be on birth control—the point of our marriage is to produce an heir; she *can't* take birth control without my permission. And I certainly won't give it. Not with so much on the line.

Everything I'm doing is for Serena. To give her a life she

deserves. But the cost is more than just my hand in marriage, as I scan the crowd and spot a red angel drifting through the hall, I realize the cost is my own heart.

If I marry Belén, I will lose Effy forever.

I won't even bother entertaining the thought of having her as a mistress. While that is a common thing in my world, it isn't common in the world Effy comes from. She's a Christian woman. And while she may have had her share of struggles and mistakes in her faith, I know she will never agree to that sort of relationship, and I would never insult her with such an offer. She's worth more than that to me.

I want to protect her for myself now, not just because of her connection to Mario. I can't lie about that anymore. Not to myself or to Serena. Though, I will admit I've never directly told Serena everything that's happened with Effy. She knows me well enough to have figured it out on her own. Which is why she dressed her up like this and dragged her out here in front of everyone.

She looks beautiful. She looks breathtaking. And she also looks like my whore.

Effy's wearing a dangerous red dress that makes her look entirely seductive. If I were at a restaurant with my friends, she would be an intriguing woman I would shamelessly flirt with. But here, at the *wedding party* of the Italian underboss, her attire is unwholesome.

The rest of the women are dressed fashionably in gowns and expensive dresses, but they're still rather modest. Even Serena, despite wearing six-inch stilettos and a tight-fitting dress, has made sure she's covered her tattoos with a shawl and chosen to wear her long hair swooped up above her shoulders to make her look youthful and demure.

Effy, in contrast, looks like a call girl on duty. Searching for the highest bidder. But the worst part is that she doesn't even know it. She has no idea why everyone is glaring at her, why all the men are stealing glances over their wives' shoulders and the women are shooting daggers from their eyes. I can see her embarrassed confusion as she tucks herself away near the ice sculpture across the room, and my heart aches for her.

I've done this to her. If I'd never touched her, Serena wouldn't have played this cruel hand. She thinks she's helping me by singling Effy out. She's hoping Belén will realize Effy is my personal plaything and call off the wedding in jealous anger. It's a sneaky little plan, and it just might work.

Mistresses are common in this business, but they're supposed to be kept a secret. They are not allowed at official functions like this. And they're certainly not allowed to prance around dressed like that. With Belén being so young, she might get angry enough to call off the whole thing. But I've met Emilio. And I know my father. They're both ready for this.

The contract is already on its way here. I have a pen in my pocket waiting to be used. Once Belén gets here, we'll sign together. In front of everyone. And there's nothing Effy's hot little dress can do about it. If anything, that dress has placed a target on her back. Which is not what I need at all. I've had my hands full protecting her from the Russians, I cannot spare the time to protect her from my jealous fiancé or angry female cousins.

Women in this business can be bitterly vicious. They hate mistresses. It's the one thing they will ban together on, to make the other woman's life a living nightmare. I get it, I do … but I've seen mistresses driven to suicide. I can't let that sort of bullying happen to Effy, so when I see her whirl around to leave the dining hall, I push my way through the crowd and go after her.

The night is crisp and chilly in the autumn evening, but I welcome the cold air that washes over me as I step onto the stone patio outside. The sun has just begun to set, spilling yolky yellow light across the horizon. In a few moments, that light will become orange and then hazel and then it will disappear as night takes over.

I watch the patio lights flicker on as I walk the length of the stone path, following the curve of the hotel building. Just as I round the corner, I spot Effy on the far end of the walkway. She's leaning against the brick wall, her arms folded in front of herself in a fragile hug. She looks miserable, but I don't miss the joy on her face when she notices me approaching.

Her happiness is hidden well, almost imperceptible behind a curtain of sorrow and confusion. But it's certainly there. The tiniest dimple appears in her right cheek as she presses her lips together. It's gone by the time she inclines her head and returns her vision forward.

I stand beside her, both of us staring into the grassy field surrounding the hotel. For a while, neither of us speak. We just exist beside each other, like two cracked pillars holding up a broken world.

Effy breaks the silence first. "Congratulations."

The word is like a slap.

"It wasn't my idea," I explain. "I never wanted any of this."

"What did you want?"

She turns to me, staring, silently pleading for a truth I can't give her. A truth I'm afraid to give her. What will she do if she realizes just how much I need her?

Every time I've killed someone on the list she gave me, I've lost a piece of myself. I feel myself slipping, feel the world tilting closer to the knife's edge. I'm walking a thin line, and if I fall over, I won't ever make it back.

The first two kills, I went back home and lay beside Effy all night. Her mere presence kept the nightmares away. But the third kill… that night I returned home and called for Isabella. When she left, I woke up screaming, covered in sweat, hands balling fists into my blankets.

Without Effy, I have no peace. But it's not fair to place that burden on her shoulders. She shouldn't be responsible for keeping my madness at bay. It's my insanity. I should handle it myself. But the only way I know how is to bury it in her overwhelming calmness or between Bella's legs. Only one of those methods has worked properly so far.

What is it about Effy that brings so much warmth into my life? So much *light*?

"Luca?"

Her voice startles me back to the moment, and I focus on

her face, on the emotion I see so clearly in her wide-open eyes. "I don't know what I wanted," I say, taking the coward's way out. If I tell her that I wanted someone to keep the darkness away, she would know how much I've slipped and how much I've used her.

This is my burden, I promise myself, *I have to bear it.*

"I know what I wanted," Effy says, shocking me. She looks back out at the grass, brushing a silky strand of her dark hair behind her ear. "I wanted to be there for you, Luca. That's what Serena asked me to do. She said I was the only one who could because of our unique connection through Mario." Her gaze slides over to me, and our eyes lock. "I wanted to be by your side, even though I didn't know how. Even though it wasn't good for me. I wanted it. Because it was the first time in my life that someone had ever needed me."

"Effy…"

I don't really know what to say to that. So instead of speaking, I take a step toward her. She turns with her hand extended, reaching for me, like she already knows what I want. But *knowing* what I want is only half the joy, it's that she wants the same thing too that sends pleasure sparking through my body.

Little shocks of happiness erupt between us in a reckless kiss.

I kiss her hard, no point in holding back, and she wraps her hands around my neck. The gesture is so small, probably something she did just to stable herself and keep from falling over. But it ignites a fire inside me and I groan as I run my hands down her body. She's so short she's standing on her tiptoes even though she's wearing high heels. As my hands run down her waist, I grip her bottom and lift her from the ground.

She gasps, jerks away, but I press her against the wall and find her lips again. Her slender fingers tangle through my hair, tugging, then massaging, like she has no idea if this feels like heaven or hell.

Only a desperate need for air pulls us apart. We're both panting when I rest my forehead against hers, and I can't stop myself from smiling.

"Is that what you wanted?" I ask.

She looks sad all of a sudden, glancing over my shoulder. I look back to see a black car pulling around the corner.

"Please let me down," Effy says.

I listen to her request, gingerly setting her on her feet again. "What's going on?"

"I'm leaving."

"Effy—"

"This is your dinner party for your *wedding*, Luca." She shakes her head. "We can't do this."

Her driver steps out and leans against the car. He doesn't speak, just stands there waiting patiently. His presence annoys me. I'm trying to save the very first relationship I've ever really had. If Effy gets into that car, she will never come back to me. Not like this.

"Effy, wait. We can work this out," I say desperately.

"How? By turning me into your mistress?" She chuckles. "You know I'll never go for that."

"Maybe not a mistress." I lick my lips, trying to think. Trying to come up with something—anything that will keep her here. She's slipping away so fast, even though she hasn't even moved.

Effy will remain in my home until the trial, but unless I can turn this conversation around, her place in my life will never be the same. She will go back to being a hostage. Nothing more. I don't want that. I can't survive that. I've had a taste of the peace she brings, and I can't live without it now. I'll lose my mind if I lose Effy.

"Luca," she says kindly, "I have no place here. We come from two different worlds. Maybe this is for the best."

"Don't tell me what's best for me," I snap.

She sets her jaw but doesn't speak.

"I need you," I say. "More than you know."

"You need Jesus."

Her words hit me like a truck. Is that it? Is that her secret peace? That blinding inner light I see so clearly? When I'm with Effy, is it Christ inside that chases the nightmares away?

I blink, trying to run from the truth that's been chasing me down since I met Effy. I know it deep inside. I know it from the conversations we've had. From the inexplicable way she makes me feel. And from the Voice I heard in that warehouse.

I love you.

Not that dry, robotic way Isabella said it. Not the way my parents have ever said it. Or even the way Mario used to say it. That Voice was different. And when I heard it, I was filled with the same otherworldly peace and comfort that I feel around

Effy.

There is no mistaking it. The peace I feel comes from God, and I feel it around Effy because she's a Child of God.

But … what does that mean for me? I'm not a Christian. If I die now, I'll wake up in hell. Effy is the closest thing I've got to salvation. To peace. To joy. To a good night of sleep.

I simply cannot let her leave now.

She seems to sense the change in my mood, taking a tentative step toward her car. "I should go," she says.

"Effy, wait—"

She shakes her head and turns around, but I grab her by the elbow and pull her back. Effy yells at me, even swats at my hand, but she's quickly silenced by a deafening scream. Both of us are thrown backwards into the brick building, so hard that my vision blacks out and the sound disappears.

When I blink back into focus, I'm on the ground of the patio, Effy is passed out in my arms. There's smoke everywhere, and something is screaming again. *No—not screaming*—I realize it's a car horn blaring. The same noise I heard before we were thrown into the building. As I peer through the smoke in front of me, I understand what's happened.

Effy's car is gone. It was blown up.

When she'd stepped away to leave, her driver opened the back passenger door—and the car exploded. Mercifully, we weren't close enough for the bomb to be lethal, but my entire body aches and Effy is unconscious.

Panic shoots through me as I blink down at her. She's

bundled in my arms, like I'd subconsciously protected her during the explosion. There's a smear of blood on her face from a cut on her forehead, but she looks fine otherwise.

I shake her. "Effy…"

She doesn't respond.

I shake her again, call her name, shake her harder. Then I full on slap her.

She still doesn't wake up.

18

Luca

Effy comes to on the second slap, slightly confused and a little angry at the buzzing pain in her cheek. I don't care. I'm so relieved I could kiss her again, but my joy is snatched away by the shouting I hear heading toward us.

A car was blown up, I shouldn't be surprised that people have come to help, but I wish I had a few more moments alone. I almost lost the only hope in my life, I need some time to digest that. I need time to swallow the fact that someone planted a bomb in Effy's car. If we hadn't gotten into an argument, she'd be dead right now.

"What happened?" Effy sits up, wincing at her cuts and bruises. She glances around and then gasps, staring at what's left of her charred vehicle.

"A bomb," I say plainly.

She visibly stiffens. "A bomb…"

Perhaps that wasn't the best way to tell her the Russians tried to blow her up. Effy isn't in the mafia; she isn't used to this sort of stuff. I can see the panic rising within her, can feel her body trembling as she turns to look up at me again.

"A bomb?" she repeats, lower lip quivering.

"Effy," I grab her face with both hands, "you're alright. You're alive."

"The driver."

I hesitate. Should I tell her he's dead? How much can she handle?

Before I can decide, I hear my name shouted somewhere in the distance.

"Luca! Luca, my love!"

I look up in time to see Belén running right toward me. Her presence is a shocking reminder of where I am, and I quickly shift away from Effy. Belén click-clacks over and helps me to my feet, only sparing a sideways glance at Effy, whose red dress has been torn and singed to reveal even more skin than before. Her legs are bare up to her thighs, and one of her straps has been burned away so it droops down, almost giving everyone a peep of her small boobs.

She notices me staring and holds her hands to her chest. Embarrassed.

"Are you alright?" Belén asks, checking me for injuries.

I kindly step away so I can shrug off my suit jacket. "Here," I say, extending it to Effy.

She stares at it.

"What are you doing?" Belén asks.

"Offering her my jacket."

"Luca—"

"Take it," I say to Effy, ignoring my fiancé.

Effy reaches for it and quietly places it over her shoulders while Belén glares at her. She can hate her all she wants, but Belén knows her place. She won't utter a word about this. Not to me at least. Emilio may get an earful, but I can deal with him on my own.

Speaking of Emilio, he runs over with my father and mother, puffing for breath. His tie is slightly askew, and his hair is disheveled like he's been running his hands through it.

"What happened?" my father nearly shouts.

"A bomb," I say.

"They tried to kill him!" Belén goes into hysterics, throwing herself into my chest and wrapping her arms around my neck. I have no choice but to hug her back since her father is right there, observing.

I run my hand through her hair. "I'm alright. I wasn't the target."

My father glances at Effy, immediately understanding. "We've got to move her. She isn't safe out here in the open." He reaches for her. "Come, sweetheart. Let's get inside."

"What will happen next?" Belén asks. "What if you had been hurt?" She strokes my cheek.

"I wasn't."

"What if you'd died?"

"I didn't."

"We should marry them here." Emilio turns to my father who's wrapping an arm over Effy's shoulders. Both of them stop and stare between Belén and me. My father looks contemplative. Effy looks horrified.

"We haven't signed the contract," I say pathetically. I can feel the engagement ring in my pocket now, nearly burning a hole through my pants.

Belén snuggles closer to me. "We can sign it now. Your life is in danger, my love. We shouldn't waste any more time."

"I'm a mafia underboss," I say flatly. "My life is always in danger."

"This is an emergency," Emilio tells my father. "We need to settle this here and now. The priest is in attendance, I'm sure he wouldn't mind performing a short ceremony, given the circumstances."

"*No*," I say, shocking everyone.

Belén stiffens in my arms, but that only makes it easier to step away from her since she doesn't have her arms hooked around my neck anymore.

I look at my father because I know he's the only one who'll understand what I'm about to say. "I'm not marrying Belén," I say firmly.

My father's gaze narrows.

"I'm marrying Effy."

"Excuse me?" Belén says, the words sound very dramatic in her Spanish accent, but I ignore her and stay focused on my father.

"They tried to kill her. They planted a bomb in her car. They won't stop until they get her."

"We will increase security," my father begins, but I cut him off.

"That won't be enough, and you know it. The only thing that will make them back off is elevating Effy to a higher status. Right now, she's just a nameless nobody under our protection. Anyone could take her out without repercussions. But if she's my wife, the Bratva will think twice about touching her."

The area falls silent.

My father knows I'm right. Effy is just some inconvenience to the Russian gangs right now. But if I marry her, she will become the wife of the Italian underboss. That means she will become very important to a lot of people. I won't have to order my guards to protect her or explain who she is for security to understand how important her life is. The entire Italian mafia of Benton will have to protect Effy with their lives because she will be my wife and the future Lady of the organization.

This is the only thing I can do to fully protect her. I've tried locking her away. I've tried keeping her at Serena's side. Sending a full security detail with her. And yet, she was nearly blown to smithereens.

"This is our only option," I say to my father.

"You're already engaged," Emilio reminds me.

"The contract hasn't been signed."

"We're at your rehearsal dinner!" he shouts. "We would be signing right now if this hadn't happened!"

"But it *did* happen," I snap.

"You would break my daughter's heart?"

I glance over at Belén. She's standing just behind me, a strangely calm look on her face. That's when it clicks. Belén doesn't want to marry me any more than I want to marry her.

I've said before, she's an obedient little princess, raised perfectly by her father. All of this has been an act. She isn't jealous of Effy, and she doesn't care about a broken heart. She probably hopes I'll refuse the contract, and why not? We just met barely fifteen days ago, and we're expected to get married and have sex by the end of the week. That car bomb is probably the best thing that's happened to Belén. I can see the nervous relief on her face as my father speaks up.

"You have a point," he says to me.

"And we have a deal," Emilio reminds him.

I step forward. "What's more important? Justice for Mario or money from Emilio Moreno? Because we can always make more money, but we have one chance to send Mario's murderer to prison. That won't happen without Effy there to testify, and she can't testify if she's dead."

This seems to do it. My father nods and takes a deep breath, puffing his chest. "I am sorry, Emilio. But we will have to cancel this contract."

"You've got to be kidding me—"

"I don't kid when it comes to my son," he says quickly.

To my surprise, Emilio nods calmly. "I heard about what happened to Mario Vittore. It seems nothing is off limits to the Russian gangs. Not even children." He pauses, and then shakes his head. "The Bratva have even caused trouble in New York City, stupidly waging war with the German gangs of Brooklyn. It's all over now, but still. I have learned what they are capable of." He looks up at my father. "That is why I will not retaliate against this betrayal. But I will not forget it, Vincent Vittore. You have broken my trust, and I don't believe it will be easily repaired."

"I understand," my father says. "Perhaps in the future we can figure something out. For now," he extends his hand, "I suppose this is goodbye."

Emilio stares at his hand before taking it. "Goodbye, don Vincent." He turns to me and only offers a curt nod, then he reaches for Belén's hand and swiftly takes her away from this awful place.

In the silence that follows, I dig the diamond ring out of my pocket and drop to one knee. I know I'm being dramatic, but I have no idea how else I'm supposed to do this.

"This ring was meant for someone else," I say to Effy. "And, honestly, I know you probably don't even want it. But you don't have a choice. I need to keep you safe, and I'm willing to tie my life to yours to do that." I swallow. "Effy, will you marry me?"

She blinks at the ring. Then she blinks at me.

And to my absolute shock—and even a little horror—she says yes.

19

Effy

Everything happens so fast. Emilio Moreno wasn't lying when he said they had a priest on the premises. He's called out into the smoke and rubble to perform a hasty ceremony with two witnesses and a very nervous couple.

I can't even look Luca in the eye as he slides the ring onto my finger. I mumble through the vows. I nod at the right intervals. And I accept a very chaste kiss on the cheek when the priest steps back and announces us man and wife.

I don't feel like myself. I don't feel like I'm living in my own skin, in this moment, in this world. Everything feels like a dream playing out in slow motion, and it isn't until Serena runs over with wide eyes and a heaving chest that I seem to snap into focus.

"The hall is empty. I managed to get everyone out," she pants, glancing between all of us. Luca's mother and father are walking hand in hand, somber smiles on their faces. I'm still wearing Luca's jacket to cover my tattered dress; I have to hold the front closed so I don't expose my boobs to everyone. I didn't wear a bra with this dress.

Security have made their way out here, picking through the rubble and sectioning off the area. We held the ceremony in relative privacy, but now there are guards dotting the grass and lot. Despite all the men and the smoke and the charred vehicle smoldering just fifty feet away, it's the sight of the elderly priest walking behind me and Luca that catches Serena's attention.

She stands in front of us so she's blocking the doorway, hands on her hips. "What the heck happened?" she demands, and I'm sure she said *heck* because of the priest.

Vincent Vittore steps forward. "Your brother is a married man now." At the sight of Serena's shocked face, the older man chuckles and reaches out to caress her cheek. The gesture is oddly affectionate, a rare act from the people I've seen on this dark side of the world so far.

Serena seems to relax at her father's touch, taking his hand and giving it a squeeze. "You're serious?"

He nods, then glances back at us. "You should congratulate them, Rena."

"Save the congratulations for later," Luca says, stepping in front of me.

I'm glad for the interruption, I can't look anyone in the eye right now. I'm too embarrassed. Too confused. I don't know if I've just done the right thing or not, but it's too late to take it back. I am the wife of Luca Vittore now, and even though I had yearned for this, now that I have it, I am absolutely terrified.

I'm in the mafia now. Mafia *royalty*. Have I just turned my back on God?

Tears well in my eyes and I clutch Luca's jacket tighter around myself, hoping no one is paying me any attention. The rest of the family is busy talking about what happens next while I stand there and shiver.

"Someone planted a bomb in my wife's car," Luca's voice—his use of the word *wife*—gets my attention. And then the rest of the statement clicks into place. Someone tried to kill me. I was nearly blown up.

"I want to find out who," Luca growls, then he gestures toward me. "Take Effy home. I'll be busy for the night—"

"Doing what?" Serena snaps. "It's still your wedding night, brother. You're not going anywhere."

"Someone tried to kill her," Luca replies. "Right under our noses."

"I can start chasing leads." Serena jerks her head at me, and even though she lowers her voice, I can still hear her words very clearly. "Your wife needs you, Luca."

Her statement is a stunning revelation. Because even though I married Luca to buy myself some extra security, I don't feel safe at all anymore. Now that I've said, 'I do,' I feel so exposed and vulnerable. And I feel like I've made an awful mistake.

Luca is suddenly in front of me, his hand touching my cheek. He looks down at his thumb and stares at a tear he's wiped away.

I'm shocked. I hadn't even realized I'd begun to cry.

"Let me take you home," he says.

I nod because I don't think I have any choice. I haven't had a choice since I witnessed Mario's murder. No choice but to run. No choice but to remain in Luca's house. No choice but to testify. No choice but to marry a mafia boss. No choice but to go home with that man.

Will I have a choice in what comes next?

I can't get myself to ask that question aloud. My throat feels sticky, and my mouth feels dry. When I try to talk, nothing comes out but incoherent whimpers which are justifiably interpreted as sobs. There are still tears running down my cheeks and I'm covered in dirt, gravel, and smears of my own blood. I just want to go home. But at the same time, I don't. Because that place shouldn't be my home.

Luca lets me cry in peace as he escorts me through the hotel and out the front doors. He doesn't say a word during the drive home and when he gingerly helps me out of the car once we're at the front steps of the estate, he simply wraps a strong arm around my shoulders and walks me to his room.

I'm shocked by the relief that washes through me when he opens the door to his bedroom. This place feels familiar. It feels comfortable, almost like the home I've never had.

Luca leaves me standing in the middle of the floor as he heads to the bathroom. I stare at the sliver of light spilling out across the carpet, warm and yellow compared to the pale moonlight washing in between the balcony curtains. There's water running in the bathroom, steam rolling out the cracked door. It opens wider in a silent yawn, and Luca appears with his tie loosened and his sleeves rolled up to his elbows.

He looks both nervous and relaxed. A muscle in his jaw tics before he unscrews it and says in a low rasp, "Come here." Then he steps back into the bathroom before I can reply.

I shuffle to the open door and peek inside. There's bathwater running, and there's also alcohol and a damp rag set out on the counter beside a sink that's full of warm water.

I glance between the sink and Luca who is patiently waiting for me to enter. "I won't bite," he says.

It's a poor attempt at a joke but I give him a tightlipped smile anyway and walk all the way inside the bathroom. He reaches around me and shuts the door. Then he locks it.

The sound of the lock engaging makes me stiffen. "What are you doing?" I ask.

"I just want to get you cleaned up." He looks at the cut on my forehead, then he raises his hand and hesitates, looking me in the eye before he goes on.

I nod, granting him permission.

He touches me as gently as he can, but it still stings. I can't help but wince, which earns me a string of apologies in a strong Italian accent. Luca doesn't sound like the sweaty men in the back of the pizza shops I grew up eating at. His accent is entirely different. Neater. Refined. The difference between a butcher and a surgeon.

He wets the cloth and dabs it on the cut, watching me the whole time. I try my best not to fidget. Then he reaches for the alcohol, and I hold my breath.

"It will sting," he says, pouring it on the rag.

I nod.

"Ready?"

I nod again and he lifts the cloth. I can smell the alcohol as his hand draws nearer, but all my senses go dark when it touches the injury. I'm blinded by the burning pain, squeezing my eyes shut and sucking in a gasp. I'm vaguely aware of Luca saying something, and his voice is warm and soothing and vibrates in his chest. It sounds so much closer than it did a moment ago.

Slowly, I peel my lids back and realize I've stepped forward—or maybe he pulled me forward—into his arms.

Luca peers down at me. "Better?"

"A little."

His eyes flicker down to my lips, and I tuck my chin and stare at his crooked tie. I feel his low chuckle buzzing in his chest, like a hum against my palms flattened across his broad frame.

He kisses the top of my head. "Let's take a bath," he says.

"*Let's?*" My voice is a mouse's whisper.

"We are married now. It's our wedding night."

Luca is already undoing the buttons of his shirt, shameless and genuinely perplexed as to why I haven't begun to undress yet. This is the same man who wanted to sleep with me despite knowing me for less than 30 days. I understand that happens a lot these days. But not with me. I can't do it. Not so quickly and easily at least.

"Luca…"

It's the only word I can say, and it seems to sum up all my fears and hesitation. Luca stops unbuttoning his shirt, leaving it hanging open so I can see his perfectly smooth olive skin. He's ripped and jaw-droppingly gorgeous. And that just makes this even harder. I feel embarrassed all of a sudden. Like an ugly ragdoll beside a beautiful male model.

Luca sighs and turns to shut off the bathwater. "We don't have to bathe together."

I exhale slowly.

"Clean yourself up, Effy. Don't take too long."

Then, he's gone, walking out the bathroom without another word. No more sweet kisses. No more reassuring words. I'm left standing in a steamy bathroom in my husband's suit jacket and my tattered dress.

I blink around the room, tempted to lock the door behind Luca, but I have no idea if that will make him angry or not. Instead, I focus on getting cleaned up, like he said. My dress peels away and falls to the floor like a pile of rags. My shoes come off easily, and my underwear is a sweaty cloth I'm happy to kick away.

The bathwater is hot and milky and I almost dunk my head underneath but then I remember my glorious silk press and I only submerge until my chin touches the water. My flat-ironed hair is tied up in a sloppy bun. I know I'll have to brush it out later, but for now, I enjoy this bath.

It takes me half an hour to scrub away the grime, but as I sit in the tub, staring at the pinkish brown stained water, I feel like I've tried to scrub away everything else too. The worries, the anxiety, the nauseating headache I have from the unease of not knowing what will happen next.

Is Luca waiting out there for me? Wearing nothing but his birthday suit. He'd so casually undressed right in front of me and had announced that we're married, as if that would make this so much easier. It isn't about sin anymore. It's about what I'm comfortable with.

How strange… When we were unmarried, I had to wrestle my flesh into submission. Staying pure for God was a literal war. But now that I'm married and have permission to enjoy my husband, I feel like I want to hide in this bathroom all night.

What is it that's changed?

I can only find out by leaving this room.

I'm wearing a bathrobe I found hanging behind the door, but I have nothing on underneath so the air in the bedroom feels cold as soon as I open the door. I shiver and hug myself, padding across the carpet on bare feet.

Luca is sitting on the edge of the bed, his shirt fully unbuttoned now, tie resting beside him like he took it off and tossed it away. He has a focused look on his face, so intense I almost don't want to interrupt him, but as I cross the room, he glances up and our eyes lock.

"You've finally finished," he says.

"I have."

"Feel better?"

"Considering I was nearly blown up an hour ago? Yeah, I feel great."

His face darkens. "I'm going to find who did this, Effy. I won't let them get away with this."

Serena's words stir in my mind. *He's got a list… He's spiraling…*

"What will you do when you find them?" I ask cautiously, unsure if I even want to know.

Luca glances away. "You know what sort of man I am."

"Tell me I didn't marry a monster."

He spears me with his gaze. "I was a monster when you met me. I kidnapped you, remember?"

How could I forget?

"And you still said, *I do*," Luca reminds me. He stands and crosses the room in three easy strides, towering over me with the tiniest smirk on his face. "You don't get to take back your vows, Effy. You can't run away again. You're mine for good now."

The way he says that is like a threat, but the way he touches me is gentle. His hand is on my face, knuckles brushing my cheek. The contact makes me shiver and close my eyes, though I want to keep them open. I want to see the look on his face, watch his smirk melt into a comforting smile.

I know he's stepped closer when I smell the dark scent of his cologne; amber and something masculine that I can't name. His voice is a murmur against the shell of my ear.

"Forget about the explosion tonight. Focus on what happened before that," he says. "Do you remember, Effy?"

Of course, I do. He'd kissed me right before that. And it wasn't the chaste little peck I got in front of the priest. Luca had me pinned to the wall, his tongue in my mouth. Just the thought of it now makes me numb down to my toes.

"I can take you back to that moment," he tells me, voice a husky whisper. "If you'll let me."

It's a tempting offer, and I find myself nodding before I can talk myself out of it. Because no matter how nervous I am, thinking of kissing Luca will always be a better thought than reliving that explosion.

Luca drops his hand from my cheek, and I feel a tug at the belt of my robe. "Take this off," he murmurs, leaning down to kiss my neck.

All the comfort from before washes away as I realize, *this is happening*. I've married Luca and now he wants to cash in on the wonderful perks of marriage. But I'm not ready. Not like this. Not right now.

I take a step back, clutching my robe. "I can't," I say shakily.

Luca stares at me. "Is it because of God?"

That's a peculiar question. I almost don't have an answer because God *is* part of the reason.

"We're married," Luca says, like I don't know that. "This isn't a sin."

"But it isn't about sin," I insist, clutching the robe even tighter. How can I explain this to him? That it isn't a sin to have sex with my husband, the sin is that I shouldn't have married him in the first place.

I don't have the words. I don't have it in me to hurt him like that. Because I can see the emotion on Luca's face plain and clear. He wants to protect me. I know that. He wants me to drop this robe, the tent in the front of his pants makes that obvious. But Luca has feelings for me. Real feelings that I hadn't noticed before. This is as new for him as it is for me. Not the sex—the *marriage*. And we're already off to a bad start. But I don't believe sex will make it better. That isn't the answer. It isn't what I want.

"Please don't make me," I whisper.

Luca exhales long and slow. That same disappointed look he wore in the bathroom shadows his face, but his voice comes out in a calm whisper. Not comforting, but not angry either.

"Goodnight, then."

I watch in cold numbness as he turns and leaves the room.

I can't believe I just rejected my own husband. And I can't believe he left me alone because of it. There are other things we could've done. We could've cuddled. We could've kissed. We could've snuggled beneath the blankets and enjoyed pillow talk. Gotten to know each other—because we're just a step above *strangers* right now!

Luca was only interested in sex. And when he didn't get that. He left.

I shouldn't be surprised. This is the same man who left me like a hot potato for a pretty Spanish woman with no warning or explanation. Why on earth am I surprised by his actions now?

Instead of getting upset, I climb into my gigantic bed alone and I snuggle by myself. Then I close my eyes and beg God to forgive me for the massive mistake I've just made.

20

Effy

The click of the bedroom door wakes me like a whisper against my cheek. I roll over in bed and blink at the sliver of light that falls into the room as someone enters. Immediately, I know it isn't Luca because the silhouetted figure is smaller and shorter. I half expect it to be Serena, or maybe even Isabella, but when the figure shuts the door and says, "How are you?" I'm stunned into silence as I recognize the voice.

"Mrs. Vittore?" I whisper.

She stops in front of the bed. In the darkness, I can make out her calm face. High cheekbones, a small nose, and the same burning eyes as Luca. Her hair is auburn and styled into a fashionable pixie cut that frames her face well. She looks older but regal. Perfectly aged, like the wine her family produces.

Mrs. Vittore smiles and reaches out to touch my shoulder; her hand is surprisingly warm. "Please, call me Aurora."

"Aurora," I say awkwardly, "is something wrong?"

"A lot of things are wrong." She nods solemnly. "I'm sure

you know that."

Of course. One of her children is dead, there was an attempt on my life at her other son's wedding party, and then that wedding was cancelled and hastily replaced with my own impromptu wedding.

It hits me, all of a sudden, that Aurora is now my mother-in-law. That revelation summons a wave of guilt, confusion, and fear all at once.

"So much has happened," I say without thinking.

Aurora nods. "That's why I came. I saw my son leave not long ago."

A thick blob of emotions gets stuck in my throat. I can't pretend I'm not hurt by Luca's departure, but that's exactly what makes this so confusing. I shouldn't be hurt. I should be upset that I've married a mafia boss. Instead, I feel tears forming in my eyes because that mafia boss isn't here by my side.

Aurora touches my shoulder again, and when I look up at her through blurry, tear-filled eyes, I see a sense of understanding forming on her face. It's in the mature creases around her mouth, the wrinkle of wisdom in her forehead. The first time I saw her, I thought she looked like a Lady of the mafia. But now she looks like a mother.

"You do not belong in this world," she says in a gentle Italian accent.

I nod, wiping at my tears. "But I'm here now. Stuck. And … I'm not sure if I'm upset about that. I'm not sure if I regret marrying Luca." I turn to her, shifting on the bed. "I want his protection. I want to be there for him. But …"

"The cost for all of it is greater than you thought."

"You sound like you're speaking from experience."

She smiles, and it bears no joy. "I was born into the mafia. This world is all I've ever known. But I realized there was more to my life when I found God."

My eyes snap to hers. That's what I saw on her face. The wisdom, the empathy. It was her faith I was seeing. The realization tugs a sob from my throat, and I bury my face in my hands. I feel Aurora rubbing circles on my back. She doesn't speak for a long time.

"I've made a terrible mistake," I say shakily. "You know what it means to be unequally yoked. You know what I'm talking about."

"I do," she agrees. "But you cannot wallow in your guilt. This world has no time for tears."

"I'm not talking about this world." I wave my hand around the room. "I'm talking about the life I've dedicated to God."

"You've made a mistake," Aurora says calmly. "A mistake God knew you would make before you were even given the chance to make it." She leans closer to me. "Do you think He cannot use your mistake for His glory?"

I blink. "What kind of glory can come from marrying a mafia boss?"

"My son needs you, Effy."

The seriousness in her voice makes my skin prickle with goosebumps.

"Luca depends on you. I'm sure you know this."

"I do," I whisper.

"But he shouldn't." Aurora glances down and shakes her head disappointedly. "He thinks he is drawn to you because of your connection to Mario. But I know the real reason."

I stare at her, waiting for an explanation. But instead of speaking, Aurora reaches up and touches the golden cross pendant hanging around her neck, and I suddenly understand.

"You think he's drawn to my faith?"

I know the answer even before Aurora confirms it with a nod. Luca is curious about God. He says he doesn't believe the Bible, but I know that rejection stems from bitter pain. Not from a true place of doubt. Luca is hurt, and he thinks he can cover his pain with any comfort he finds in me. But that will never be good enough.

There is no such thing as peace without God because God *is* peace. Until Luca gets to know the Lord for himself, he will spend his days surviving off nothing but his mother's fervent prayers. While that may help him through the worst of things, it won't be enough to get him into heaven. Salvation is a conscious choice. It isn't something that falls onto your shoulders because of someone else's prayers. But it is something that can be offered to you because of someone else's prayers.

"I believe you were dragged into my son's life to introduce him to God," Aurora says.

I shake my head.

"He responds to you, Effy. You're the only one who can—"

"What about *me*!" I say quickly. Serena wants me to be there for Luca. Luca has convinced himself that I'm his light. And now Aurora wants me to introduce him to Jesus.

All of that is wonderful. All of that is evidence of how close this family truly is—how much they care about each other. But none of that takes my own feelings into consideration.

"You said it yourself," I tell Aurora. "I don't belong in this world. How can you ask me to spend any more time here than necessary?"

"Because if my son accepts Christ, he will reject this world. He will want to leave the mafia."

I laugh bitterly. "You didn't."

"I *couldn't.* And now I see why."

I tilt my head to the side.

"I spent many days and nights in prayer, wrestling with God for an escape from this world. I've fasted. I've sowed seeds. I've spoken in tongues. It wasn't until Luca told me of your faith that I realized why my prayers went unanswered." Aurora smiles. "I was kept here because God knew you would need someone of faith to stand by your side and help you through this."

I sniffle, feeling defeated. "This isn't fair. How on earth could it be God's will that I marry someone like Luca?"

"It was His will for Hosea to marry a prostitute," Aurora says. "I don't think it was His will that you marry Luca. I believe you are right by saying you made a mistake. You acted without His guidance or permission. But I also believe He knew you would make this mistake and decided to use it for His glory. He's using your mistake to save someone else's soul." She reaches for my hand and grips it tightly. "To save the soul of my son. My firstborn son. My last living son."

The tremble in Aurora's voice makes me realize just how much this means to her. She probably spent more time praying for Luca than she did praying for her own escape. This is surprising because Aurora doesn't strike me as a particularly affectionate mother. At the garden party, she hardly spoke to either of her children. Even at the wedding dinner, she was oddly aloof—if not cold—for the mother of the groom. But now I see how wrong my assumptions were.

Aurora may not be the most affectionate woman in the world, but it's clear how much she cares. Even from a distance. Because only a mother who cares would overlook the kidnapping of another woman if it meant saving the eternal soul of her own child.

"This is too much," I whisper, shaking my head.

Aurora stiffens, then stands from the bed. "If that is how you truly feel, then go, Effy."

I frown, watching as she walks to the door. She opens it behind her and then turns back to face me. "If you really think God has a greater purpose for you out there, then go find it. I won't hold you back."

"Aurora—"

"I won't beg you to stay," she says crisply. "God knows I've wanted an escape for years. I cannot blame you for wanting one too."

I hesitate. Now it feels like I'm being put out.

"I thought you wanted me here."

"I do. But it must be your choice. I've done what God has asked, and I have expressed my own personal desire for you to stay, But I can't hold you hostage, Effy. I'm not like my son."

I almost chuckle, but nothing is particularly funny.

Aurora jerks her head at the open door. "No one will stop you if you leave. I'll make sure of it." Then she turns and walks out, leaving the door open behind her.

I wait exactly ten seconds before I toss the covers back and make a beeline for the door.

21

Luca

The guest bedrooms in this house are particularly small. I feel trapped whenever I try to sleep in them—that's why I decide to take a walk through the gardens tonight. I can't sleep. I can't relax. And apparently, I can't romance my own wife.

It's strange to think that I'm a married man now. Something I've never wanted to be.

Tonight is my wedding night. I'm supposed to be sweat-soaked and breathless right now. But instead, I'm walking around in the cool evening, staring at empty grape vines.

When I was a boy, I loved walking through the vineyard after the harvest. The plucked vines were like barbed wire when it got cold, and they stiffened for the winter. Sometimes I would pretend to be a soldier on a mission, crawling on my belly through the wire, tiptoeing around trip mines.

So much of my life revolves around wine. They say wine represents the Blood of Jesus—during communion, I think. I wonder what that means today.

I remember enough from Catholic school to understand that wine is sacred in the Church. It's something Christians drink as a representation of the sacrifice of Christ. Of the redemption they've been given. Now, we drink wine because it makes us feel good. It numbs our senses. It melts away our problems. Those are the things God is supposed to do. And that's why He hates when we drink alcohol. Because we're not supposed to depend on anything but Him to relax, unwind, or whatever excuse we feed ourselves as we tip the bottle.

Wine used to be sacred.

I stare at the prickly vines, wondering what Effy would think of all this. She doesn't drink, yet she married a mafioso who runs a vineyard. I shouldn't care what Effy thinks—most men in this business don't care what their wife has to say. Or what any woman has to say. But I do care.

I care that I've forced her into a life where she will always have to choose. Decide between honoring her faith or loving me.

My eyes widen at that thought. Is it possible that I love her?

I dig the toe of my shoe into the stiff dirt and sigh. It doesn't matter what I feel because I know how she feels. She didn't even want me to touch her earlier. On our own wedding night. That says an awful lot about the prospects of our marriage.

It shouldn't bother me. But it does.

With a sigh, I turn and start down the rest of the path through the garden. The deeper you go, the hardier the plants get. I pass Christmas cacti, snowdrops, and Dutchman's Breeches. My mother picked out the Dutchman's. I can't help but think of her when I see them, but the memory is bittersweet. She picked them out, but it was Mario who helped her plant them.

I can still see him kneeling beside her in the garden, covered in soil, dirt smeared across one of his cheeks. His smile that day had been infectious. We'd all eaten in the garden to celebrate how well he'd done. I don't think he was more than five years old.

I turn away from the Dutchman's and step through a patch of witch hazel, but once I'm on the other side, I freeze.

My mother is sitting on a bench ahead.

She looks striking in the moonlight, like a woman who'd once been a queen in another life. Maybe a life outside of the mafia. Who knows what she could have been if she hadn't dedicated her life to serving her husband. Imagine what *any* woman could be if their husbands were as dedicated to serving them too.

"Mom?" I say.

She turns her head, and I see the doleful smile on her face. It looks like it's there as an obligation. "Come." She pats the empty space beside her, and I walk over but I don't sit.

"What are you doing out here?"

"Thinking." She checks her watch, it's a silver band with diamond studs surrounding the face. I think my father bought it for one of their anniversaries.

"Thinking about what?"

"You. The choices you've made. The choices you'll make later."

"I don't understand."

"I've done something, Luca. Something terrible."

I squint, my heart beginning to beat rapidly.

"Tell me plainly," I order.

She looks up at me, her eyes just as brown as mine. Just as burning. "I let her go."

For a second, her words don't click. I have no idea what she's talking about. And then she checks her watch again, and I feel my breath fall short.

"What have you done?" I whisper.

"She doesn't belong here, Luca." My mother starts to speak quickly, like she's afraid she won't get the words out. "She should be given a choice—she should be allowed—"

"This isn't just about her!" I nearly shout.

She flinches. "Luca—"

"Have you forgotten?" my voice cracks, breaking as I see those stupid Dutchman's in my mind's eye.

SEE YOU LATER. SEE YOU LA—

I squeeze my eyes shut. "She married me for protection. She's here because of Mario."

"Luca…"

"How could you take that away from me?"

"She is not your redemption," my mother says sharply.

When she finally raises her vision, I see the pain in her eyes she's kept hidden so well. My mother is just as broken as I am. And I had convinced myself she'd never loved us. Perhaps I was wrong. Maybe she grew to love us. Maybe she loved us after losing Mario—after realizing our power did not make us invincible.

Whatever the case, her words are like a strike of lightning to my heart. I'm not sure if it stops or starts when she speaks.

Redemption. A term that feels like glue in my throat. Is that what I've been seeking in Effy? A chance to make things right. As if I could somehow wipe away my sins by protecting her. I know it doesn't work that way, but I don't want it to work the way it does. I want to find my own redemption. My own way. In my own strength. I want to finally be enough.

"I'm not sorry," my mother says, snapping me back to reality. Her callous words turn my heart to stone.

"You should be," I say.

She lifts her chin. "She has an hour on you. And she's good at hiding. You should know that."

"I'm good at finding things," I turn away, "you should know that too."

"What will you do, Luca?" she calls behind me.

I stop walking, but I don't turn back. "I'm going to bring her home. Where she belongs."

22

Effy

My feet hit the pavement with a slap. I'm walking as fast as I can in a pair of UGG minis that were clearly *not* designed with *dangerous escape* in mind. They're warm and delightful, like walking on a field of cotton balls, but they also make my feet feel heavy and flat and two sizes larger than they are.

Or maybe I'm just a little anxious because I'm running away from my mafia husband and his dangerous family and the crazy Russians who've already tried to kill me via car bomb a mere few hours ago.

Considering all that's happened, I should sprint back to Luca and never let him go. He wants to protect me. He wants to keep me safe. And I want the same. Except, I see two monsters in this story.

When the dust has settled, and the trial is over, who will protect me from *Luca*?

He can't keep me safe when he's a monster too.

But I'm not escaping because I think Luca is dangerous,

I'm running away because I believe his *world* is dangerous. I believe the connection we've developed is dangerous—and not just as a threat to my life, it's dangerous because it's a threat to my *spirit.*

"I shouldn't have married him," I blurt, shaking my head as I walk as quickly as I can.

I'm going toward the downtown area to catch a Greyhound out of town. I hear New York City is pretty much lawless these days. Ruled entirely by the mafia. That could be very good or very bad for me. I could get lost in NYC and no one would ever find me unless I wanted them to. But in NYC, no one would help me if I faced the same dangers I've seen here. Law enforcement is nearly nonexistent over there, and I doubt there are many mafia bosses with a heart like Luca's. If some other mafioso picks me up, they won't be as charming as him.

But I've got to try. I've got to get out of here. I can't spend the rest of my life living as Aurora did. Under my husband's thumb, completely at his mercy. I can't sign a contract and commit myself to a man who could murder me as easily as he could love me. Whether Luca himself would behave that way isn't the question, it's the fact that no one would stop him if he did.

Why, God? I wonder, wiping tears from my eyes. *Why didn't You stop me from making this stupid mistake?*

I know the answer already. Because God has given us free will. Every human on earth knows right from wrong. God has instilled that within us—the world calls it the little voice in our head, but the Word of God says it is His law written on our hearts. That means we all know what we ought to do, and God gives us the strength to make righteous decisions, but the decision is still ours.

I knew I'd be unequally yoked with Luca before I said, 'I do.' But I still said it. And now I'm running away, praying that God will somehow fix a situation I knowingly walked into.

"Jesus, You are merciful," I say desperately. "Please help me. I can't get out of this alive without You."

The Russians want to kill me. They *really* want to kill me. And I don't know what Luca will do if he ever finds me. I'm in worse shape now than when this story first started, and the only One who can truly help me now is God.

"I should have depended on You from the beginning," I say earnestly.

I'd placed my faith in myself, living on the run for months. Then I'd placed my faith in Luca, marrying him despite what it would mean for me as a Christian woman. I have made mistake after mistake.

"But I still trust You, Jesus. And I still believe You love me enough to help me. Even when I don't deserve Your outstretched Hand."

I stop walking so I can wipe away all the tears that've blurred my eyes, and when my vision clears, I see a black car sitting at the end of the street.

A solid rock settles in my stomach.

Without hesitation, I pivot, and begin walking down the street in the opposite direction. I'm wearing a backpack I found in the back of Luca's closet, stuffed with clothes and supplies I took from around the house.

Aurora hadn't been lying. No one had tried to stop me when I packed my bag or when I walked out the front door. I don't know how she did it, but she managed to put what little power she has to use on my behalf. Maybe I should've taken a car too because I can hear the rev of an engine creeping up behind me now and even as I break into a sprint down the sidewalk, I know I won't be fast enough to outrun whoever is pursuing me.

The sound of tires screeching is like a scream cracking through the air, it tears a gasp from my lips and makes me run harder. My bag bounces against my back with each step, but I don't slow down. Not even as I see the car whip around me and jump the curb.

I turn right at the corner, holding onto the sticky brick wall so I don't lose momentum. That's when the sound of the engine is replaced by the sound of pounding feet.

They're coming! They're going to—

Someone grabs me by my backpack before I can even finish the thought. With a grunt, he jerks me backwards so hard that my feet fly up from under me. I feel my body sway to the side, and it takes me a moment to realize my attacker has thrown me. I am weightless for exactly two seconds, then I collide with the ground and stars burst into my vision.

I wake with a headache, blinking back little bursts of light that speckle my vision. The room is grey and brightly lit from overhead. It takes me a moment to realize I'm in a warehouse. The information isn't given to me from anyone in the room. It isn't written on the concrete walls. It is a sudden knowing that overtakes me with a wash of fear so great, I gasp and backpedal until my back hits the cold wall.

"Don't worry—"

I snap my gaze to my left to find a tall man sitting on an overturned crate just a few feet away. He's wearing a black suit with a crimson tie, white feathery hair combed back from his aged face. The lights reflect off his shiny shoes as he stands and clasps his hands together in front of him.

I shrink like a child, raising my hands in defense—only to realize they are tied at the wrists. My eyes bulge and my mouth drops open.

"What's going on?" I say in a whisper.

The man walks toward me.

"What's going on!" I repeat.

He stops in front of me and stoops, reaching behind his back to pull something from his waistband.

A gun! My mind blanks out and I close my eyes, biting down hard on my lower lip. The last thing I say in this life will not be a scream or a plea for mercy. I will die with dignity, in silence.

But death never comes. Instead, I feel something tug on my wrists and then relief floods through my hands as my blood flow returns to normal. I peel my lids back to find the ropes around my wrists have been cut away.

In front of me, the tall older man tucks away a pocketknife and stands again. He offers his hand. "I am not going to hurt you."

"Hard to believe when I've been kidnapped."

Which seems to be a trend lately.

He smiles, but it isn't handsome; it looks like a sliver opens in his face to reveal sharp teeth and a snake-like tongue that whips out to wet his lips.

"We had to take drastic measures to get our hands on you," the man says. "Measures which we hope you will forgive."

Forgive?

I raise my eyebrow. Judging from this man's expensive clothes, his sharp accent, and the fact that I've been kidnapped, I'm going to assume he's from the Russian Bratva. That isn't entirely surprising, but what does catch me off guard is the fact that he wants me to forgive him for his actions.

"What's going on?" I repeat once again.

"My name is Pavel Stepanov, the boss of the Russian Bratva." He inclines his head as I try to hide the gasp I'd sucked in. "And you are Effervescent Storm—" that slivery smile returns, "or should I say, Effervescent *Vittore*."

I blink, understanding blooming in my head. He isn't going to kill me because of who I am. Luca was right. The Russians can't touch me now because I'm the wife of the Italian underboss. They might have gotten away with killing Mario because Vincent wants peace, but I'm *Luca's* wife. If they hurt me, my husband will burn this city down—no matter what

Vincent wants.

This is what it means to be a Vittore. The realization makes my throat painfully dry; I wince as I swallow, staring up at this murderer.

Pavel takes a step back, mercifully giving me space to breathe. I feel sweat bubble on the back of my neck, I swipe it away with a shaky hand and glare at him.

"I need to know what's going on. You've wanted me dead since you murdered Mario, now you've kidnapped me, but you aren't going to hurt me." I shake my head. "I don't understand."

"Do you know why Mario Vittore was killed?" he asks.

"Because you're a monster—"

"You think your pretty husband isn't?"

"He's never killed a *child* before," I hiss.

Pavel's smile slithers across the rest of his face so he looks like the Cheshire Cat. "Says who?"

I squeeze my eyes shut. I won't believe anything this man says. He is evil—I've witnessed his evil firsthand.

"Mario was murdered because he made the mistake of hurting my daughter."

My eyes pop open. "He did what?"

"He hurt my daughter," Pavel repeats, and the pain in his voice makes me pause. "Mario Vittore hurt my only daughter, and I didn't find out until it was too late."

"How did he hurt her?"

Pavel turns and says something loudly in Russian. I hear the squeak of a rusty door and then soft footsteps. I'm not surprised to see a beautiful teenage girl step around the corner, but my stomach twists at the bundle in her arms. At first, I think I'm seeing things, but the shaky wail that fills the air is unmistakable. That girl is Pavel's daughter, and in her arms is a baby.

I stare between the nameless girl and the Bratva leader, a million questions running through my head. I can't pick a single one to voice.

"He raped her," Pavel says, confirming the nightmare I'd suspected. I can't help but close my eyes again, as if to block out the truth.

This can't be true. The kid I saw in the alley was not a rapist. He wasn't. He was just a teenager. A high schooler. And he looked so broken and miserable. His last words weren't the venomous hisses of a predator. They were the defeated words of a child who knew his life was over.

I wasn't enough…

That's not what a rapist would say when facing judgment. But Pavel seems convinced of Mario's guilt. I can see it in his eyes. I can hear it in his voice as he speaks, even though he's talking in Russian again.

The young girl steps forward and looks down at me with tears in her eyes. She nods when I shake my head. "It's his baby," she says in a gentle accent, clutching the wailing child to her breasts.

"Why are you telling me this?"

"Because I want to make a deal with you," Pavel offers.

"You should be making this deal with Luca, not me. He's

the one who wants to avenge his brother's death."

"He will not listen to me."

"I don't blame him." I can't stop myself from glaring at the girl too. My eyes are filled with hatred toward everyone in this room except the infant. The only innocent one here.

I don't believe Pavel's story, but *they* have a baby and *I* have nothing but a feeling. It won't be enough.

"Here is the deal," Pavel says, regaining my attention. "We wanted to kill you to stop you from testifying in court. Then we got word that you married Luca Vittore."

"Already…" I say aloud. It just happened a few hours ago.

Pavel shrugs. "Word travels fast in our world—when you want it to. And Luca Vittore certainly wanted everyone to know about you because your marriage means we cannot touch you without guaranteeing years of war."

I nod.

"My men just so happened to see you on the street today. That was pure chance, but I am glad it happened. We picked you up so I could speak to you … as a father." Pavel looks at his young daughter, at the child in her arms, and then glances at me. His face is dark, filled with anger and hatred, but he cools those boiling feelings down with a sigh. "I am asking you not to testify. And in exchange, I will allow Luca to have a relationship with his nephew."

I gasp, eyes flicking to the baby. It's a boy.

"I've named him Mario," the girl says. "After his father."

It almost sounds blasphemous, but as I gaze at the warm, tear-streaked face in the bundle of blankets, my heart melts and breaks for the innocent child born into this chaos. His life is already over, filled with promises of violence, darkness, and misery. Just like everyone else in this mafia world.

Still… No matter what his life holds, Luca would want to be part of it. He would want to hold on to this last bit of his brother. If I testify, he will lose this child. But if I don't testify, he'll never get justice for Mario's killer.

"What a cruel choice," I say darkly.

Pavel grunts. "This world is cruel. Rape is cruel."

I want to lash out at him, scream that he's wrong about Mario. But how do I deny the infant right in front of me? How can I argue against the teenager with brimming eyes who holds her young child? She's a mother at this precious age because of Mario Vittore.

My shoulders drop in defeat. "I'll need time to think about this."

Pavel offers his hand and I take it, climbing to my wobbly feet. "The trial is still a few weeks away."

I nod.

"Until then, my men will return you to your home. Please apologize to your husband for this ordeal and be sure to remind him that we did not harm you."

I nod, though I doubt Luca will take any of this kindly. Even though I wasn't hurt, I was still kidnapped. But only because I ran away. That part was my own choice.

Choice… it seems I have a difficult one to make. How do I tell all of this to my husband? How do I explain that Mario's justice and vengeance and judgment has been placed at my feet? What would Luca want from me?

Shockingly, it's Luca I want to see most right now. I'm not afraid of what he will do to me for running away. I suddenly want to run back to him and climb into his bed, pull up the blankets and let his brave confidence lull me to sleep. He might be a monster, but he's the monster I need right now.

So when Pavel's men drop me off two blocks from the estate, I practically run home. *Home*, I can't believe I'm calling it that now, but it's how I feel. I have no place else to belong except here, and I've somehow brought this place more trouble than it had before.

How can I tell Luca that his precious little brother is a rapist? How can I tell him he's got a beautiful nephew hidden away in the Bratva? How can I tell him that I must let go of Mario's justice to give him a life with Mario's child?

Serena's words ring in my ears as I climb into Luca's large bed. *Will you be there for my brother?*

Right now, there's so much drama to unfold, I need him to be there for *me*. We need each other. As twisted as our lives have become, it's suddenly clear now that maybe we were made for each other.

23

Luca

There's no point in being subtle or careful anymore. Effy's life is seriously in danger. I could lose her now.

The first thing I want to do is run down to my warehouse and interrogate the Russian we've kept locked up for the last 24 hours. He's the last one on the list. There are questions I have, and I know he will provide the answers. He must if he wants to live. Or at least die with all his limbs intact.

But something is bothering me. Something about how this whole thing has played out. It started as an itch in the back of my head. Like the tiniest feeling of discomfort you simply cannot ignore—a wrinkle in a perfect sheet of paper. It could be nothing, it could be overlooked, but once you know it's there, you cannot ignore it.

That wrinkle is not a Russian in a warehouse. It isn't a hint that maybe my little brother was involved in business I didn't know about. That wrinkle exists in my conscience. It's a feeling, a knowing that, somehow, something has been off all along. And all the little wrinkles it's created has formed a map back to Louis Valentino.

I don't knock when I arrive at my cousin's home. He knows I'm here. He's expecting me, so he leaves the porch light on and the door's unlocked. A wise move. Despite the warm welcome, I still walk in with my gun drawn because if any of my suspicions are true, then my cousin could likely kill me.

Louis has a modest home, making an honest living as a cop and all that. He has plenty of opportunities to earn extra cash from the family business, but he turns most of them down. Says he wants to live a life as close to normal as possible. His two-story home is proof of what's possible with hard work on the other side of the law. But I'm not impressed by his IKEA furniture. I'm only interested in one thing right now.

I half expect to find Louis standing in his living room with a shotgun, waiting for me to round the corner. Instead, my cousin is sitting at his kitchen table with his head in his hands. A mug of steaming coffee rests in front of him.

It's an odd, humbling scene. Watching everything unravel from his point of view. I wonder how messed up I look. If it's obvious that I'm as broken as the world around me.

But this isn't about me.

"You knew I would come," I say.

He clears his throat and lifts his head. His face is serious but calm. Not an ounce of fear anywhere—I don't know what to make of that, but it doesn't change things.

"I'm going to give you the chance to explain yourself."

He simply nods.

"Effy never escaped, did she?" I ask. "After the initial arrests, you let her go. But you didn't expect her to be so good at hiding. So instead of getting picked up by the Russians—like you planned—my men had the time to join the hunt. And we found her first."

Louis doesn't speak.

"The car bomb. That's what got me curious. It's what put everything into perspective. Because Effy didn't get her own car. *You* led her outside—and *you* arranged for her car to be brought around." I take a step forward. "Have I said anything wrong?"

Louis sighs. "You've said everything wrong, cousin. Do you really think I'm a traitor?"

He looks at me with a stern expression, his brows drawn together, his jaw set. I've never seen him more serious. The sight makes my heart melt a little.

I'd hoped this would be his response.

Louis says, "Believe it or not, I didn't let Effy go. She legitimately escaped from custody on her own. She's slippery. Which I'm sure you've learned by now."

I set my gun on the table to keep from shooting him.

"I'm a crappy cop in that regard, but I'm not a traitor, Luca. I have nothing to gain from stabbing my own family in the back. You know that."

"Go on," I say.

"I escorted Effy out of the party, but I didn't bring her car around. I got a call from my wife—" he stops to swallow, and I understand his emotion. Louis has always had issues with who his family is and what we do. Part of it is his job but the other part is his family. His wife isn't from the mafia, she's a normal woman he met in college and fell hard for. Hard enough to try to detach himself from the organization as much as possible.

If she called him at the party, he would have answered. And I'm positive she did call because they've got an infant child together. It could have been an emergency.

"Is everything alright?" I ask, momentarily setting our differences aside.

Louis nods. "The baby had an allergic reaction to a new formula we're trying." He waves his hand around. "It's all good now. But I convinced my wife to take our child and stay with her mother for the night."

"Good."

He clears his throat. "Well anyway, I got a call from my wife, so I stepped away to take it. While I was gone, I asked Isabella to fetch the car for Effy in my place."

My stomach knots up.

"Isabella…" I whisper.

Louis is right. He's a Valentino, cousin to the Vittore name. Even though he doesn't like his connection to the mafia, he knows he has nothing to gain from betraying our family. If we fall, he goes down right with us. But Isabella isn't in the family. She isn't anything except a maid and a pretty face to warm my bed when I deem it necessary. I know she has deeper feelings for me, which I've never acknowledged, but did that hurt her enough to resort to such drastic measures?

"Why?" I wonder aloud, and Louis scoffs in response.

"Because she's been in love with you for years and the most you've offered her is shame and neglect, Luca. What did you expect?"

"I expected loyalty." I lift my chin. "I don't care if I stripped her naked and put her on display, I'm her *underboss.* She owes me her respect for that fact alone."

Louis clenches his jaw but doesn't dare disagree.

"She wanted to kill Effy because she knew it would hurt me. Fine. But why team up with the Russians?" I ask. "Did she help them kill Mario?"

He shakes his head. "I doubt it. She only reached out to them recently, and only because she wanted to hurt Effy for personal reasons."

For petty jealousy.

"How do you know all this?"

Louis sighs. "When I heard the explosion, I knew it would only be a matter of time before you came looking for me. I was the last person you saw walking out with Effy, it made sense that you would be suspicious of me. But I knew I was innocent, and I knew Isabella had been the last one to handle the car arrangements. So I left the party to find her as soon as I saw the flames." He rubs the scruff on his chin. "She was walking up the street just a few blocks away, carrying a duffle bag full of money."

"Payment from the Russians."

He nods. "She was disappointed to learn her bomb missed its target."

"You have her?"

"Locked up with the Russian in our warehouse. I'm sure you have a lot you want to say to her."

I shake my head, a strangled laugh tumbling from my lips. It sounds like the wild cackle of a madman. Someone on the verge of losing his mind. That's how I feel right now, like my body is welded in place but my mind is slowly slipping.

"I still need to find Effy," I say.

Louis slides his phone across the table. There's a text on the screen from the head of my security detail. I squint at it, almost unsure that what I'm reading is real.

MISTRESS IS SECURE. RETURNED SAFELY.

My heart nearly stops as I fumble for my own phone. I'd been so caught up in trying to learn the truth from Louis, I hadn't checked my messages. Then again, I hadn't expected anyone to find Effy so soon. I'd honestly believed she was gone for good. But as I read the same message on my own phone, from my security and one from Lorenzo, I realize … maybe there is a God.

Did You protect her? I wonder inside. There is no answer, but I'm not angry about it. I don't expect a holy God to acknowledge the prayers of a filthy man like me. But I do expect Him to protect the innocent life of my wife, so whether He answers me or not, I'm grateful He was there for Effy.

Why weren't You there for Mario? I wonder bitterly. *Was he not worthy?*

I shove away my emotional questions as I race out of Louis's home. I suddenly don't care about the Russian in our warehouse. I don't care about Isabella's betrayal. I don't even have time to think about Mario's case anymore. The only thing on my mind is seeing my wife again. Making sure it's her. Making sure she's real and alive and safe.

I burst through the front doors of my home and storm down the hall, rushing toward the guest room where her stuff was stored before we got married. My heart slams against my ribcage when I throw the door open and find it empty.

Is someone playing a cruel joke on me? I let out an angry growl as I slam the door, but my assistant's voice cuts through my temper.

"She's in your bedroom, sir."

I whirl to stare dumbly at Lorenzo. He shifts uncomfortably and then straightens his bowtie. "I escorted her there myself."

"Why?"

I don't understand. She came back … and went to my room. Did she miss me? Did she come back *for* me? Does she feel safe there in my personal space?

Lorenzo answers nervously, "It's where she wanted to be."

Without another word, I rush to my room. I feel like I'm flying down the hall, my steps so harried, I almost trip over my feet.

When I reach my room, I don't snatch the door open like before. I pull it open slowly, like a perfectly timed reveal. I'm almost afraid of what I'll see. If I'll find my light or be met with another room shaded by darkness. Just like every other corner of my life. But my hopes are not put to shame.

Effy is there, sitting on my bed, wrapped in a blanket. She's wiping her eyes and staring ahead, so she doesn't hear me enter, but she looks up in time to see me cross the room to the bed. Our eyes meet and a storm crackles between us. I have no words for what I feel—for what her return means to me. I could be furious about her leaving in the first place, but I just want to make sure she's really here before I allow myself to feel anything other than relief.

I need this. I need her. And I want her to know that.

So instead of yelling or starting a fight, I grab her and kiss her before she can even speak. She shocks me by kissing me back. It isn't a romantic exchange—it's desperate, needy, and only broken by a gasp of air.

Panting, Effy places a hand on my chest, and for a heart-stopping moment, I fear she's pushing me away. Instead, she starts to unbutton my shirt. The gesture tugs a groan from my lips, and I push her into the blankets as I climb into bed.

She can stop me if she wants. If she says the word, I swear I'll let it all go. I'll forget about my needs and put her first. It'll hurt. It'll tear me to pieces, but that's what it means to be a husband. You bear your pain with a smile so she can hand you hers without worry or guilt. If you can't put your wife first, then don't marry her. Because her burden becomes yours the moment you say, 'I do.' That's what it means to be her protector and provider. It means you're there for her, even when she isn't willing to be there for you.

But Effy *is* here. She's right here in my arms, and she's willing and she's ready. But I've just got to hear her say it. I want her to speak the words.

So instead of tearing her clothes off like a madman, I lean away from Effy and look into her eyes. My hand finds her chin, my thumb runs along her jaw. "Let me make love to you," I whisper.

She leans into me, and her words are as sweet as a kiss. "Please, Luca…"

24

Effy

This is not the way I thought my night would end. Then again, it is my wedding night. Technically, this is the most normal exchange Luca and I have shared since we met.

For the first time, things are clear between us. We're both being honest. We know what we want, and we aren't putting up a front anymore. No more subliminal messages. No more hiding our emotions. This is us. This is what love looks like.

It's a dance with tangled limbs and breathy whispers. It's a poetic ritual. It's an act that cannot be recreated with anyone else. Because no one else could ever satisfy but him. Luca Vittore.

I'm not sure if what we have is love, but it's stronger than lust. It's stronger than the bullet that took his brother's life and the bullets that claimed vengeance on the Russians he hunted down. It's stronger than my testimony. It's stronger than the tension I feel building inside of me.

It flows like a storm, lightning crackling in a fiery kiss.

Thunder echoing through the groan he releases. I fit beneath him like I was made to be there, an extension of his own body. We move in sync with one another, performing this lovers' dance. But it quickly becomes clear that I don't know all the moves.

I try to compensate. Close my eyes, whisper his name, cling to him like a newlywed would. But Luca sees through the act. He is hyper-aware of everything I feel, and the moment I gasp in pain, I know he learns the truth.

The tension between us snaps as realization rumbles through the room. Every muscle in Luca's body freezes and he leans away to look down at me. I can't meet his gaze, but I don't want to look down either. There's a smear of red staining my inner thigh. Proof of what I've just given my husband. Something no other man could ever have.

Luca sucks in a gasp, but it sounds more like a hiss. "Why didn't you tell me?" he whispers.

I can't answer. I just squeeze my eyes shut and turn my head to the side. I don't know if I feel embarrassed or angry.

Luca kisses my temple. "I would have been gentler."

But he's been gentle enough already. He didn't hold it against me for running away, he hasn't even mentioned it. Even though I rejected him earlier, he didn't let that come between us. He ran through the door and took me into his arms. He asked me for permission to make love. He left the choice in my hands, and every bone in my body knows he would have honored my choice if I'd said no.

But I said yes. I knew I was a virgin. I knew what it would

mean to say yes to him. And I said it anyway—because I wanted this as much as he did. I can't fight it anymore. I don't want to. And part of me believes this is for the better; because we've got a bigger fight ahead of us and we won't be able to tackle it apart. Luca and I are married now, whether I like it or not. From this point forward, we will face everything in this world together. As one.

This is the first hurtle, but it hardly feels like a challenge or a chore. In fact, the pain I feel melts at Luca's next kiss, and as he whispers in my ear, I feel only the overwhelming flood of passion between us. It storms through the room and washes over me before I can even attempt to tame it. Luca only withstands a few moments longer, hissing through his teeth before he buries his face in the crook of my neck. And then we drown together.

In the aftermath, I lay beside Luca and teeter the line of pleased and ashamed. I feel my ears burn red and my cheeks turn pink as he pulls me close with a satisfied sigh.

"Thank you," he says.

"For what?"

"For coming back."

It's the first time either of us has officially acknowledged what happened earlier.

"I didn't just come back for this." I gesture to our surroundings, at the pile of clothes on the floor by the bed.

Luca actually blushes. It melts my heart.

"I came back because I have something to tell you," I say, then I take a long breath and pour out the story. Every detail flies from my mouth, beginning with my conversation with Aurora, and ending with him bursting through his own bedroom door. Luca listens in silence, his jaw clenching and then unclenching. I'm not sure what to make of his expression, but I know he's listening. I know he hears every word. And when I'm done speaking, he closes his eyes and nods to himself. A long moment of complete silence passes before I can't take it and have to ask him, "What happens next?"

Luca looks at me in shock. "Effy, it's your statement. That means it's your decision to recant or not."

I shake my head. I don't want this to be my decision. What happened to the overbearing underboss I knew a few hours ago? I thought women didn't get a choice in this life. Not that I'm complaining about Luca's willingness to pass me the reins. Still, this decision is too much for me to make alone. It will impact more than just me—or even our marriage.

"If I recant my statement, Mario's killer will never be brought to justice." My voice is a whisper when I speak, so soft, I'm not sure Luca's even heard me at first. But then he clears his throat and says, "That child is my nephew. The only part of Mario I have left in this world. He's worth more than bitter vengeance."

That's all Luca has to say. I understand where he's coming from. I understand the desire to hold on to family. Even though I've never had one. Maybe because I've never had one.

I nod and snuggle closer to him. "Then my decision is made. I'll contact Louis tomorrow."

"Louis?"

"He's one of the detectives who first interviewed me. And I know he's mafia, he'll help us."

Luca smiles. "*Us*."

"That's what we are now. A team. That means I'm in this with you," I say seriously, then I sit up and reach for the bedside table. I'm not surprised to find the Bible still in its place, resting inside. "Even together, we're not enough to face the demons of this dark world, Luca."

I can feel him glaring at me, but I hold the blankets to my bare breasts and flip through the Bible anyway. If I can put up with the madness of the mafia as the wife of an underboss, then Luca can put up with prayer time as the husband of a Christian woman. That's the one thing I won't allow this world to take from me—my faith.

I look at Luca, hoping he can see how serious this is for me. "Pray with me?" I ask, holding out my hand.

He stares down at it. "What do you want to pray for?"

"For peace. And for God's wisdom in this situation."

He hesitates but takes my hand anyway. It's warm and large and as calloused as his heart, but my fingers fit perfectly between his.

I turn one more page in the Bible, searching for the scripture I want. Then I begin my prayer. "Jesus," I say aloud, "You said where two or more are gathered together, You would be in the midst. I invite You into this storm, Lord. I'm handing this problem over to You. And I invite You into this marriage too. I don't know if this was part of Your will, Lord. I don't know what purpose I serve here, but I'm here now.

And I'm asking You to make me a beacon light in this dark world. Help me and Luca carry out Your will as one, and protect us as we go on our way. In Jesus' Name I pray, amen."

When I look up, Luca is staring at me. He doesn't say *amen*, or even acknowledge my prayer, but he squeezes my hand before he lets go. I suppose that's a start.

25

Luca

I should be halfway across town right now, but instead I'm meeting my cousin in my office because he's got information I *must* hear. I'm positive he's just being dramatic because Effy recanted her statement.

She wasn't kidding when she said she'd made up her mind. The morning after our wedding, Effy woke up and made the call to police. There was a lot of anger and paperwork but in the end, the police had no choice but to go with it.

I understood how they felt. Effy has been the key to Mario's justice and vengeance since this story began, and now she is the one undoing it all. It breaks my heart. But it also stitches it back together again. Because losing Mario's killer means gaining Mario's son.

That is the secret behind this entire nightmare. My little brother had a child with the princess of the Russian mafia. According to Effy's story, the child is a product of rape. I refuse to believe that. I know my brother. I know what he was capable of, and sexual assault is not on the list. I won't lie and say he wouldn't hurt a fly, but killing bugs doesn't make you a rapist.

Still, my wife believes the child is his—she believes it enough to recant her statement just to give me a chance to see the child. That's exactly what I want. I need to look at this child with my own eyes, and the only way I can do that is by letting go of Mario's killer. For now.

The thing is… without Effy's statement, the case falls apart and Mario's killer can expect to have his charges dropped within a week. That means he'll be a free man. A man I can hunt down myself.

So, no matter what the real story is, I will have my vengeance.

Effy doesn't need to know this. It's hard enough that she's carrying the guilt of recanting her statement. I don't want to place an emotional burden on her shoulders by telling her I plan to hunt down and kill my brother's murderer as soon as he's set free.

Honestly, this works in my favor. Mario's killer will not rest easy in prison for the next 50 years of his pathetic life. He will die screaming—whether I get to see my nephew or not.

But before any of this can happen, I've got to meet with Louis and hear his urgent news. He's in my office when I arrive, pacing back and forth before my desk. Lorenzo wisely leaves us alone without so much as a goodbye.

"What is it, cousin?" I ask, leaning against the large wooden door.

Louis pins me with his gaze. This is the most intense I've ever seen him; his mood is even darker than when I stood in his home with a gun in my hand. Ready to kill him.

"Your wife recanted her statement—"

"I know," I interrupt, "and I fully support her decision."

"Why didn't you speak to me about this first?" He runs his hand through his hair and exhales so hard, spittle flies from his mouth. I watch him unravel, wondering what it is he knows that I don't.

"What's going on?"

"Mario's killer will go free by the end of the week," Louis replies, "without Effy's statement, we have no real evidence on the guy. The case was entirely circumstantial!"

"Why do you seem more upset than I do?"

"Because I was busy on your wedding night." He splays his hands on my own desk, leaning over it like he owns the place. Like he's an underboss and I'm a measly two-faced cop. I don't like the position he's taking, on the other side of my desk, but I keep my mouth shut and make a mental note to deal with this later. For now, I want to know what my dear cousin has to say.

"While you enjoyed your new wife, I was torturing a Russian Serena kidnapped for you." He glances away, face going pale. That's when it becomes clear just how removed Louis is from all of this. He really wants nothing to do with the mafia. He can't even handle one simple interrogation. I won't say torture is easy, but I've had worse things on my to-do list.

Louis wasn't raised for this life, but he was raised in it. So

I have no sympathy for his dewy forehead or his trembling hands. This is the life we live, whether we like it or not. He's had it easier than the rest of us with his 9-5 job and his pretty wife and his simple house. A small part of me even envies him and his tiny slice of happiness. I wonder if I can emulate that life with Effy. Somehow. Someday.

Unlike my cousin, she wasn't born into this life, and she wasn't made for it either. She shouldn't have to suffer in this world because of one mishap that wasn't even her fault. She had the misfortune of being in the wrong place at the wrong time, and her life is forever changed because of it. But I'm the Italian underboss, I have the power to change her life again. I have the power to shield and protect her from this madness. So that's what I'm going to do.

The first step is dealing with this nonsense.

"What did you learn from your interrogation?" I ask Louis.

He clears his throat, then momentarily presses the back of his hand to his mouth. "I learned about the baby. And what really happened with Mario."

My eyes widen… and the rest of his story knocks the wind out of me.

26

Effy

I'm wearing a warm sweater dress and fashionable booties. My hands are clasped together in my lap and my purse is resting beside me. I fit perfectly between casual and professional. I'm not entirely sure how a mafia wife should dress, but no one has complained so I guess I'm doing something right. The only opinion I really care about anyway is Luca's. But he isn't here right now.

Luca is still in his office. I've been waiting in the car for almost half an hour now. I don't know if it's okay for me to go back inside and see about things. Am I allowed to tell him to hurry up? There are so many rules in the mafia, I understand why everyone here is so unhappy—despite their wealth and power. Now I see this world for what it truly is, and it scares me.

Luca makes me feel safe, but that's only when I'm wrapped in his arms, and we're tangled in his bed. A blush forms on my cheeks at the thought of us together. It's official now. We're connected in every possible way. I haven't had much experience with men, but I have no complaints about our wedding night. It was everything I hoped it would be—minus the attempt on my life or the great escape, plus getting kidnapped by Russians and then having a bombshell dropped into my lap.

That's why I'm in the car now. Luca and I are supposed to go deal with this bombshell. But his cousin desperately wanted to speak and now Luca hasn't returned. I have no idea what to make of this or what to do right now. Should I just sit here and wait? What if Luca doesn't return for hours?

I clear my throat, twisting in my seat to peer out the window. "What am I doing here?" I wonder aloud. That seems to be the question of the year for me. "Where are You in all of this?" The prayer is raw and honest. I can't even begin to imagine what great plan God has for me here as Luca's wife. Am I a positive influence on him? Or is there an even bigger picture? I have to believe that I'm serving a purpose or else it means I've backed myself into an awful lust-filled corner that I won't be able to get out of very easily. If at all.

Before I can sink myself into depression, the double doors to Luca's estate open and he stomps out with a scowl on his face. Whatever Louis had to tell him clearly didn't leave him in a good mood.

I can feel the anger radiating around him as he slides into the leather seats beside me. He surprises me by immediately reaching for my hand. I let him take it and squeeze it, blinking at him in shock. I don't know which is more surprising, the fact that Luca finds comfort in being close to me like this, or the fact that he's holding my hand at all.

Who is this man? I wonder as the car peels from the curb and starts down the long driveway. Is this the side of Luca Vittore that he's kept hidden for his wife's eyes only? The side that enjoys holding hands and needs this physical connection to keep him anchored.

"What did Louis say?" I ask in a quiet voice.

The driver clears his throat and then slides the partition closed. I'm guessing that's his way of giving us privacy; it's a kind, respectful thing to do, but it makes me nervous. And to make matters worse, Luca doesn't speak once the partition is closed.

I steal a glance at him, taking in his clenched square jaw and his sharpened eyes. He's staring at the floor, a scowl on his face that makes him look rigid. He's like a coiled snake, waiting to strike. The look of him only makes me dangerously curious, I cannot help but ask him again.

"What did Louis say?"

"Don't worry about it," he grinds out.

"Whatever," I huff, which I quickly learn is a bad idea because now I have Luca's full attention. His gaze is like a torch burning right through me. I feel my skin prickle with sweat, and it intensifies when he squeezes my hand almost to the point of discomfort.

"Come again?" he questions.

I'm smart enough to know he isn't looking for an answer. I keep my mouth shut and stare down at my free hand gripping the thick material of my sweater dress.

But Luca doesn't let it go. He turns in his seat to look at me fully and demands a response. "You have something to say."

I glance up at him, trying to find my husband in this storm of anger. I know who Luca really is. I know *what* he is. That's never been a secret to me. But this side of him is new. Even when we wrestled each other down on my first day here, he'd gotten angry and shouted that he wasn't there to hurt me.

But what about now?

Now, I've recanted my statement. He doesn't need to keep me safe anymore. He doesn't need me anymore. Which makes me feel like I've married him for no reason. The Russians aren't after me anymore. So what was the point in all of this?

Where are You? I pray again in the stiff silence. I get no answer, and my hesitation only makes Luca even angrier.

"I don't have time for your attitude today," he snaps, letting go of my hand.

I stare at it, wondering what the heck is going on. Should I say something and calm him down? Or just let the anger fizzle out? I've no idea what to do.

We finish the ride in silence, pulling up to a very normal looking home in the suburbs. I was blindfolded the last time I came face to face with a Russian Bratva, but I could tell from my surroundings that I was not inside a two-story family home like what I'm walking up to now. That encounter had played out in a warehouse, the sort of place they use for torture and executions.

The change in location for this meeting eases my nerves a little. Being in someone's home sets the tone for a much different encounter than the last one. Maybe things will turn out better than expected today. I can only hope.

I glance around at the other nice houses as Luca rings the doorbell and then grumbles about how he hates to wait. This neighborhood is beautiful. Upper-middle class with front lawns dotted by piles of freshly raked leaves, driveways with mailboxes waiting at the end, and two-car garages attached to a cozy-looking home. This was the sort of neighborhood I dreamed of living in while I roamed the streets as a sad orphan.

Now I live on a private estate worth millions of dollars, and this place seems like a dressed-up nightmare. I bet none of the plucky soccer moms on this street have any idea their neighbor is a member of the Russian mafia. I wonder what they would do if they found out.

A slender woman opens the door and inclines her head at Luca, then does the same at me. She greets us in Russian but then speaks in English, though her accent is quite heavy. Luca seems to understand what she's saying, nodding at the right intervals and then stepping into the house behind her when she walks away. He only stops to reach back for me. I hesitate for half a second before grabbing his hand.

Like a hawk, he notices my delay and glances down at me, but I pretend to be distracted by the décor of the home. We're led through the living room and then down a hallway toward a back room I thought would be a study or office of some sort. But when we walk inside, I'm shocked to see it's a nursery.

Luca is just as shocked. He's so stunned he actually stops walking and freezes right there in the doorway. His hand is clammy now, and his eyes are wide open. He's blinking around the room, staring at the blue curtains, the white crib, the chest full of stuffed animals and the rocking chair in the corner. Beside the chair is a small table with a framed picture resting on it. Even from my distance, I recognize the smiling boy in it.

It's Mario Vittore. He's wearing a lightning yellow backpack and a beautiful grin. It's so huge it splits his face in half—I'm convinced the only thing keeping him safe from decapitation is his set of nickel-deep dimples. In that moment, captured forever in that photo, he is the cutest teenager I've ever seen. Boyish and innocent and full of the sort of joy you only see on television. He's throwing up the peace sign to whoever is holding the camera, but his other hand is holding someone else's.

That girl's hand. The one I met earlier. The mother of his child. She's standing beside him in a cute school uniform, smiling just as wide. They look happy. The sort of youthful love you read about in diaries and dusty journals. High school sweethearts full of dreams and fanciful ideas of love.

Their story ended in murder.

I swallow, but my throat is sticky, and it feels like I'm choking. What a cruel tactic. The Bratva know what they're doing. The child isn't even in the room, but the sight of this nursery is enough to leave us both shocked. Luca Vittore, the underboss of the Italian mafia, is stunned into silence by just standing in the room of his supposed nephew.

Maybe this is a testament of how much he loved Mario. Or maybe this whole thing is a big mistake, a gesture that only serves to stoke the flames of rage burning inside my husband. I feel it the moment his mood blackens, like a curtain snaps shut on his emotions, blocking out everything except dark hatred. It comes off him in dangerous waves which threaten to drown me. The room is suddenly stifling. My eyes begin to water, like my body knows death is waiting for us, but my mind hasn't caught up yet.

"Luca," I whisper, but the lady who walked us into the room returns with guests before I can say anything else.

Pavel Stepanov and his daughter are here, along with the baby. He's bundled in the girl's arms but that doesn't stop Luca from glaring at him. The tension in the room is palpable, if I reach out, I bet I could grab a handful of it. Carry it around like a living burden. But nothing happens. Instead of flying into a rage, like I expect us to, the room melts into a dark shade of calm when the baby in the girl's arms releases a little giggle.

The anger pops like a bubble of madness and we're drenched in a wave of momentary peace. A nervous chuckle bubbles up my throat like a dirty burp. "Thank you for inviting us," I say, well aware that I'm speaking out of line, but I don't care. I can't live by mafia law right now. There's too much out of line. Too much I don't understand to care about talking without my husband's permission.

Luca doesn't seem to mind anyway, he's still staring at the baby, eyes filled with an emotion I can't name. *This is too much for him…*

I squeeze his limp hand, but he has no reaction. Instead, his focus snaps to Pavel.

"How dare you…" the words come out in a gritty whisper. Luca steps forward, his hand slipping from mine. "How dare you call me here and insult me with this child and these lies."

We're all stunned. I have no idea what Luca is talking about, and both Pavel and his daughter are wearing matching expressions of shock. Their brows are high on their foreheads and their mouths are gaping open, forming perfect O's. But then Pavel recovers and his surprise melts into a calm sort of smugness that makes my throat go dry.

What is going on here?

It's obvious Pavel knows something, and Luca has managed to figure it out. Even his daughter no longer looks surprised. She looks *worried. No*, I realize, studying her closely, she isn't worried. *She's terrified.*

And then Luca reveals something I never saw coming.

"My brother wasn't a rapist," he says slowly, his eyes narrowing to slits of fire in his face. He's so angry I'm sure he'd burn me if I touched him. "But he was a teenager. One who had strong feelings and emotions. And no mentor to teach him how to handle those things." Luca glances away for a single moment, passing me the most fragile expression I've ever seen on him before. He looks broken. But just as quickly, he pieces himself together and his face goes back to the rigid anger he'd been wearing a moment ago.

"Mario and your daughter, Nadia, were in a relationship. I can't say whether you knew, but I had no idea," Luca admits.

"I'm also sure no one had any idea that Nadia was in a relationship with another man at the same time. An older man in your organization."

Luca's hands curl into fists. A vein on his right hand pops out over the middle knuckle, I stare at it as he speaks.

"That man was Oleg Petrov. Mario's murderer."

I audibly gulp, and nearly choke on it afterward. I can't believe what I've just heard, but as I glance at Pavel and Nadia, it becomes very clear that I'm the only one who was left out of the loop. Father and daughter look very calm together right now. Nadia's terror is gone now. She looks stoic, unmoved. Pavel looks like he's holding back a grin. It makes me want to take Luca's gun and shoot him myself. How my husband manages to remain calm is beyond me.

Oleg Petrov is the man who pulled the trigger that night. I know because I watched him do it. And now Luca is saying Oleg had been in a relationship with Nadia Stepanov, but Mario was somehow killed because of it.

"Oleg is the father of that child, isn't he?" Luca demands.

No one moves or speaks for a moment, so Luca starts yelling, "ISN'T HE!?"

Nadia jumps, her baby whimpers and then threatens to wail but she immediately begins to bounce him in her arms, and he seems to quiet down. Meanwhile, Pavel stares at Luca like he's looking at a feral animal. The two of them glare at each other, waging a silent war that I barely understand.

"If Oleg is the father, then why was Mario murdered and branded as a rapist?" I say.

"You allow your wife to speak out of term?" Pavel says, not even looking my way.

Luca ignores the question entirely. He retrieves his gun from his hip and points it in Pavel's face. "Oleg was sleeping with your daughter. When she found out she was pregnant and unmarried, she befriended my little brother. Then she cried rape to cover up the pregnancy and the fact that she was no longer a virgin." His gun begins to shake. "You had my brother murdered based on a little girl's lie. And you had my wife recant her statement to release the real father of that bastard."

"Luca…" I whisper, tears brimming in my eyes.

He ignores me. "Say it," Luca tells Pavel. "Tell me my brother was innocent."

Pavel smirks, and I hold my breath, wondering if Luca will pull the trigger for it. But my husband keeps his head.

"Mario didn't rape your daughter," Luca says. "She got pregnant by Oleg and panicked." He glances at Nadia, shifting his aim so the gun is pointed at her instead.

Nadia cowers, the teenager in her finally surfaces with a sob that shatters her resolve. She ducks her head and leans away from the gun, crying, "Please! I have a baby!"

"I don't care about that child!" Luca shouts, shaking his gun.

I feel my hands start to sweat and rub them on my dress. This isn't good. Luca is losing it. He might actually shoot Nadia or her baby. That cannot happen. That child is innocent, no matter how much pain his birth has caused, it isn't his fault. Nadia is the one who got pregnant. Oleg is the one who murdered Mario. That baby is innocent.

"Say it!" Luca screams, clutching the gun tightly. "Tell me my brother was innocent!" Spittle flies from his mouth as he makes his demands, keeping a white-knuckle grip on his weapon.

Pavel lifts his chin. "My daughter told me he forced himself on to her. I believe her."

"She lied," Luca says plainly.

"Your brother raped her."

There's a loud *pop!*—and then silence. My ears ring as gunpowder clouds in the air around me like a puff of silvery-white vapor. The air smells burnt, but all I can register in my head is the look on Pavel's face as he falls to the floor. His mouth is open, but it's the cries of the baby that I hear instead of his own. That's what snaps me back to reality, the fact that my husband just killed someone in front of an infant.

He points the gun at Nadia who screams and drops to her knees, clutching the wailing child. "Please!" she sobs. "I'll admit it! Mario was innocent! I had a secret relationship with Oleg behind my father's back—when I found out I was pregnant, I befriended Mario long enough to have a one-night stand with him." She sniffles, hiccups, and then keeps going. "I told my father Mario forced himself on to me to cover up the pregnancy with Oleg. I didn't know it would lead to all this."

Luca cocks the gun. His voice is a rasp. "You knew exactly what you were doing," he says. "You're a mafia princess, touching you is punishable by death. You knew Mario was dead the moment you let him kiss you." His voice cracks. "You told him about the pregnancy, didn't you?"

Nadia's eyes grow so large, I fear they'll pop from their sockets.

Luca nods. "You did. And you let him die thinking he was the father of your child. You let him *die* believing he would leave a fatherless child behind in this world." His voice drops an octave. "How could you…"

I agree. As Mario's final moments replay in my head like a nightmare, I understand my husband's pain as much as his anger.

I wasn't enough…

Now I know what he meant by that. Nadia told Mario about the pregnancy, and he'd tried to step up and do the right thing about it. But it hadn't been enough. He ended up murdered. And he died thinking that he hadn't been enough. That he couldn't be a good father to his child. That he couldn't save Nadia from this mafia world. He died a broken young man, over a child that isn't even his.

"You killed him," Luca says, and the heartbreak in his voice nearly brings me to my knees. There are tears streaming down both his cheeks; he wipes them away with the back of his free hand while the other holds tightly to his gun.

"You killed him because a mafia princess cannot have sex before marriage. But the organization will make an exception in the case of sexual assault. When you found out you were pregnant, you had to cry rape or face the wrath of your father." Luca sniffles. "But now you're facing *my* wrath." He steps forward, but instead of pressing the gun to Nadia's head… he aims it at the baby.

"Don't!" I scream, running forward. I squeeze myself between Nadia and the gun, daring my husband to shoot me instead.

He blinks at me like he's just realized I was even in the room.

"Step aside," he says calmly.

I shake my head. "I can't do that, Luca. I can't let you make this mistake."

"It won't be a mistake. A life for a life."

"You've taken more than one life for this."

His face darkens. "Those other men deserved to die."

"This is the end of the road, Luca. If you hurt that child, you can't blame it on the mafia code. That's all *you*. This is *your* decision." I swallow thickly, trying to keep my composure, but that's hard to do when you're staring down the barrel of a gun.

Holy Spirit help me… I pray inside. No one can get through to Luca but You, Jesus. What do I say? What does he need to hear to change his mind right now?

I almost gasp as the truth hits me. *This* is the purpose I serve. This is the reason God allowed me to walk down that jagged path and fall into this mafia world. Everything I've been through has led to this moment. And now I'm thankful for it—because I'm the only person in the world who can save this innocent baby.

Nadia can hardly speak around the sobs that wrack her, the baby can do nothing but wail, and Pavel is already dead.

It's just me and Luca right now. In this moment. Sharing the same pain and trauma—like two halves of the same nightmare. Except this time, I can't heal his wounds. I can't kiss him and make everything go away. Luca must turn to God for this. He must learn to trust the Light of the world instead of depending on me to be his conscience.

What do I tell him, Lord?

Tell him I love him.

It seems like the most ridiculous thing in the world to say right now. Luca has a gun in his hand that he's already used once. I don't think he wants to hear about how much Jesus loves him in this moment, but it's not my job to dissect everything God says. It's my job to simply obey. So I say the words without even thinking.

"Luca, Jesus loves you!" I practically shout at him. It's such a random statement, even Nadia glances over at me, a bewildered look on her tear-streaked face.

Luca frowns. "Effy—"

"Jesus loves you," I repeat. "Even right now with that gun in your hand and a dead body at your feet. He loves you." I step forward until the gun is pressed to my own forehead. "If Jesus could love you, a murderer, then He could certainly love that innocent child. And He wouldn't want you to pull that trigger."

Luca drops his gaze.

"For the love of Christ, don't hurt that baby."

Silence stretches on like a wire ready to snap, but God is here with us. Luca lowers the gun and releases a long sigh that

I feel deep in my bones. For a moment, we all stand there, not really knowing what to say. Even the baby is quiet now. But then Luca holsters his gun and turns toward the door.

"I will spare the baby," he says, "but when your men come after me, I will show no mercy."

My breath freezes in my chest. This isn't over. The baby is unscathed but the rest of us have been marked for death. Because Nadia and her son made it out alive, but Pavel Stepanov did not.

Luca just murdered the boss of the Russian mafia. That will not go unanswered.

27

Effy

The estate has been on lockdown. No one has been allowed to leave and visitors are searched and then monitored while on the mansion grounds. I'm used to being locked up like this, but seeing everyone else walk around in this misery is foreign. It's so odd, I feel a cavern of sympathy open in my stomach like a pit.

Aurora looks like a ghost drifting through the manor, her hair is thinner, her eyes have dark circles beneath them, and her skin has lost its natural olive glow. She looks awful, a wisp of a woman weighed down by a million worries and even more fears.

I understand why she's broken down like this. A week ago, the boss of the Russian Bratva was murdered in one of his own homes. In front of his own daughter and grandson. We are sitting ducks now, waiting for the bloodshed and violence to hunt us down. Waiting for vengeance to find us.

I remember staring at Nadia, watching her wail as loudly

as her infant child. A bit of blood spatter had gotten onto the sleeve of her white cashmere sweater, a dark red stain on pure white wool. In that moment, I realized what'd truly happened.

Luca opened the doors to death and left us in an impossible situation. It was a miracle we even made it out of Pavel Stepanov's home alive in the first place. As reckless as my husband's decision seemed, I learned that he'd entered that home with every intention of murdering someone and walking out alive.

The house had been surrounded by his men. Even before we'd gotten there, he had people in place—thanks to arrangements he made with Louis. To say I was surprised to see all the men with weapons and cars parked on the side of the road as we rushed out the front doors would be an understatement.

For the first time in this entire ordeal, I felt thankful for the fact that my husband is the underboss of the Italian mafia. And then I immediately felt guilty. Because I shouldn't depend on him in those dangerous situations. I should place my faith in Christ. It was God who directed my path, even used my mistakes to my own advantage. He made a way for me in this wilderness. Not just to survive, but to impart His goodness and mercy onto others.

Before I walked out of that house, I spoke to Nadia Stepanov. As her child wailed and tears streaked her own face, I stepped away from my husband and spoke from my heart.

"Thank you," she had sobbed in a wobbly voice. "Thank you for letting us live."

I'd glanced at her father's corpse, his blood still running red along the floor. "Thank God instead," I told her. "It was Him who saved you and your baby."

She'd blinked at me. "God? What does God have anything to do with this?"

"It was God who brought me here. I made my own mistakes. I'll admit that. I got myself thrust into the valley of the shadow of death, but God's Word is true. He was there with me, and He used my mistakes for the glorification of His Name."

Nadia's eyes widened like she was looking at a crazy person.

"The reason I'm here is because God knows I'm the only one who can reach my husband. I'm the only voice he will yield to in this darkness. God trusts me to use my voice to guide Luca to Him. The true light in this world." I somehow managed to smile. "When your child is older, tell him that Jesus loves him and died for him. Tell him that God used me to save both of you from the monster inside my husband. Because your child matters to Him."

"Did my father not matter?" Nadia had asked, almost angrily.

"Of course, he mattered. But you and I both know Pavel Stepanov never would have changed. If he was alive, he would go on spending the rest of his life spreading evil in this world. It had to end here."

"And what about your husband's evil?" Nadia jutted her chin toward the door where Luca had left through. "He's a mafia underboss. He murdered my father. When is his judgment coming?"

My stomach had twisted with pain and guilt. "Soon," I'd whispered. "He will be judged soon."

I thought I was speaking from my heart, but as I lie in bed going over the events now, I think maybe that wasn't from my heart. Maybe I was speaking the words God had given me, poured into my Spirit.

"Did you really use a worthless street rat to save an innocent child?" I ask aloud. I don't know why God saw fit to use me. I don't have, or even want, any children. I'm not even a very good Christian, and I've barely kept the straight and narrow.

I did not choose you because you are good.

The words ring in my ears, almost bringing me to tears.

I chose you because you were willing.

That does it. I feel the dam keeping my emotions at bay break in two, and then a flood of guilt, remorse, fear, and so many other feelings rush down my cheeks like a storm. I'm crying so hard; all I can do is roll over and scream into my pillow.

God chose me… of all the 7.8 billion people in this world, He chose me to accomplish His will. I wonder how the heroes of the Bible feel when they look down from heaven and see how deeply their willing obedience has impacted the entire world. I have a tiny inkling of understanding of what that feels like now. But somehow that feeling of overwhelming joy is muddied by all the negative emotions I feel too.

Why am I so sad, then? I wonder. *Jesus, I don't get it.*

Before I can listen for God's reply, the door to my bedroom opens and Luca appears. He blinks at me like he's surprised to see me, then he closes the door behind himself. The silence that fills the room is so stifling, I want to run across the room and open the balcony doors to let in some air.

We haven't spoken much in the last week. Luca's been busy making arrangements for the coming war. Trying to make up for the huge mistake he made. If we can even call it a mistake. So far, only the women seem surprised and miserable during this lockdown. I get the feeling that everyone else knew this would happen. Or maybe they knew Luca well enough to figure this was coming.

"You're still in bed," he says in his raspy voice. He crosses the room and opens the blinds. I am shocked by the bright afternoon light that rushes into the room.

I close my burning eyes for a moment. "I didn't feel well this morning. So I stayed in bed."

He nods and then stares at me. Watching in silence.

I squirm beneath his gaze.

"Get yourself cleaned up," he says. Then he walks toward the closet and starts digging for clothes.

The one thing I will say about Luca is this: he takes care of me. I've never missed a meal, never wanted for anything, never had to ask for anything. He isn't the husband I would have chosen, but he's the one I was given. So far, he's made me as happy as I can be in this gloomy world. So I try my best not to give him any trouble. He's already got a lot to focus on, a whiny wife should not be added to the mix.

In silence, I climb out of bed and pad across the floor to the bathroom. I smile at my toothbrush sitting beside his on the counter. The place is still incredibly masculine, but seeing these little changes is heartwarming. I want more than this to change in our lives, but I don't know how to implement those changes.

Will You help me, Jesus? I pray in my heart. *I know what my next mission is. You want me to share the Gospel with Luca. But how? How can I reach him?*

I brush my teeth as I pray, searching for the wisdom and guidance of the Holy Spirit. I don't get an immediate answer, but I have no doubts that He *will* answer. So I don't let myself get distracted by worry or fear as I peel off my pajamas and step into the shower. I'm reaching for the soap when I'm suddenly smacked by a blast of cool air.

The frigid sensation makes me whirl around to search for the culprit. I freeze when I see Luca entering the bathroom. He shuts the door behind himself and stands there, silently looking through the glass shower door.

I'm not ashamed to be naked in front of him. But I feel weird with his silence and his mystery looming around us. I feel like I never know what he wants, but his motives right now are clear as he takes off his suit jacket and then his dress shirt, slowly peeling every layer of clothing from his body as he watches me. His eyes never leave mine, not even when the steam from the shower threatens to block his view.

Once he's free of his clothes, he stands there for a

moment, as if to see my reaction. The only response I can give him is submission.

I open the shower with a click, and he grabs my wrist. It's a rough gesture, followed by him stepping into the small space and pressing me against the wall. The water is hot and threatens to burn me, but it's nothing compared to the look in Luca's eyes. They are marbles of fire in his face, scorching me with every blink.

His lips are like flames, burning, singeing, growing hungrier with every heavy breath. I let him kiss me until I can't breathe, but when I pull away, he demands more, his need almost overwhelming.

"Turn around," he growls.

I stare up at him and find myself growing bold as I shake my head in defiance. Submission begone.

"No," I say, stunning both of us. "I want to see you this time."

I say *this time* because there have been others. In the last week, we've barely spoken, but we have communicated in other ways. Sharing each other's pain and confusion. Bearing our burdens the only way we know how.

Now I get it, as Luca moves so close that we're nearly one person now, I understand where my confusing sadness is coming from. We're married. We're truly as one. In mind, body, and spirit. The things I feel are an extension of my husband's feelings. That's what it means to have a marital covenant with someone. To be soul tied.

It makes me love him even more. Makes me love him so

much that it hurts—because he's hurting, and the only relief he can find is this. This dance between us, this carnal satisfaction. A momentary distraction.

But I don't want our passion to be a distraction, something that keeps his mind busy for a little while. I want everything between us to mean something. To last beyond eternity.

When he grips my hips, I bite down on his shoulder and let him bury his troubles again. Everything feels as good as I imagine it would. Each time it gets easier to love him, it gets easier to understand *how* he loves me. But this time I want to show him how *I* love him.

I give my husband every part of me in that shower. Not just for his benefit—this is a two-way street, and I've got pain I want to unload too. But it's different for me. I have a Light inside. I have hope. I can share that with Luca too. So, when he slaps his palm against the shower wall and lets out a long groan, I hold him close, panting, breathing in unison.

"I love you," I tell him, almost trembling. "Through all of this, I love you."

Those are almost the same words I told him in Pavel's house, except I'd been talking about God's love. I know he remembers because I feel his arms stiffen as he holds me. But he doesn't pull away. We remain like that, tangled in an embrace, until the shower runs cold. Only then do we pull apart and reach for the soap.

When we're dressed, Luca kisses my forehead and tells me

lunch will be served in the small dining room. I nod and watch him leave, but I never make it down to the dining room. I spend the next hour reading my Bible and writing in a prayer journal Aurora gave me, and when I'm done with that, I pack everything away and head to the door to leave. Except a sudden wave of sickness stops me in my tracks.

I feel like I'm going to vomit.

It's a miracle I make it to the bathroom in time to scream-puke into the toilet. I don't know how long I'm there, but when I rinse my mouth at the sink and step into my bedroom, I see Aurora sitting on the edge of my bed.

I could complain that she's overstepped her boundaries by entering my bedroom without permission, but I like Aurora. There's no need to challenge her authority as the Mistress of the Vittore mafia. So instead of complaining about the lack of privacy, I plaster on a smile and hope my breath doesn't smell like vomit.

"Afternoon," I say.

She nods, eyes vacant and ghostly.

"You don't look well. Have you eaten?"

That seems to shake her from her stupor. "I haven't been able to eat all week. I don't know how anyone can eat, honestly. It feels like we're all waiting to die."

"Want to pray about it? That's the only solace I have in this world."

She smiles, and it looks genuine. "We can pray, but first I wanted to check on you. I didn't see you for lunch. Luca said you would be there."

I glance down at my socked feet. I'm wearing a simple pair of black leggings and an oversized sweater that's probably cashmere. I don't know. It feels expensive.

"Sorry, I wasn't feeling well all of a sudden."

"Hmm." She nods, making me wonder what's going on.

"Did Luca say something?"

"No," she chuckles, "I doubt he knows any more than you do."

"Knows what?"

Aurora raises her eyebrows at me, a knowing expression on her face. "About the pregnancy."

My eyes pop. I want to laugh at her foolishness, but another wave of sickness hits me, and I clutch my abdomen instead. The nausea puts everything into perspective, leaving both of us in a very stiff silence.

Aurora sits there on the edge of my bed with a motherly smile on her face while I swallow and wince at the dryness in my throat.

Oh no… Oh no no no…

The thought bounces around my brain like an alarm on repeat. I cannot be pregnant. I can't be. I just lost my virginity a week ago! How could I possibly be pregnant?

Aurora seems to read my mind. "It's none of my business, but did you and Luca use protection?"

I almost scoff. "Once. But it came off and he didn't bother to put on another."

She rolls her eyes. "Men."

I laugh, but it's cut short as I groan and cover my mouth

with the back of my hand. "I don't understand. We've only had sex a handful of times."

Aurora raises one eyebrow like she knows I'm lying. We've rolled around this room more than twice a day every day, despite the stony, painful silence between us. Sex seems to be the only way we willingly and easily communicate these days. Sometimes it's all we can offer each other, and lately it's been all we've needed.

But now I'm faced with the consequences of our carelessness, and it scares the crap out of me. I am not fit to be a mother any more than Luca is fit to be a father. The world we live in isn't built to nurture children.

Look at what happened to Mario. Look at what almost happened to Nadia.

Tears prick the backs of my eyes and I clutch my stomach, but not out of illness. I know Aurora is right. I know it the way a woman knows the moment her period begins—recognizes the tiniest of cramps in the deepest parts of her. You just know.

I am pregnant. And it makes me want to scream and cry.

"I can't do this…" I whisper, wiping my wet eyes. One challenge after another in this world. They hit me like an unending storm. "I can't have a child."

Aurora holds out her hand. "We'll call a doctor to take a test and be certain. But you know I'm here with you. And Luca will be too."

That makes everything worse. How on earth do I tell this to my husband? He's gone right now, trying to fight a war he started. Trying to keep me safe. What will a baby do for this situation? How will it affect him?

He'd been willing to change the world for a chance at seeing his nephew, maybe he'll be willing to change himself for a chance at being a good father. A father who isn't a mafia boss.

Is this from You? I pray inside. *Is this our way out of this world?*

Could it be possible that Luca would leave this all behind if he knew there was something better—something more important—out there for him?

I won't know until I tell him.

28

Luca

I lie beside my wife in silence, listening to the sound of her peaceful breathing. I wonder what she's dreaming of—if she dreams at all. I imagine she would dream of a better life, where she isn't living in a lockdown, where her life isn't in danger. Where she isn't married to me.

This is the sin I carry.

Like a parasite, I latch on to those around me, feeding off them, infecting them, dragging them down into the depths of hell with me. I got Mario killed. And now I've put my entire family at risk. Now I've put Effy in even more danger.

The death of Pavel Stepanov will not be overlooked. All I can do is wait for the Bratva to retaliate. Will they shoot up my home? Try to set it on fire? Infiltrate us the way they used Isabella to plant that car bomb?

My hand balls the blankets into a fist as I think of Bella. What were the nights between us worth? How did we end up like this?

I won't even pretend I ever loved that woman, but I cared enough to keep her in my home and take care of her. I thought she knew her place. I thought what I gave her had been enough. But I was wrong.

She betrayed me, in the worst possible way. And she paid for her sins the only way this business allows.

I wasn't the one who pulled the trigger. Louis did. He tortured her and the last Russian on my list to get the information I needed to piece together the truth behind Mario's death. Then he finished them both off while I put a bullet in Pavel's head.

All of that careful planning—gathering my men to surround the Stepanov home, keeping constant surveillance so we made it out alive, making sure Effy knew nothing about it at all—was for naught. I got the vengeance I'd been chasing. I killed the man who issued the order for my brother's death. But I'm still unhappy. I'm still lying here in the dark trying to figure out what to do next.

I'm still afraid.

What if everything falls apart and I get Effy killed?

I shake my head. I can't think about that right now, it'll drive me insane. As if I haven't already lost enough of my mind. The visions of Mario don't happen as often as they used to, but I'm not comfortable at night. I hate going to sleep, and I hardly pass a day without a drink. It helps with the nightmares.

Think about the good things, I tell myself. I'm sure there's a scripture about that, but I can't remember it now and I don't want to wake Effy over it. She looks too peaceful right now.

I shift on the mattress to stare at her, my gaze traveling the round curve of her nose, the cupid's bow of her full lips, the tiny dimple in her right cheek—like she's smiling in her sleep. In the early morning light, her brown skin is the color of mahogany wood. Her curly afro hair is soft as cotton. Her mouth is perfect for kissing.

She glows, like the light for which she's been named.

Just the sight of her puts me at ease, and staring at her peaceful face makes me wonder if there is a God after all. Because only a comforting Father could give someone such a peaceful slumber in the midst of all this chaos.

I want that peace. I want a good night of sleep. I want *something more* than what I've been living. I just don't know how to get it. I think maybe Effy's God could give it to me, but I don't want to try that. I don't want to trust God. Because what if I trust Him and the same thing happens to Effy that happened to Mario?

Trust is dangerous. Hope is even worse. At least in this world I know death is always waiting. I expect the violence, so it never catches me off guard. In Effy's world, it's different. But I don't fit into her world any more than she fits into mine.

Yet … here we are.

We made love again last night. And she told me she loved me forever. In a breathy whisper, the words came out like a song against my sweaty cheek. *I love you forever, Luca…*

What does that even mean? How could she love me. She watched me kill someone. She was forced into this life against her will. And it's not like I've even tried to romance her. I don't even take it easy on her in bed. But she clings to me like I'm all she's got. Like if she lets me go, I'll drift away. And maybe I will. Maybe when I get out of bed today, I won't return. I could die at any moment. This war could end us. But I've got to go out and fight anyway. I have to protect my wife and family.

It's not going to be easy, but I don't think about that. I think of the good things. Like how Louis managed to keep Mario's killer in prison. With the confession from the Russian he tortured, Louis was able to look into the claims over the paternity of Nadia's child.

If Oleg is truly the father of that baby, then he could be brought up on charges for statutory rape. Nadia is only fifteen, like Mario. She shouldn't be a mother at this age, no matter who the father is. But if the father *is* Oleg, he's about to face another set of charges he won't easily escape. The best part is that there is no statement to recant.

Due to the seriousness of the accusations, Louis got his hands on a court sanctioned DNA test. Once the results come in, we'll know if any charges can be filed.

That's the good I think about. The small blessing I've been given, despite all the sin I've brought into this filthy world.

I look at Effy again—at the light of my life—and I think of the scripture she quoted in her prayers before bed. She says them aloud so I can hear. I try not to listen, but the words catch my attention without warning.

A thousand may fall at your side, ten thousand at your right hand, but it will not come near you.

That's **Psalms 91:7**. Despite my years at a private Catholic school, I never heard that scripture before. It stuck with me the moment I heard Effy say it. I've memorized it, replayed it in my head, wondered if that verse can be applied to a sinner like me.

Now, more than ever, I need God's protection. The kind that will keep me standing even as everyone around me hits the ground. I don't deserve the Lord's protection, but for the sake of my wife and her desperate faith, I close my eyes and try to pray for it anyway.

Effy's God, I say in my heart, *help me.*

That's all I've got. I've no idea what else to say. But if He's really all-knowing, then I suppose there's nothing more for me to say. He already knows. But is it right for me to pray for protection in a war I started?

I've got men waiting for my call so we can move on the Bratva today. We're setting up a perimeter to lure them in and push a counterstrike. They won't see it coming. But how many bodies will fall?

I wonder if Effy will see me differently after today. After I storm the Stepanov mansion and murder the rest of the Bratva. After I burn their home to the ground and dance on the ashes. Will she love me for what I've done to protect her? Or will she recoil from me, unable to accept the man she married.

I can't even begin to imagine the answer to that question. I barely survived Mario's sudden absence from my life. I will die if Effy leaves me too—I'll die screaming if she leaves by *choice.* But can I blame her if she doesn't want to stay?

Effy told me she had something important to share, maybe she'll stick around long enough to deliver the news. That's what I hope, at least. She could have told me last night, but we were busy. For a while.

I'll make that my new goal. Come back alive so my wife can share her news with me.

A tired sigh puffs my cheeks as I roll over and gingerly get out of bed. I walk around to my wife's side, staring down at her, then I brush her coiled hair from her face and plant a kiss to her forehead. Her brows crinkle, but she doesn't wake.

"I love you forever, Effy," I whisper. And then I walk out the door and hope that I'll return.

29

Effy

I should be used to waking up alone, but when I see the empty space beside me this morning, my heart breaks a little. It doesn't break for the loneliness; it breaks for the worry. It breaks at the mystery of my husband's whereabouts and his motives. It breaks because I still haven't gotten a chance to tell him the news. I still don't know how.

We're in the middle of a mafia war now, and according to Serena, the first casualty has finally occurred.

"They killed one of our guards while he was on patrol last night," she says, staring at her untouched food. We've both been served fluffy omelets and coffee but neither of us has an appetite. I can't eat because of morning sickness; Serena lost her appetite because of the conversation.

"Bullet through the back of the head," she continues with a sigh. "The good thing is, there were no signs of torture. That means they've got nothing on us."

"You mean, they won't know our movements?"

Serena smiles like a proud mother. "That's right. You're learning."

I don't know how I feel about that. Do I want to learn the rules of this world? It's beneficial to know what's going on, but the more I know, the more deeply involved I will be. It's hard enough just knowing that Luca is part of all this. I can't imagine the stress I'll have to endure if I start actively participating in the organization. Not to mention how much it will impact my relationship with God.

"Is Luca fighting?" I ask without thinking.

Serena hesitates but nods.

I feel myself getting angry. "This is so stupid."

"They killed Mario," Serena argues.

"And Luca killed how many others in turn? Plus, Pavel Stepanov himself. I think he's done enough."

She bristles, eyes narrowing. "Whose side are you on?"

"I will always be on Luca's side."

"You don't sound like it."

"You don't understand—"

The room tilts as I'm hit with a sudden bout of nausea. The effect makes me grip the edge of the table as I try to wait out the wave. I feel my eyes begin to burn with frustrated tears, I blink away the emotion and focus on my breathing. Serena is talking somewhere in the background, but I can't hear her over the pounding of my heart. Her voice sounds like she's underwater. Her hand on my own feels like a Brillo pad scraping over my skin.

I jerk away from her touch and the sound comes back with

pop! I feel a migraine starting at the base of my head.

"Talk to me," Serena demands. The look on her face is the perfect mix of concern and anger, like she isn't sure what to feel right now.

I may as well tell her the truth since she just witnessed me nearly passing out. I know she won't let this go easily.

"I'm pregnant," I say in a shaky whisper.

Serena curses and then immediately apologizes, her eyes drifting toward the cross-shaped pendant hanging around my neck.

I wave her off. "It's alright."

"I'm happy for you. I'm just…"

"I know. I feel the same."

She brushes a thick lock of hair behind her ear. I notice the polish on her long nails is chipped. That isn't like her at all, it's the only sign that she isn't as okay as she seems. Serena's wearing a black sweater with black ripped jeans and combat boots. Her hair is stylishly messy, like she's mastered the windblown look, but her polish is chipped and there's a smudge of liner in the corner of her left eye. As if she forgot she was wearing makeup and wiped her eye.

Since I met her, Serena has been the image of perfection in this business. Beautiful, confident, strong. As intelligent as her mother and as ruthless as her brother. I'm sure her father is proud of her. I'm sure he wishes she were a man so he could entrust more of his organization to her. But the mafia is still a hundred years behind; if it weren't for the war, I'm sure Serena would be trying on wedding gowns today, preparing for the marriage she had no say in.

As it stands, she's here now. And for the first time, I see her as a worried little sister, not a mafia girl boss.

"I want to tell him," I say, unsure if I'm talking to myself or to Serena at this point.

"Luca doesn't know?"

I shake my head. "There hasn't been much time for talking lately." I can't help but blush, hoping my brown complexion covers the tint in my cheeks.

"Well, that's how you got pregnant a week after your wedding." Serena laughs, lightening the mood. "I don't blame you. Spend as much time with Luca as you can. Love him as much as you can." She sighs. "If I could see my lover, I wouldn't let him go."

My heart breaks for her, for the woman in love with the man she couldn't marry. I remember the tattooed guy at the bar she took me to. I remember the way she couldn't stop ogling him. And now I realize she hasn't seen him since the lockdown started. She likely hasn't been able to contact him at all. Luca had everyone's phones confiscated to make sure we couldn't be tapped or tracked. I'm sure Serena fought it, but there are limits to even her influence over her brother. And now she has no idea when she will see or hear from her lover again.

"I need to see Luca," I say urgently. "I need to tell him."

Serena shakes her head. The way she drops her eyes makes my stomach sink.

Something's wrong.

"What aren't you telling me?" I ask.

"Luca isn't just fighting; he's making plans to assault the Stepanov mansion today."

"Their *mansion*?" I may not know much about the mafia as a whole but living on the estate has given me *some* understanding of how this world works.

The homes of mafia bosses are like safe zones. They are off limits for attack. No matter what. It's considered a mafia code of honor. Don't touch the women, children, or civilians. And don't target personal homes. Businesses, warehouses, and other property are fair game, but homes are private. They're safe havens.

To attack the Stepanov mansion is to run through the gates of hell. If that happens, the Bratva may be offended enough to send in reinforcements *from Russia.* We'll be dealing with the real mafia then.

I stand so quickly, my chair nearly topples over behind me. Serena blinks in surprise and then gives me a pitiful look. "Effy, don't do something crazy."

"You know I have to try to stop him." I turn away before she can respond. *God, please help me*, I pray. *Please protect Luca. Even though he doesn't know You yet, will you show him Your mercy for my sake?*

The words I spoke to Nadia come back like the toll of a bell, singing its song of death over an empty graveyard. *When is his judgment coming?* she'd asked. My response had been…

Soon.

And now, here we are.

Luca has a choice. He's had so many choices all along. Show his enemies mercy they don't deserve or let his emotions drive him toward vengeance. Each time, he chose vengeance and God withheld the punishment he deserved. But now his chances are over. He's down to his last decision.

Luca cannot attack that mansion, or else he will never make it out alive.

Serena runs up and grabs me by the elbow. "Effy, you can't go out there. Not only is it a crazy idea but we're on lockdown."

"Tell me you haven't thought about sneaking out," I challenge her. With the way she misses her bartender boyfriend, I know she's got plans.

I twist my elbow free and take her hand in mine. It feels sweaty. "Help me, Serena. He's not just my husband, he's the father of my unborn child and he's going on a suicide mission." My voice cracks. "I have to stop him."

Serena stares at me for a long moment, and then her shoulders sag as her dissolve melts away. "Alright," she says. "But you follow my orders. Got it?"

I nod without hesitation. "Lead the way."

30

Luca

I stare at the wreath hanging on the front door of the Stepanov mansion. I'm sitting in a truck just a few yards from the estate. It's bigger than my own home with a rolling lawn and a massive wrought iron gate. There are guards out front, but not as many as you would expect. The Bratva might be ruthless, but they honor most of the mafia code.

Most.

The one rule they didn't obey is the very reason I'm here right now. They killed my baby brother. A child of fifteen who was undoubtedly innocent in all of this. And then, to twist the knife, they tainted his reputation, lied to free his killer, and kidnapped my wife.

I'm going to burn their house to the ground today.

It'll make me the same as them. Betraying the code we live by. But they broke that code first.

Judging from the lack of sufficient guard detail, I'm guessing the Stepanovs have underestimated the lengths I'm willing to go to for vengeance. They've probably focused their forces on their trucking station, where they ship out most of their cargo. It's a smart defensive measure, something I would've done if the shoe were on the other foot. Because attacking their supply stations would cripple their business beyond repair. But I'm not interested in hurting their money flow.

To be honest, the Bratva hasn't harmed the Vittore business at all. They stabbed us in our hearts, where it mattered most. So I plan to do the same. I'm going to take as much from them as I can before they end me.

I don't think I'll make it out of this attack alive. All I can do is try to cause as much damage as possible before they retaliate.

I think about Effy as I see the signal from my men who've finally gotten into position. I know what she would say about all of this. I can hear her quoting scriptures like a preacher, trying to get me to see the Light. But *she* is my light. I only see her. If I cannot protect her from the monsters of this world then what good am I as her husband?

I had almost all the power I could obtain in this business, and it wasn't enough to protect someone I loved. I can't risk that happening again. I won't survive the pain of losing Effy, so I'm going to end everything here and now. The Russians can't hurt anyone else if they're all dead, and everyone who matters is holed up in that house right now. If I take them out, the war will end. Like cutting the head off a snake. Or a rat. Take your pick.

God… the One Effy trusts… I exhale into the cold afternoon around me as I walk toward the estate. Frost crunches beneath my boots, signs of an early winter, but the only sound I hear is the whistle from my man ahead. We've got the clearance to move forward. As I walk, my prayer pours out of my heart. It shocks me that I even care to pray right now, but what else are you supposed to do when faced with certain death?

If there is even a chance that God is real, I'll take a moment to speak to Him.

The only thing I want is for Effy and the rest of my family to be safe. I don't care about what happens to me. Quite frankly, I deserve the fate I know is coming.

A Voice reaches out to me, freezing me in my tracks.

Who is to say what you deserve?

I don't know how to respond. I don't even know if what I heard was real or not. But I can feel the certainty in my bones—in my marrow—and then the Voice speaks again.

My Son, Yeshua, died so that you can place your fate in My hands. Not your own. If you accept Him, you will receive mercy.

I squeeze my eyes shut. The Stepanov mansion is right there in front of me. A few steps away. I could reach out and grab vengeance by the hair. Why would God speak to me now? When my goal is so close…

I know the choice I should make. I know the choice Effy would want me to make. But my own desires win this battle.

Rolling my shoulders, I exhale a foggy breath and walk forward.

The back entrance has already been cleared by the time I walk up the paved walkway. Bodies line the cold concrete ground, taken out by our first team that'd been armed with silenced weapons. We have a sniper to watch our backs, but he's a last resort. Snipers make too much noise. We need to keep things hushed for as long as possible.

I can smell the gasoline when I step through the back door. It leads to the garage and then to a mudroom which is wet with gas. One of my men pours a trail through the house while two assassins move in with silencers and knives. I watch as they enter rooms, and just as quickly return to the hall. One of the assassins cleans a knife as he exits a room right beside me. Before the door closes, I get a peek inside. The décor is plain, and the bed is small—a servant's room. There's a body in the bed, but from my distance I can't tell if it's a man or a woman. The only thing I see is the large red stain on the white pillow. And then the door shuts.

My men are moving ahead of me, swiftly taking out my enemies. Following my orders. I could stop them. I could end this silent massacre, but I am not a man of mercy. That offer is off the table now. My fate is in my own hands. And in that fate, I find chaos. It isn't pretty, but it is familiar. I'd rather die in the world I know and understand than take a chance at living in Effy's unknown world.

I know how ridiculous that sounds but it's the truth and I won't deny it for your sake. I don't care if my sins make you uncomfortable, you should know who I am by now. You should understand that a man born in darkness will always squint at the light, burned by its uncomfortable brightness.

The burn is too much for me, so I'll remain in the shadows. Where it's safe. As safe as it can be for a mafia underboss.

A shot rings out in the hall, followed by a shrill scream. One of my guards was caught off guard by a maid rounding the corner. He's holding her limp body in his arms now, but it's too late. Our cover is blown.

I retrieve my gun from its holster and signal the guard nearest to me. He knows exactly what I want and holds out a match for me to take.

"At your cue," he says in Italian.

I nod and strike the match, staring at the flame. Once I drop this to the floor, the house will ignite and burn from the inside out. We made it deeper into the mansion than I ever expected us to, past the staff quarters, toward the main foyer. But this is it. For my men, at least. There's one more room I want to check before I run out of time.

"Go. Don't break protocol," I order, still holding the match.

My guards hesitate but follow my command anyway. I think they know what I'm telling them, that this is likely goodbye. They don't question it. I may have their loyalty, but I don't have their hearts. If I die in here, they'll go on about their business, taking orders from my father or Serena instead. After murdering Pavel Stepanov and starting this war, there aren't many who would miss me besides my wife and immediate family.

It's funny, when Mario was first killed, the rest of the Italian mafia had cried out for blood. War. Vengeance. They loathed my father for his complacency. Hated that he valued such a frail thing as peace more than he valued the life of his youngest son. But now that I've done the dirty deed and started this war, those same shaking heads from before are now being shaken at *me*. The tables have turned, but it's too late for me to care.

I wait a few moments before I drop the match. When I do, the heat is so intense I have to take a step back. Fire bursts to life on the carpeted floor, flames crawling up so high that my cheeks are kissed with little sparks. I stand and watch the trail of heat run down the hall, devouring the house as it moves. Exacting my vengeance.

Shots ring out through the house as my men make a hasty escape. I would've expected more chaos than this but there weren't many guards to begin with, and with the fire growing, the Bratva forces will have to choose between fleeing or shooting. Judging from all the screaming ahead, they're trying to do both.

When the heat grows too intense, I cover my nose and step away. The smoke is getting thicker, so I jog into the foyer and make a sharp turn. I was given a rough layout of the house from intel my men were able to gather. I doubt it's completely accurate but if Pavel is anything like my own father, then I know his office should be somewhere nearby.

Vincent always went on and on about keeping his office on the first floor. The tactic was a double-edged sword; easily accessible to us and to enemies if they ever entered the home.

That's exactly what I'm counting on.

Pavel's office will have all of his documents and reports for personal and business deals. With that information, I won't have to attack his truck station. I can end their organization by sending those documents to the right people. For the right price. It's a win-win situation for me.

The only problem is that awful double-edged sword. A first-floor office allows me to stumble to the door moments after running through the foyer—it's the largest door in the hall and has an intricately designed *P* carved into the wood. *Of course*, this is the office. But its convenient location also allows other people to reach the room just as quickly and easily.

A smart person would run straight to the office as soon as the first shot rang out. So I expect someone to be inside when I get there, frantically trying to pack or shred all the paperwork before any enemy arrives. What I don't expect is for that person to be Nadia Stepanov. Or for her to be armed.

When I open the door to the office, a shot screams through the room. I gasp and take a step back, blinking through the smoke and the sudden blurriness of my own eyes. It takes me an extra moment to realize I've been shot.

The pain is delayed by surprise. Even Nadia looks stunned, like she can't believe she just shot me. Then her stunned expression sears into anger and her nostrils flare.

"I'm glad it was you," she says, slinging a fat duffle bag over her shoulder. She's wearing a warm sweater dress with a pair of mismatched boots. I guess this whole thing really did catch them off guard. But she kept a clear head and managed to make it here. Her father raised her well.

I slump against the wall, clutching my ribs. The smoke is getting thicker by the second, but Nadia doesn't seem to be in a rush. She watches me with narrowed eyes that blaze as hotly as the flames eating up her home. There is nothing but hatred on her face, and I don't blame her for it.

The gun in her hand trembles as she raises it to my forehead. She doesn't speak. She just glares at me. Her knuckles are bruised, like she's been in a fight. And there's a tear in the right shoulder of her dress. I wonder what she went through to make it to her father's office. Not to mention she had to get her son out of here first. Somehow, I doubt I'm the first person she's shot so far. I'll probably be the last.

"Do it," I rasp, staring over the barrel of her trembling gun. "Enjoy your vengeance. It's what you want."

She chuckles. "What I want is for you to suffer. And you can't do that if you're dead." She lowers the gun. "So, if you're asking for death, then I'm going to give you life."

"You've already shot me. Kind of hard to give life when there's a bullet in my lung."

"You'll live. I'm sure an ambulance is on the way. The smoke will draw them—thanks to you."

She moves toward the door, but I weakly reach out for her. "Nadia… Please—"

"*No*," she hisses. "You will spend the rest of your life knowing that I am a better person than you. Knowing that I showed mercy when you deserved nothing but vengeance."

Vengeance. That pretty little word again.

Nadia is gone before I can reply. I watch the door shut in slow motion and then I slide down the wall to the floor. I don't know how much mercy she thinks she's given me. I'm bleeding out on the floor of a house in flames. I'm dead with or without her precious mercy.

Still… She had a point. Nadia Stepanov, a teenager who watched her father die in one of his own homes, while her infant child was in the room, had the strength to move her finger from the trigger. She showed more self-control than me. When she had every right to put a bullet in my head, she chose to be the bigger person.

I wonder if God is proud of her. The thought is bitter and filled with venom. *Nadia can afford mercy because she doesn't know pain the way I do—*

"She lost her father. She does know pain."

The voice snaps me to attention. My eyes open with a *pop* and I see a familiar face across the room, leaning against the grand wooden desk in his school uniform. That acid-yellow backpack strapped to his shoulders.

He smiles at me. "Hey, Luca."

"Mario…" My eyes burn with tears. "*Mario?*"

His grin widens. "You're in bad shape."

"Am I dead?"

"No. Almost, though."

"Good."

He shakes his head. "You can't die here, Luca."

"This is my punishment. I failed." My voice is a sob. "I

wasn't enough, Mars."

"You were. You've always been enough, Luca."

I stare at him, wondering how on earth he can say this to me. I won't even entertain the fact that he's dead and we're still speaking. Or maybe this is a hallucination from my injuries. Either way, my emotions are real. My words are real.

"I wasn't enough," I repeat miserably.

Mario crosses the room and squats in front of me. "Those were *my* last words. Not yours."

The revelation hits me like a clap of thunder.

"Even if those were your last words, they're still true about me. I had a choice, and I made the wrong decision."

Mario laughs his boyish laugh, and when I blink at him in confusion, he points to my right hand. "You *almost* made the wrong decision."

"I don't understand."

"Yes, you do." He looks serious all of a sudden. "You had a gun too. Just like Nadia."

He's right. I got shot when I walked in, but I'd been armed too. I could've fired back. I could've killed Nadia, taken her duffle bag, and maybe even made it out of this house alive. Bleeding, but alive.

Instead, I'd kept my gun at my side. Finger off the trigger.

"You spared the daughter of your enemy. The girl who tricked me. The one who shot you." Mario smiles warmly. The sight breaks my heart. "You made the right decision, Luca. You showed mercy. Now God will show you His mercy."

I drop the gun to the floor. "But I still burned down the

house. I gave the order that claimed the lives of so many others."

"Do you know what mercy is?" Mario asks.

I blink away my hot tears, trying to understand where he's going with this. It doesn't make sense that God would save me after everything I've done. Like the lives of all those people meant nothing to Him.

"Mercy is what happens when God withholds the punishment you deserve," Mario explains. "He doesn't do it because you're a good person. Or even because you made the right decision, Luca." Mario leans away so I can see him fully. "He does it because He loves you. And I'm willing to bet He would've saved you no matter what decision you made. That's how merciful He is."

I let out a strangled sob. "I don't deserve to be saved. I don't deserve God's mercy."

"None of us do." Mario chuckles and rises to his feet. "Wait until you discover God's grace."

"Grace?"

"You'll see in time. I think that's why He saved you. Because some people only appreciate God after they've been broken." He sighs. "Like the Apostle Paul. He was a murderer; worse than that, he specifically hunted down *Christians*. He persecuted the Church. But why do you think God waited so long to stop him? Why not reveal Himself to Paul sooner and spare the lives of so many of His beloved?"

I want to shrug, but I feel too weak.

Mario answers anyway. "Because some people don't

appreciate God until they can look back and see the damage they've caused. Until they realize just how much He has forgiven." He shakes his head. "The Bible says it better, *Whoever has been forgiven little, loves little.*" Mario shrugs. "I believe the opposite is also true. Those who have been forgiven for much, love very much. That is what God wanted for you."

I deflate, and not because of the bullet in my body. It's because I'm overwhelmed by everything that's been revealed to me. People were killed tonight. And I'm supposed to believe it was to show me mercy in the end?

"I don't know if I can accept that," I say in a scratchy, tired voice.

"You don't have to," Mario replies. "God is asking you to accept *Him.*"

"And those people who died? What about them?"

He shrugs. "Those people might have died unexpectedly, but everyone in this house was part of the mafia. No one here was innocent. Not even Nadia."

Don't I know. She just shot me.

"God knows best," Mario says firmly. "Perhaps those people were like the Pharoah of Egypt. People whose hearts were hardened and would never accept Him, so God allowed them to be used as an example for a man who *could* accept Him."

I stare at the floor, thinking.

"If it bothers you so much, ask God for yourself. Seek Him, Luca. Don't let their sacrifices be in vain." He glances at the door now. "They're almost here."

"Who?"

"The one who prayed for God to show you mercy."

"Effy…" her name comes out as a breathy whisper—and at the same time, I hear her voice.

"Luca!" She's calling out for me. Searching for me.

That brings everything into focus. Effy is here, in this burning house.

I gasp, and then choke on the smoke around me. I feel like I've just come back to reality. The room is suddenly dark, almost black. And it's hot in here. Mario is nowhere to be found. It's like I just imagined that entire conversation while the mansion burned down around me.

Suddenly, I'm thankful Nadia shut me in here. The closed door kept out the smoke for a little while. Otherwise, I may have succumbed to smoke inhalation by now. Instead, I find myself shakily getting to my feet. Pain screams through my body as I move, but it only gives me more energy.

I have to get to my wife. I have to make it out of here. I have to find a reason for the mercy I've been given. Countless people were murdered here tonight because of me, yet, God saw me worthy to save. If Mario is right, it wouldn't be the first time He's shown mercy to a killer. But what is the point? What did the Apostle Paul do with the second chance he'd been given?

I won't know until I leave here—and get my hands on a Bible.

"Luca!" I hear Effy's voice again, and it sends a shock of adrenaline through my body. With a grunt, I rise and fall into the wall, my hand grasping the doorknob beside me.

Effy calls my name again. And again, I get a surge of determination.

With strength I didn't know I had, I yank the office door open and stumble into the smokey hallway. I take a deep breath that nearly chokes me and answer my wife's call.

"EFFERVESCENT!"

Everything stills as I see a figure moving through the smoke. I can't make out any features. I can't even tell if it's a man or a woman. But I know it's my wife. I know it with every fiber of my being, and it leaves me with a sense of peace as I finally give in to my injuries and drift away from this world.

31

Effy

The room is quiet. The only noise that disturbs the silence is the sound of Luca's breathing. I'm lying beside him in bed now, something I wasn't sure I'd ever get to do again. But God is merciful.

Serena and I made it just in time. I'm positive Luca would've been dead if we'd arrived a moment later. The mafia princess came through when it mattered most. We'd been too late to stop the initial attack, but we made it to the estate in time to control the damage.

Getting out of the house had been relatively easy, getting to the Stepanov mansion was the hard part. That was because we had to take nearly every available guard with us. Serena had managed to get by them with a charming smile or a menacing threat—depending on the guard—but they'd proven their loyalty by insisting they come along. So we arrived at the Bratva estate with an Italian army, a mafia boss lady, and a pregnant wife.

The smoke billowing into the sky had already attracted the attention of first responders so traffic was terrible and anxiety was high. We could've gotten arrested just for showing up, but I finally understood the benefits of having a cop in the family.

Louis showed up with a team of officers who were loyal to the Vittore name. They sectioned off the area and gave us access to the house—some of them even went inside with us to help search for survivors. A few members of the Stepanov staff were rescued, and two of Luca's guards stumbled out in a daze. They told us where to look for Luca, right before getting grilled by Louis on why they'd left him in the first place.

I understand the mafia code of honor, but I don't blame those men for escaping while they had the chance. The mansion was covered in flames when we arrived. It looked like a living nightmare from the outside, I couldn't imagine the horrors they'd experienced behind those closed doors. But I went inside anyway.

Serena had tried to stop me, being the only one there who knew about the pregnancy. But I wasn't about to wait outside while everyone else searched for Luca. I had to find him myself.

It wasn't until I had him in my arms that I realized the size of the risk I'd taken. The place was filled with smoke and death, and I was just a week into my pregnancy. I could have caused irreparable damage to my own child. I could have killed him/her.

But, like always, God is merciful.

Luca was shot in the ribs—took a bullet straight through

the lung. But he survived his surgery and is expected to have a full recovery soon. I inhaled a lot of smoke, but I'm fine. So is the baby. I finally got an official doctor's report, not just Aurora's motherly intuition. I'm really pregnant. And I've decided that I'm really happy about it.

This baby gives Luca and me something to look forward to. It gives us both a reason to change. To do better for ourselves. What exactly will we change? I know I want to take my relationship with God seriously and teach my child everything I can about the One who saved me and my husband from certain death. But I want another sort of change too.

I want to get out of the mafia. But that isn't something I can do alone. I'll need Luca's help and cooperation for that. Will he be willing to make that change? Luca was born into the mafia; he's never had a chance to be anything else except what he's become. He's never known any other life except one in darkness. And now, he's been unconscious for over a week, recovering from his surgery and the damage to his lungs from all the smoke. The doctors say he'll be on bedrest for a while, but I know Luca. He won't be able to stay like this for long.

Forget the bedrest, I think, lifting my head to gaze up at my husband, *the real question is whether he'll want to stay in this organization for long.* So much has happened in the week he's been gone. The Bratva have rallied what remains of their forces. They're calling in men from their motherland and even rallying with allies from NYC. I have no idea what's going to happen next, and I'm not sure we're prepared to handle it.

Serena has been the spearhead of the Vittore organization

since we rescued Luca. Vincent's health is steadily declining, and with his chosen heir in the hospital, he's had no choice but to let his daughter take the reins, despite her gender. He's even called off her arranged marriage, much to the Caruso's dismay.

I'm happy for her. Happy that she's finally attained the authority, freedom, and power she deserves, but I'm also worried. I hope this world doesn't turn her into the monster her brother used to be.

I use past tense because I believe Luca has changed. The man who entered that home is not the same one who emerged from the flames. Something happened in that house, something that's impacted Luca on a level deeper than flesh and bone. I'm too afraid to call it *spiritual* because I don't want to get my hopes up. What if I'm wrong? What if Luca *is* the same man from before?

I shake my head. *I can't think that way. I have to have faith.*

Luca stirs beside me—it startles me so much, I almost fall off the bed, but I suddenly feel his strong hand at my side, stabling me and pulling me closer. His grasp is weak, I could easily break away if I wanted to. But that's the last thing on my mind.

"Luca?" I whisper, blinking back desperate tears.

His eyes are still closed, but he lets out a low groan and I can't stop the sob that spills from my mouth. I cling to him, crawling closer in the bed, hugging him like my life depends on it. I must be crying loudly because after a moment, a bewildered nurse runs into the room to see what's going on.

When she sees Luca peel his tired lids back, she gasps and

runs back out. I assume she's going to alert the doctor, or maybe even call Serena. I don't care. I'm just happy my husband is finally awake.

"Can you hear me?" I say, staring at his tired eyes.

He looks like he hasn't slept in a week, even though that's all he's done lately. His skin is dewy, but his lips are dry, like his body doesn't know how to react to everything he's been through.

Luca nods at my question and groans, shifting slightly in the bed. "How long—"

"Over a week," I say quickly. "But don't worry, Serena has been handling everything."

He swallows and his eyes dart around the room.

"We're at a safehouse just outside New York City. Serena doesn't think the estate is safe. Since you attacked the Stepanov home, she suspects they may try to attack ours in retaliation."

He swallows again, still looking around. That's when I realize he isn't thinking about Serena or the Russians at all.

I gasp and roll over to grab the cup of water on his bedside table. There used to be ice cubes in it, but they melted an hour ago. The straw the nurse gave me is on a tray beside the cup, I grab that too and gingerly place it between Luca's lips.

He takes slow sips at first and then summons the strength to grab the cup, toss the straw aside, and gulp down the rest.

"Careful!" I insist. "You could get yourself sick."

He grunts, and his voice comes out in a rumbling rasp. "I need to regain my strength."

"For what?" I prod carefully.

"For the war."

"You still want to fight." It's not a question. I know Luca's answer before he even looks down to nod at me. The realization deflates me, and I sink into the heavy pillows beside him.

We both fall silent, unsure what to say, unsure what to think.

I decide this is the best time to tell him my news.

"I'm pregnant," I whisper.

I feel Luca stiffen beside me. The tension in his body isn't the reaction I wanted, but at least he didn't shift away from me on the bed.

"Are you sure?" Luca finally asks.

"I'm positive. The doctors tested me while I recovered from smoke inhalation."

He exhales slowly. "How…"

"We never used protection, Luca."

I think the growl he releases is supposed to be a chuckle. I can feel the laughter bubbling through his body as I lean against him. It vibrates in his chest and hums against my shoulders like a massage.

"Are you happy?" I ask in a quiet voice, but before Luca can respond, the door to our room opens and Serena enters with a smile on her face. She looks strong and confident in a black trench coat and thigh-high boots that make her six inches taller than her already ridiculous height. She's back to her bold red lipstick and all of her thick wavy hair is caught up in a slick ponytail that bounces down her back as she walks to stand at the edge of the bed.

"Welcome back," she says with a grin—it's sisterly, but also teasing.

Luca grins back as best he can. "I hear you've been running things."

"Someone had to step up after you got shot."

He lets go of one of those rumbling growl-chuckles again. "Did you miss me?"

"More than you know." Serena glances away for a moment, the only sign she'll give us of just how worried she was for her brother. "Louis has stepped up too," she says after a moment. "He's filed official charges against Oleg for statutory rape. The DNA test results came back positive. He's the father of Nadia's child."

We all sigh in relief, feeling some small sense of justice for Mario. Oleg won't be serving time for his murder, but he will serve for his inappropriate relationship with Nadia. That DNA test also cleared Mario's name. He never raped the Stepanov princess. They were in a consensual relationship, though Nadia's part was all an act.

Speaking of the girl…

"Where is Nadia?" I ask.

Serena looks disappointed. "No one has seen her. Not since the fire. It's possible she's hiding out, or maybe even returned to Russia. No one knows."

Luca stares at his blankets but doesn't speak. I wish I knew what he was thinking but I know it's pointless to ask right now. He'll tell me when he's ready. So instead of questioning him, I decide to change the subject. "I told him about the pregnancy," I say to Serena.

Her grin returns. "Papa Lulu, can you imagine that?"

"I can't," Luca admits. I'm not sure if I'm offended or not, but then Luca surprises me by adding, "But I'll learn to."

Serena places her hands on her hips. "You'll have to learn away from home."

"Serena," Luca begins, but she cuts him off with a shake of her head. "No. You started this war—"

"So let me end it."

"This *is* you ending it."

"By running away?"

"The Bratva will not stop until you are dead." Her words are thick with emotion. I feel her pain down to my bones, but I also feel Luca's pain and his shame. This entire ordeal is his fault, and now he's being ordered away. I know it's for the best, but for the underboss of the Italian mafia, it's a serious blow to his ego and reputation—especially since the person who'll replace him will be a woman.

"You got shot, Luca," Serena says. "And the Bratva won't rest until they put another bullet in you. You can't stay."

"I will not run," he growls in his shredded voice. The sound is so gravelly and deep, I almost flinch as I listen to him speak. "I am not a coward—"

"No. But you are a husband." Serena nods at me—at my belly. "And a soon-to-be father."

Luca doesn't respond. I'm happy for his silence because it means he's thinking about what she said. It means he's considering her words, instead of snapping back in anger.

"Dad isn't getting better," Serena's voice cracks. "Let him die knowing you're alive somewhere."

"Let him die," Luca repeats slowly, tasting each word, acknowledging that his father is truly an old man. And there is nothing he can do to save him. Just like there was nothing he could do to save Mario.

I touch his hand. "It's okay, Luca."

He seems to understand what I'm really saying, glancing down and giving my hand a gentle squeeze.

It's okay for him to walk away from this. It's his mess, but the best way to fix it is to let go. If he continues to explore his faith with me, he'll learn that's the key to a great relationship with God. Let go and let Him handle it.

I want to say this to him now, but I know with all the tension in the air, the conversation will go over his head. So I store up this revelation in my heart and ask God for His perfect timing in the future. I ask God to soften Luca's heart toward His wisdom. Because I can't share this revelation with him if he's dead, and he will certainly die if he stays here to fight.

Luca swallows and winces. I debate calling the nurse for more water.

"I have connections that can get you out of the country in a few days," Serena says. "They'll put you in touch with some good people—ex-mafia just like you."

"I'm not ex-mafia," Luca corrects, but Serena talks right over him.

"It's got to be done soon. So think on it and get back to

me."

Without another word, Serena turns and strides out, her black coat flowing behind her.

Luca and I sit in complete silence for a while, staring at nothing, thinking about everything. I have no words, so instead of speaking, I begin to pray inside.

Jesus, please soften his heart.

It's the only prayer I can think of right now, but I'm sure it's all I need.

32

Luca

So much has happened, and so much more is about to happen. Once again, I have a choice to make. This is the first time I've truly felt torn.

When I sought vengeance, I knew it was wrong. But I made the decision anyway because it was what I wanted to do. Now there's another set of choices and I don't know what's right or wrong. I don't know what I want anymore.

I can stay and defend my family. End the war I started, as any responsible underboss should. Then again, a responsible underboss wouldn't have carelessly murdered a rival boss without a follow-up plan in place. That's why I want to stay. To fix the mess I created.

But if I stay, I'll put Effy in even more danger. She's married to a mafia underboss. To an extent, she will always be in danger. But it's different now. She's pregnant. My wife is pregnant and we're at war because I made a stupid, impulsive decision. And now everyone else will suffer while I tuck my tail and run.

If I stay, my wife may end up paying for my sins. But if I run, I will ruin my reputation and leave that stain on the Vittore name.

What am I supposed to do?

I blink as I stare at the ceiling, lying in bed. It's been a few days since Serena showed up and gave me this ultimatum. She hasn't been back since, and Effy hasn't brough it up either. But I know it's on her mind. I can see the thoughts churning behind her pretty eyes, each time she blinks is like the thoughts pause—momentarily hidden from me. But then I see her furtive glances, I hear her sighing in her sleep as she rests beside me. I see her hands tremble when she clasps them in prayer. And I know what my choice must be. I just don't want to make it.

I can admit that. I don't want to do what's right. It's hard to do what's right. I'm comfortable in this life. I've never done anything else. Leaving and living my life as a normal man is a scary thought. What will I do? How will I live?

I suppose I could ask my wife; she spent her life as a normal woman. *This* life is what's foreign and scary to her. She probably doesn't understand my hesitation at all. But when you've only existed in the dark, the light isn't a beacon drawing you in, it's a burning pillar of fire that scares you mad.

Effy's gentle love helped me understand. She helped morph that pillar of fire into a streak of luminescence. An effervescent storm. And now, I'm still scared, but I know the fear will pass. If I'll be brave enough to take this chance.

For the first time in a long time, the decision I make won't be about my little brother.

In the flames, he told me to let him go. Now I know what he means. Because my vengeance had been for Mario, but this change will be for my wife. I have to let all that pain go if I want to move forward.

A raspy groan fills the air and I roll onto my side. It hurts like crazy, my bruised ribs and punctured lung feel like they just got turned around inside of me. I lay like that for about five seconds, then I give up and lay flat on my back again. All the movement stirs Effy.

With a flutter of her lashes, she wakes and blinks up at me. The room seems to still and spin at the same time. I don't know what to say to her, and she seems content with the silence. We stare at each other until she sits up and rests a hand on my chest.

I try to stifle the grunt, but it seeps between my lips like a leak and Effy pulls away. "I'm sorry," she whispers.

"I'm getting better," I say.

She nods.

"I've been thinking…"

I don't want to say the rest. Once I make the decision, it'll be real. I'll be leaving the mafia. Abandoning my family when they need me most. Turning against everything I believe in.

Is this the right decision?

"What were you thinking?" Effy pokes at the bubble of mystery hanging over our heads.

It pops with a question. "What will you do if I turn down

Serena's offer?"

At first, Effy just stares at me, then she answers truthfully. "I would stay by your side."

She must see the surprise on my face because she leans closer to me and lays her head on my shoulder. Her hand reaches for mine. "I'll always be by your side, Luca. Even in a world I don't want to be in."

"What…" I clear my throat. "What about the baby? You wouldn't be safe here."

She pauses. "God will keep us safe. He has so far."

I almost can't keep it together. The fact that Effy is ready and willing to make such a sacrifice for me solidifies my resolve. I can't expect my wife to make all the sacrifices. To set everything aside for my sake at all times. That isn't a marriage, that's enslavement. That's not a husband and wife, that's a man and his servant.

If Effy is willing to stay, then I should be just as willing to go. For her sake. And for the sake of our child.

And … in my heart, I know she is right. God has protected her all this time. He's protected me too. I can't help but think of Mario in that smoke, and everything we discussed about God now. About His mercy. About His grace.

If God would extend a hand to me in the midst of a burning building—right in the raging storm of my sin—then I know He'll be there in our peace as well.

That's the change, I tell myself. *I'm not abandoning my family; I'm leaving the war to find peace.*

"I'm going to accept Serena's offer," I tell Effy.

She snaps her head up at me, her eyes filled with surprise.

"Did you really think I would force you and our unborn child to live in this hellish world with me?"

"You wouldn't have forced me," she says firmly. "I would have chosen to stay."

I almost chuckle. She is a master escape artist after all. If she wanted to leave me, she could. But she's here right now. And she's promised to remain here—by my side. I remember telling her she belonged to me. That there was no escape. And now she's *chosen* to stay. I suppose we both had decisions to make. And it seems we've both finally made the right ones.

"I love you," I whisper.

She squeezes my hand. "I love you too. And I've missed you."

"I've been right here."

She shakes her head. "Only physically."

Effy is right. Even before the shooting, I was there but I wasn't present. I heard her when she spoke, but I wasn't listening. I'd been consumed by that world and all the trauma it brings.

"I'm here now," I offer sheepishly. "If it's not too late."

"It's never too late, Luca."

I get the feeling she isn't talking about our marriage. I know she's talking about God. That He's always there waiting for me to go to Him. I get the sudden urge to tell Effy everything I saw in the flames. Everything that confused and inspired me.

It spills from my mouth like an uncontrollable flood, a

string of words strung together in one long sentence. Effy doesn't interrupt, she just listens with this concentrated look on her face, like she's digesting it all.

When I'm finished, she swallows and lays her head on my shoulder again. "Wow," she whispers.

"Wow?" Her response is a little anticlimactic.

"Luca, you learned the truth about God and how much He loves you. And you made peace with your brother's death. Everything that needs to be said has already been said. You know what you must do next."

"I'm ready to do it," I say faster than I expect to. I'm shocked by how much I mean those words. Effy is too. She smiles warmly at me, and the sight of it melts away all of my anxiety.

I can't stop myself from leaning down to kiss her. It hurts and my ribs cry out in protest, but Effy's kiss is worth the pain. I feel everything between us. The pain, the joy, the anger, the confusion. And I know I'm the cause for so much of it. This isn't just my chance to escape the mafia, it's my chance to fix things with my wife. To right the wrongs I committed against an innocent woman.

I love my family, and it will shred me to leave them. But they are not innocent. They've chosen this world as much as I did. For over 30 years. And they will continue to choose it when I'm gone.

Effy leans into me, and I groan into the kiss, hands groping her hips. We move slowly, gingerly pushing our blankets aside so there's nothing between us. Her nightie slips off easily, my shirt is more difficult and once I'm exposed, Effy pauses. Staring.

I'm black and blue, wrapped in cloth from the surgery.

"It's okay," I say as her eyes fill with tears.

She gulps, and when she leans toward me, I think she's going to kiss my lips, but she ducks her head and kisses one of the bruises on my sore skin. It's cool to the touch, soothing to the burning pain I feel all day.

"Let these be your last scars," she whispers, tickling my chest with her words.

"I can't make that promise," I admit. "I can't promise I won't mess up again."

"We'll always make mistakes. I'm not asking you to be perfect. I'm asking you to love yourself as much as you love me. Make this choice because *you* want better, Luca."

This woman always knows what to say.

I cup her chin so I can capture her lips again. "Tell me you love me," I murmur. And she does, in every kiss, every touch, in her hands that cling to my shoulders, in the nails that dig into the flesh of my arms, in the hiss she lets out when I take her slowly, in the hiss that becomes a whisper, in the whisper that becomes a cry on her beautiful lips.

Effy gives herself to me, and I give her all that I can in return. It's a slow act that hurts with every grunt, but the pain is washed away in the pleasure, the passion, the love. Every other time had been desperate and frantic, but this time is different. This time, we're not having sex, we're making love. Despite everything.

"I wasn't expecting that," Effy says, lying beside me. Her face is glowing, the way it always does after we make love. A few strands of her thick, curly hair are stuck to her dewy forehead. I should brush them away, but I gather the last of my strength to shift just enough to kiss her.

"Good morning," I chuckle.

She laughs against my lips. "A *very* good morning."

Someone knocks at the door, making us both scramble to grab our clothes again. Since I'm still weak, Effy slips on her black lace nightie and walks barefoot to the door. She cracks it open and explains that we're busy, then she closes it and turns toward me with a grin.

"Breakfast will be sent up in half an hour."

"We've got time for another go." I grin.

She grins back but walks toward the bathroom instead of joining me in bed. "Or we can shower and get dressed."

Not as exciting, but certainly necessary. And besides, she said *we*. *We* can shower. So I drag myself out of bed and slowly walk to the bathroom. Effy's in the middle of her first lather, covered in suds, by the time I pull the curtains back. The look of surprise on her face is worth the ache in my ribs as I step in with her.

It isn't until we're dressed and done with breakfast that either of us grows serious again. Effy is sitting on the windowsill, staring out at the late morning sun. It's the color of yolk, spilling across the sky, illuminating the frosted lawn that stretches out around the house. This safehouse is a modest home my father built years ago. My mother would come here after they had a huge fight. I remember hating this house because it wasn't big and luxurious like the estate. Then I remember sneaking girls over here as a teenager.

I've never appreciated this house until now. I like it's simplicity. I like that it's a normal family home, housing very abnormal people. It's a reminder of the life I used to live in Italy, the beautiful lie that's slowly becoming a reality. And the best part is that Effy is here.

She looks lovely in her oversized sweater and cozy leggings. She's wearing a bit of blush on her cheeks and her lashes are painted in mascara. Her lips look perfectly kissable in the subtle pink lipstick she dabbed on while I finished off the omelet she picked around.

When she glances up at me, I smile and lean back in my chair. There's a small table for two set up in the room. Effy arranged for it to be moved inside when she started sleeping in here. I take all my meals here because I can't walk much yet, so she eats with me.

"You look beautiful," I tell her.

She dips her head. Blushes. "Thank you."

"I'm going to call Serena soon."

Her eyes widen, and I can't tell if the tears that fill them are of sadness or joy. "Are you sure?"

"Of course I'm sure."

"I meant what I said earlier. I don't want this to be a decision you make in the heat of the moment. It must be a change you want, Luca. For yourself." She glances away and whispers the last part so quietly, I almost don't hear it. "And for God."

Her words root me in place. This isn't for Mario, it will certainly benefit Effy and our child, but it's not enough to want this for them either. I've got to want it for the only One who matters.

Every good person in my life lives for Christ. This is clearly a change that won't hurt me. It's something my wife and my brother both want for me. Something I want for myself now.

"I'm sure it's what I want," I say, and Effy glances over at me. "Not just moving away and getting out of the mafia. I want to make you proud of me, Effy. And I want Mario to be proud of me. And our child too."

She smiles. It's the first time I've addressed the pregnancy, and I'm sorry I let the silence on that go on for so long. But I'm sure of it now. I want this. I really do.

"I want to change," I confess. "And I don't really know how. But I know I must."

Effy stands and walks over to me; she sits on my lap when I open my arms to her. Up close, she smells like peaches. I inhale her scent deeply, wrapping my arms around her as she speaks.

"I'll be here. God is here. And whoever Serena's connections are will be there with us too. We're not alone, Luca. We never are."

Serena's connections. I'd almost forgotten about that. She knows some other ex-mafia who are living different lives now.

People who got out, just like us. We can learn from them. We can grow with them.

Effy kisses my cheek. "The first change you make shouldn't be a change in location. It should be a change from within."

I know what she means, and I exhale slowly as I let her take my hands. "Have you ever heard of the Sinner's Prayer?" she asks.

I nod mutely.

Effy smiles. "Pray with me."

So I do. I make a commitment that scares me, but as the words leave my mouth, the fear escapes too. It's like the words wash them away, scrubbing me clean from the inside out, until all that's left is a sense of peace I cannot describe. A comfort that has no words.

I hug my wife, murmuring into her puffy, afro hair. "Thank you for never giving up on me."

"Thank you for never giving up on yourself."

I lean away, my gaze drifting to the cellphone on the table. It's my new one, brought up with breakfast by one of the staff members.

Effy sees me staring and reaches for the phone. She types in my passcode and then opens the text messages. I watch her punch out a question to Serena's number.

Got a minute? Want to talk.

She replies almost instantly. **I'll drop by soon. We can work everything out together.**

She sends a heart and a smiling emoji, and it summons

tears I didn't know I had inside. Serena isn't trying to get rid of me. She wants this change too. For the better. For the brother who lost himself to vengeance and hatred. She'd been in pain too, dealing with Mario's death. But I'd taken all of her grief onto my shoulders. I'd taken the pain from everyone around me. Wore it around my neck like a pendant of sorrows.

I didn't give anyone else the chance to heal or find peace. I told myself that vengeance was the only way to peace, and I chased after it so obsessively that it never crossed my mind that anyone could possibly heal any other way. The only way past pain was to inflict more pain onto others. I was living in a cycle of misery. And through my wife, God saved me. Jesus saved me.

One day … I think He'll save my sister too. I think He'll heal my father and restore the marriage of my parents. I think He will protect my child and give me and Effy more children to raise. I think He'll work everything out.

I close my eyes, exhaling slowly. And when I open them, I see my brother again. Leaning against the wall beside the window across the room. Effy is still staring at my phone, rereading the text messages from my sister, totally unaware of his presence. But I see him, and I see the smile on his face. He doesn't speak this time. He simply winks at me, and then he vanishes.

I lost him. I know I did. I almost lost Effy. I almost lost myself. I failed my family.

This is the sin I carry—wait …

No.

Christ carried that cross. All that's left for me to hold is His peace. I've grabbed onto it, and I promise I won't let go.

Epilogue

Mario

18 Years Later

Sweat makes my shirt stick to me. The short sleeves hug the cures of my arms, squeezing my biceps. I think about taking it off, but then my mother would yell at me. She's sitting at the kitchen table now, pretending she isn't just as hot as I am. Her curly hair has relaxed into a sad mop that flops against her forehead whenever she glances up at me.

I hate the summer heat. Normally, my family goes somewhere chilly in the summer, but this summer is different. I'm going to college in a few weeks, so my lovely mother decided to skip the vacation this year and enrolled me in preparatory courses instead. I still haven't forgiven her for that. But I don't know if I'll *ever* forgive my father for breaking the A/C. We need it now more than ever.

It's the beginning of August in a Portuguese summer. I'm convinced I could die without the A/C now. But my father is fine. Says he'll hire someone next week, after he's done trying to fix it himself. He's always trying to fix things himself. And he's awful at it.

Apparently, that mindset got him into crazy trouble when he was younger. He's never gone into detail and my dear mother acts like talking about their life before Portugal is a great forbidden sin. It all happened before I was born, so I don't know everything. From what I've learned over the years, and through gossip with extended family, my father was some sort of mafia boss back in the day.

You know the story.

Now he's nothing but a farmer.

Correction… He owns a vineyard. Which, apparently, *isn't* farming.

The Vittore name owns tons of vineyards in Italy, where my father is originally from. But when he left the mafia, he started over here in Portugal with some other ex-mafia couple. One of them is sitting across from me now, staring at his glass of iced water.

"Better drink that before the ice melts," I grumble, walking toward the fridge. I yank it open and then sigh as the cool blast hits my chest. "Any more Coke?" I ask, glancing back.

Amory Jäger looks up from his sweaty glass. His grey eyes are as cold as the ice in his cup. But I know him well enough to realize his steely gaze isn't personal. Neither is his hard jaw or straight mouth. That's just how he looks.

I grew up with Amory. Even call him uncle sometimes. He's ex-mafia like my father, and he's just as secretive about it.

Everyone around here is so full of secrets, it makes me sick.

I slam the fridge harder than I mean to, making my mother jump. "Mario!" she snaps.

I roll my eyes. "Now you guys wanna acknowledge me."

Amory is still staring at me. Now, I really can't tell if his icy eyes are personal or not.

"We're not ignoring you," my mother says.

"I asked a question."

"What do you want?" Amory grunts.

"Is there any more Coke?" I point to the fridge. "Didn't see any."

"Then I guess we're out."

I feel anger rise inside me, but before it can spill from my mouth in a string of words my mother would scold me for, the patio door opens, and my father walks inside.

Luca Vittore.

He kisses my mother on the top of her head before nodding at Amory and then glances over at me. "No classes today?"

"Nah," I grunt, turning to leave.

"Mario," he calls, and I stop but don't turn around.

"I'm glad you're here. There's something we all need to discuss."

I should have been more suspicious over Amory's presence, but he's *always* here. The vineyard my father runs used to belong to him. My father purchased part of the property when I was a toddler and named the farm after my mother—Effervescent. Amory is his business partner, so I see him all the time. And his annoying wife. But she isn't here now, which my mother quickly points out.

"We shouldn't start without Rosa," she says, glancing at Amory.

"She'll be here soon." Amory's voice is a rumble. "She's picking up Uwe."

I snort. Uwe hates his parents.

I got sacked with fancy preparatory school for the summer, but Uwe was incarcerated. His mother is grabbing him from jail right now. He got released this morning after serving time for some stupid crap I won't tell you about. That's his story to share. But if Rosa's late because of Uwe then my parents might as well start now. There's no telling how long this will take. Uwe is likely to get himself arrested again within the hour just to annoy his parents.

It's been like this for years now. The thick tension, the heavy emotions. I can see the stress on Amory's face, in the dark circles beneath his eyes, in the way he runs his hand through his chocolate brown hair. He used to be the one who dealt with Uwe, but Rosa convinced him that his strongarming only made things worse. So she stepped in with some gentle parenting routine she learned on TikTok.

Uwe got arrested two weeks later. Been locked up for, like, nine months.

I remember when the cops came to the house to pick him up. It was so dramatic my mother almost fainted, bless her soul. We were having dinner together, both families. And then the cops knocked on the door and barged in as soon as my father cracked it open. They rushed past him and slammed Uwe onto his roast beef.

Rosa cried. Amory glared. I couldn't stop laughing.

These perfect Christian parents did everything they could to escape the mafia and live for God. They even started their own businesses and helped other mafiosi get out over the years.

And then they raised two little monsters.

I can see the regret on my own mother's face as she sighs and then pushes from the table to pour herself a glass of ice water. When she reaches up to open the cupboard, I see pit stains on her pretty baby blue dress.

It's not all bad. My parents are secretive and overbearing. But I get why. They came from a dark world, and they've spent the last eighteen years doing everything they can to keep me away from that darkness. I get it. I just don't like it. All the secrets make me question everything. All the mystery makes me curious.

I want to know about the world my parents come from. I want to see it for myself.

So, I don't hate my parents like Uwe does, I resent them. But beyond the resentment is a tiny dot of appreciation. It stains my heart, reminds me that I am loved. In an odd, exhausting way. I'm a little unhappy with how they've raised me, but it could be worse. I could be like Uwe, in full-blown rebellion.

Uwe isn't unhappy or resentful, the only word I can use to describe him is …

Angry.

On cue, the door opens with a *bang!* Everyone jumps as Uwe strolls inside, shoulders back, chin up, a crooked grin on his face. He's got his father's dark hair and charming smile, but there's a gentleness to him that I know he took from his mother. I can see it in the sparkle that lights up his eyes, in the dimple in his cheek. I can see it because Uwe is like a cousin to me. A brother. To everyone else, he just looks cocky.

He walks right by his father and almost shoulder checks my own mother on his way across the kitchen—that's too much for anyone to ignore.

Amory and my father both growl at his backside. "Hey!"

Uwe stops and turns around, feigning confusion. "What's wrong?"

"Watch it," Amory says. "You almost bumped Mrs. Vittore."

He looks at my mother. "My apologies, Effy. Please forgive me."

She just nods and sits down with her empty glass. I don't even know if she realizes she never poured herself any water. I don't comment on it.

"Where's your mother?" Amory asks.

Uwe scowls. "Why are you asking me?"

"Because she went to pick *you* up."

His eyes pop. He grabs his chest. "My God. She did? I had no idea."

"Uwe—"

"I got a ride from a friend," he says, turning to leave again.

"Wassup, Mars." He fist-bumps me. "Miss me?"

I grin at him. "Of course."

Uwe really is like my brother. He's about a year older, raised right beside me in this Christian refuge. Both of us are sons of former mafia bosses. Both of us are living in the mysterious shadows of our parents' past. We're the only ones who understand what this life is like. How the curiosity eats away at you each day. Uwe's never handled the frustration very well. He's spent his entire life in rebellion, trying to learn more about the mafia, trying to become the man his father left behind in NYC.

I don't think he realizes how much his parents hate his attitude or his rowdy behavior. He's always been a problem child but going to prison may have been the last straw.

At Uwe's nonchalance, Amory shoves away from the table, but both of my parents reach for him, so he only makes it two steps before they're dragging him back. "Where is your mother!?" he shouts.

"I'm here…" an exhausted looking woman enters through the patio door, left open by Uwe. She slides it shut behind her and nearly collapses onto the table, dumping a pile of envelopes and papers on the wooden surface. "I grabbed your mail for you. And those are letters from Uwe's lawyers." She points.

"What happened?" Amory almost immediately calms down at the sight of Rosa. My parents let him go so he can sit beside her. He pulls her into a hug without hesitation. "What happened?" he repeats.

"What do you mean?" Rosa pulls away. Confused. "I picked up Uwe and we drove home together. He hopped out as soon as I pulled into the driveway. I hadn't even parked yet."

Everyone turns to stare at Uwe who's crammed his hands into his pockets now. He looks back at us. "What?"

"You said you got picked up by a friend," Amory reminds him. "You said you didn't know where your mother was."

"No, I didn't."

Instead of fighting, Amory accepts that his son is a liar and turns to his wife. "Let's start the meeting."

"What meeting?" Uwe and I both ask.

"We wanted to talk about your options for college," my mother explains, but I cut her off.

"I already got accepted into a school in America." They don't like the idea of me going so far away, but it's my decision. I'm eighteen and this is my future. Not theirs. I want to attend school in the States. The place where they're from. Uwe just wants to get away from his folks. I don't even know if he applied to any colleges or if he's just going to use his parents' money to rent an apartment in the States while I attend school. I don't care as long as we get to go together.

My father takes a deep breath. "There's another option. I'm sure they'll be reaching out to you pretty soon."

I blink at him. "What do you mean?"

Rosa reaches forward and digs through the mail to retrieve a matte black envelope. She holds it up. "Actually, they've already reached out." She holds up another envelope taken from her purse. "Ours arrived yesterday."

"What is it?" Uwe demands.

"It's a welcome letter, from *Heights & Shadows*."

I stare at Rosa Jäger, having no idea what that phrase even means, but Uwe gasps and lunges forward. Amory lunges too, but his son is faster. He snatches both envelopes from Rosa's hands and skips back over to me where it's safe before his father can pummel him.

He tears open the envelope with his initials on it. The letter inside is handwritten on thick, rich paper. It's expensive, and even from my stance beside Uwe, I can smell that it's scented with something robust and … old? Like the smell of a fancy attic.

Uwe scans the letter, a grin slowly peeling away the frown on his face. It's replaced by a grin that's lopsided and almost scary. "No way," he whispers.

"Tell me," I say, almost annoyed.

"Heights & Shadows is a university for kids like us."

"Kids like us," I repeat dumbly, and Amory Jäger speaks up.

"Children of mafia royalty." He lets that sink in before he speaks again, his voice no longer a growl but a shameful purr. Almost a mouse's whisper. "I went there."

Rosa snaps her head up, staring at him with wide eyes. Clearly, she didn't know that little tidbit. But she doesn't confront him on it now. They stare at each other in silence until Uwe lowers the letter and finally passes me mine.

"I don't get it," I say.

My father sighs. "Where do you think the children of

crime organizations go to learn about the business? Where do you think assassins are trained? How did I learn about drug shipments before the clipboard was placed in my hand?" He swallows. "Heights & Shadows is a private academy specifically for the world we used to live in. Almost everyone from a high-ranking family sends their children."

"And not just mafia," Amory adds, ignoring the shocked expressions on the faces of our mothers. "Children of billionaires attend the college, heirs to business gurus, political stars. The school accepts the elite from every corner of the world. Anyone with dirty hands learns dirty business at Heights & Shadows."

"Is that even legal?" my mother asks breathlessly.

My father nods. "It's a private college from overseas. On the outside, it appears as a trade school with a focus on business and leadership. But those inside know what it truly is."

"What kind of degree do you graduate with?" I ask dumbly. The question makes Uwe snort.

"At Heights & Shadows, you don't graduate. You survive."

I gulp.

"They want us to go," Uwe says, still clutching his black letter. "Because of who our fathers are."

"*Were*," my father corrects him. "We *were* mafia royalty, but we *aren't* anymore. I got out eighteen years ago. And I never looked back." He glances around the table. "None of us did."

"Well, good for you," Uwe declares. "But I want to attend.

I'm going to accept their offer of enrollment."

"Uwe," Amory says, but Rosa touches his hand, and he cuts himself off.

"This is probably the best offer I'll get," Uwe says with a shrug.

No one can argue against that. The man just got out of jail. And before that, he was held back for a year because he got kicked out of his last school. It's not like the mail on the table is a pile of letters from any prestigious schools. I don't even think there's a community college that'll want Uwe Jäger to attend.

But they would want me. I told you I'm not like Uwe. I want to get out of here too, but I haven't fought my parents at every turn to get there. I've cooperated as much as I could. I've given them everything they've asked.

I stayed out of trouble. I stopped asking questions. I did my best in school so I could get into a good college. But the agreement was that it would be a college of my choosing. They didn't like the idea of me going to school in the States, but it was my choice.

And now I have another choice. One that seems just as enticing.

From the look of horror on the faces of my parents, I think they know what choice I'm going to make before I even clear my throat and say it.

"I want to accept their offer as well."

My mother's shoulders drop. My father slowly closes his eyes, then he sighs and opens them again. "Son—"

"It's my choice," I remind him. "You can't take that away from me."

"I don't want to take your choice from you," he says, and I believe him. But I also believe he cares enough to intervene. To try everything he can to change my mind. "You don't know what that school is like."

"It's mafia school," Uwe says with a drawl. Then he shrugs. "Sounds cool to me."

"I'm sure you'll fit right in," Rosa says crisply.

Uwe winks. "You know it."

"No, she doesn't." Amory glares at his son, his gaze unwavering, his voice a baritone tremble. "You have no idea what Heights & Shadows is like. You have no idea what the *mafia* is like. It isn't *fun.* It isn't *cool.* It's real life, Uwe. It will take you for all you're worth without caring if you even survive."

"I'm not stupid—"

"Yes, you are."

"I've been to prison!" Uwe shouts, like we don't know.

His mother replies in a voice that is feather soft. "So have I."

We all stare at her, and she lifts her chin as she goes on. "I've served time for murder."

I swallow. That information is news to me. I never would've guessed this innocent Christian woman had once been a murderess mafia queen. Then again, there's no telling how much someone can change once they accept Christ into their lives. But all this does is stoke the flames of curiosity burning within me and Uwe.

My best friend jabs his thumb into his chest. "I want to go to this school. I'm not scared."

Amory chuckles and leans back in his chair. "You should be."

"This is a chance to learn about the world you've all tried so hard to keep us out of." Uwe raises his letter like a flag. "And it's a chance to learn about grandpa."

The room falls silent because we all understand what he means. Even me. That's another thing Uwe and I have in common. We're both named after dead family members. How fun.

Uwe Sr. was Amory's father. From what I've heard, he was murdered while serving as the boss of the German American mafia in New York City. That was before Little Uwe was born—before Amory and Rosa got out of the mafia. Back then, Amory was still the underboss of the organization, and Rosa was a mafia princess. Their marriage united three different gangs and made the Jägers a powerhouse that went to war with two rival mafia organizations.

Uwe Jäger died in that war.

That's the man my best friend is named after, and his death is just as tragic as my uncle's. The original Mario Vittore was murdered at just age fifteen. Killed by a rival gang—because, apparently, mafiosi are not allowed to die any other way.

My father nearly lost his life seeking vengeance for his little brother's wrongful death, but God intervened. My mother got pregnant, like, right after their hasty wedding, so I was born here in Portugal just a few months after they escaped from Benton, New York.

At least, that's what they always told me. I don't know much more than that, they've always kept the details close. I learned nearly everything from my aunt back in Benton on family visits, or from my cousins.

After my parents left the States, my Aunt Serena took over the organization. She had her hands full fighting a war and taking care of my ill grandfather. But she eventually settled down once the war was over. She got married and had four children, all of which my grandfather lived to see.

Apparently, he was going to die from cancer when my parents left New York. But my mother says God healed him and he ended up living ten more years, instead of eighteen more months like the doctors had predicted. My grandmother is still with us, she's one of the sources of information I've had over the years. Grandma Aurora has always believed it was better for me to know the truth rather than keep everything a secret. I'm glad she felt that way.

The only reason I know this much about my parents and their past is because I'm close to my relatives in the United States. We write and chat online sometimes; when we were younger, and my parents had more control over me, I couldn't ask many questions. My phone was monitored, and my mother read all the letters that came in. Family visits were closely watched, and no one was allowed to discuss 'the business.'

But now I'm older. I can contact my cousins and my grandmother whenever I want, and we can discuss whatever we want. My parents can't control me anymore. They can't force me to be the good Christian boy they so desperately want me to be.

And maybe that's who I really am. Maybe I'm *not* built to handle *Heights & Shadows University*. But I'll never know until I get out there and see for myself.

I clear my throat. "It's my decision."

My father looks at me for a long, silent moment. "Take it from someone who's made a lot of bad decisions," he says, "you don't want to do this."

He couldn't be more wrong.

I give him a grin that rivals Uwe's. "Yes, I do."

Enjoy these mafia love stories!

Want to know how Amory came to Christ and escaped the mafia? Read his love story with Rosa in **Withered Rose!**

Also check out these other Christian mafia books!

Fractured Diamond

The Woof Pack Trilogy

HEIGHTS & SHADOWS is in the works! Mario and Uwe discover the past their parents tried so hard to protect them from at this mafia university. Will it break them or make them stronger? Only time will tell. Only God can keep them on the path of righteousness.

More books by Valicity Elaine & TRC Publishing!

Christian Fantasy

Cross Academy

The Scribe

Christian Post-Apocalyptic Fiction

The Barren Fields

The End of the World series

MAGOG saga

Christian Science Fiction

I AM MAN series

Christian Romance

The Living Water

Withered Rose Trilogy

Fractured Diamond

The Woof Pack Trilogy

Singlehood

Christian Children's Fiction

Too Young

ACKNOWLEDGEMENTS

Thank You Jesus for blessing me to finish another project You assigned to me. Thank you to my lovely, supportive family. And thank YOU so much for reading Beautiful Lies! I remember being SO excited for this project when God first gave me the idea. I should have written this earlier, but I delayed and delayed. Then I felt like I was running out of time! But God is merciful. He was there through every part of this journey, and I simply cannot thank Him enough.

Not everyone understands, or is willing to understand, the sort of books I write. I'm okay with that because I know I have the support I need in Christ Jesus and I have you, the reader who made it this far! Thank you so much for sticking with me through this journey. It was quite a story, wasn't it? I plan on writing more fiction like this in the future. There is a real need and desire for dark romance for Christian women. I want to write books for women like myself. Christian ladies who love dark romance but want to see a story that isn't drowning in sex and lust.

The connection between Luca and Effy is real. It is built on love. And it is something made stronger because Christ is at the center of their lives. Books like this are encouraging to me, as well as entertaining. But I am officially OBSESSED with Mario's story! If you enjoyed the epilogue, keep your eyes peeled. I plan to write a legacy series on his journey through Heights & Shadows University. I hope you enjoy it as much as I will!

In the meantime, please take a look at my other books! I write more than romance, and I would love it if you gave those books a try! **Follow me on Amazon** to get updates on new releases, pre-orders, and reduced prices on my books. Also, follow me on TikTok! I love meeting readers and discussing new ideas. See you there!

Please take the time to sign up for my newsletter; and get access to dozens of free Christian books ready for you to download today!

The Rebel Christian Publishing

We are an independent Christian publishing company focused on fantasy, science fiction, and romantic reads. Visit therebelchristian.com to check out our books or click the titles below!

The Beta Rises
A. Bean

The Bite Of The Alpha
A. Bean

Decipis
Valicity Elaine

Exodus
Valicity Elaine

Cross Academy
Cross Academy Book I
VALICITY ELAINE

The Howler's Cry
Valicity Elaine
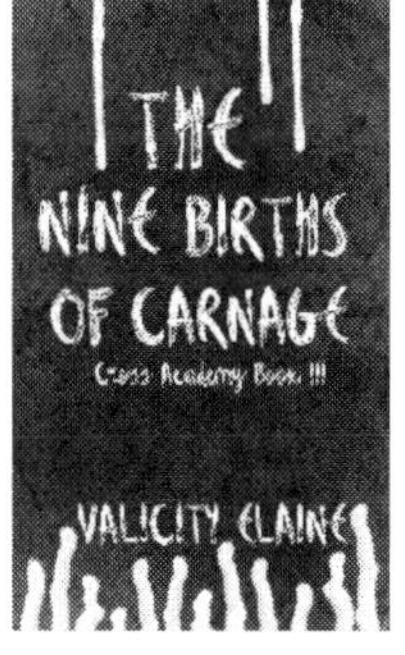
THE NINE BIRTHS OF CARNAGE
Cross Academy Book III
VALICITY ELAINE
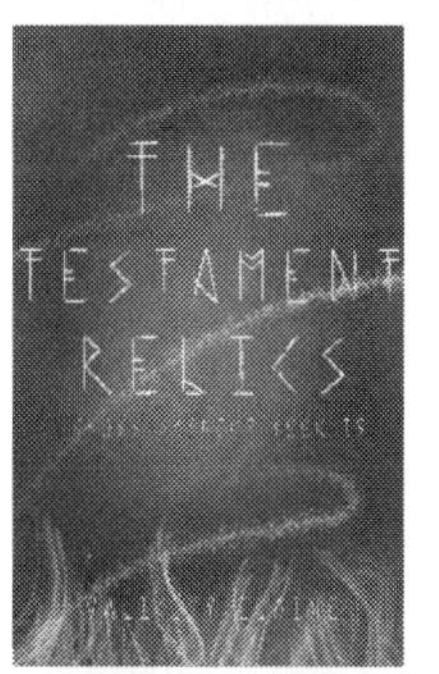
THE TESTAMENT RELICS

Shifting Tides
Cross Academy Book V
VALICITY ELAINE

I AM MAN
Valicity Elaine
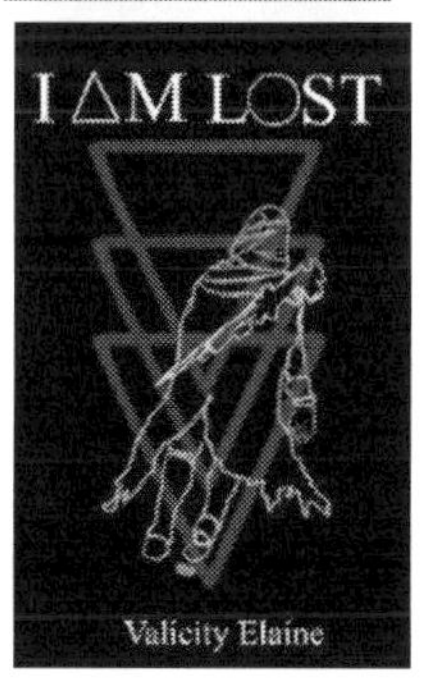
I AM LOST
Valicity Elaine
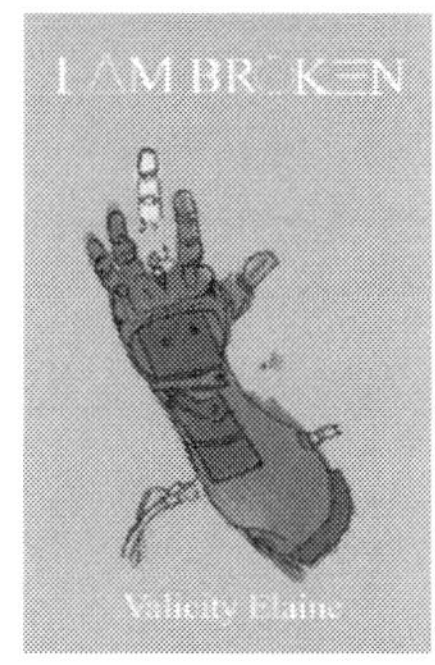
I AM BROKEN
Valicity Elaine

I △M FR≡≡
Valicity Elaine

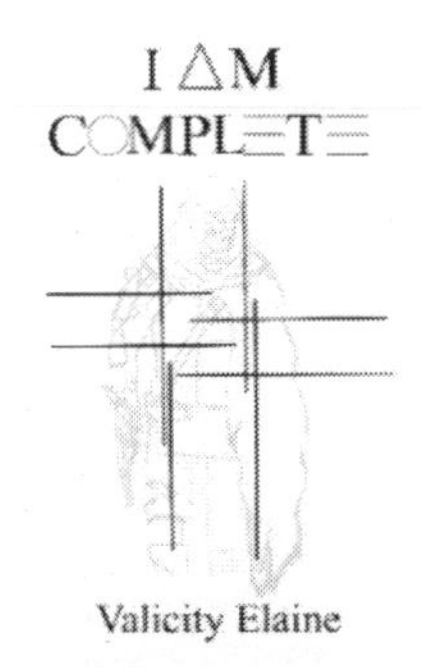
I △M
C○MPL≡T≡
Valicity Elaine

The Barren
Fields
Valicity
Elaine

The dead in Christ will rise ...
MAGOG
A. Bean

The Rise of
Desolation
BOOK II in the
Ordained Catastrophe Saga
A. Bean

The One Who is
Man and Beast
A. Bean

The
End
Of
The
World
A. Bean

The New World Order
A. Bean

SAVING
THE
WORLD
A. Bean

THE LIVING
WATER
A. BEAN

The Scribe

SINGLEHOOD
A CHRISTIAN ROMANCE
A. BEAN

PATCHES
Valicity
Elaine

The I Word
Valicity laine

Made in United States
Troutdale, OR
12/24/2024

27230895R00217